Once Upon A Summer

Various Authors
Foreword by H. L. Macfarlane

Copyright © 2023 to each anthology author and licensed by Macfarlane Lantern Publishing

All rights reserved.

ISBN-13: 978-1-914210-05-1

Published by Macfarlane Lantern Publishing, 2023

Glasgow, Scotland

No parts of this publication may be reproduced, stored in a retrieval system, or transmitted in any form or by any means, electronic, mechanical, photocopying, recording, or otherwise, without the prior written permission of the copyright owner.

This book is sold subject to the condition that it shall not, by way of trade or otherwise, be lent, resold, hired out, or otherwise circulated without the publisher's prior consent in any form of binding or cover other than that in which it is published and without a similar condition including this condition being imposed on the subsequent purchaser. Under no circumstances may any part of this book be photocopied for resale.

This is a work of fiction. Any similarity between the characters and situations within its pages and places or persons, living or dead, is unintentional and co-incidental.

Cover Art Copyright © 2023 Hayley Louise Macfarlane

TABLE OF CONTENTS

Foreword	12
The I Scream Van	13
What Big Geese You Have	29
The Forest at the End of the World	65
It is Written	83
These Burning Bones	100
Vespertine	113
The Last Roses of Summer	128
Love, Pride, Virtue and Fate	145
Juniper and the Upside Down Well	159
Love in the Time of Volcanoes	183
Bluebeard's Beach House	203
The Knucker of Lyminster	222
Summer Dreams	234
The Witches of Dogtown	240
Contract with a Mermaid	255
Acknowledgements	285

For the sun, and all the stories we've told because of it.

PLEASE NOTE: The formatting in Once Upon a Summer follows Macfarlane Lantern Publishing's house style. However, in order to preserve the voice of each contributor in the anthology, the version of English the individual authors chose to write in has not been changed. As such some discrepancies in spelling, punctuation and language between stories should be expected.

On a bank of flowers, in a summer day,
For summer lightly drest,
The youthful, blooming Nelly lay,
With love and sleep opprest;
When Willie, wand'ring thro' the wood,
Who for her favour oft had sued;
He gaz'd, he wish'd,
He fear'd, he blush'd,
And trembled where he stood.

On a Bank of Flowers (Robert Burns; 1789)

FOREWORD

H. L. Macfarlane

Summer lacks the deep hiding places and roaring fires of winter. It lacks the new beginnings of spring, and the decay of autumn. There are no golden leaves or delicate blossoms or flurries of snow to be had in summer.

But there is heat. There is the sun.

And there is light.

Summer is a time for revels that go on through nights that never get dark. It is a time for young romance, forbidden trysts beneath a blazing sky, and promises made and broken. It is a time for scorched earth. Parched tongues. Creatures that do not need to hide in the dark to be terrifying.

In this anthology, dear reader, you will find a host of wonderful, magical tales that evoke all of the above and more. Winter may be the time to listen to stories, but summer is the time to live them.

The I Scream Van

Caroline Logan

I go to my granny's house every summer.

Well, she's not technically my granny, but the old woman owes my mum a life debt and this is how she's paying it back. When I was wee, she'd lock herself in her bedroom as soon as I arrived, only emerging when I headed out. Nowadays she's gotten used to me. Mostly, we both keep to ourselves. It's fine, I like being alone. We are a solitary species, inhabiting the dark and the quiet.

Honestly, I have no idea why my mother insists I come every year, but thankfully this is the last time I'll be forced to spend the summer months in this village. I eye the squat little cottages, their white paint flaking, as I trudge down the cobblestone street. Most people are away, either working in the fields or fishing boats. That's good. I'm not exactly welcome. I've learned to arrive during the day to avoid the stares. I may look human but the villagers know I am not.

I weave down the roads, past the post office and the run-down cafe. My granny's house is near the pier; an old bungalow with a cracked chimney. She really needs to get that fixed. I thought she had a mate a while back but I think I scared him away. She's too old now to climb on roofs herself. Shame.

I come to a stop at the cottage's gate, taking deep breaths and inhaling the pungent lavender. The only sound is the incessant buzz of the bees and for a moment I wonder if she's in. But then there's movement in the frosted glass window attached to the kitchen. My shoulders curl inwards as I open the gate and finally ring the doorbell.

There's a soft humming and then the door opens. The old woman who stands there has her hair up in rollers and is wearing a housecoat and a pleasant smile. As soon as she sees me, her face crumples into one of fear and loathing.

"You're back."

"Hello, Granny," I say without a smile.

She grunts. "Stop calling me that."

I want to lash out, to bite and claw, but I roll my eyes, just like I've seen other teenagers do. "Permit me entry. Remember your debt." These are words my mother taught me, words I say every year.

There is mutiny in the old woman's eyes and she makes a great show of resisting, as she always does. But, inevitably, she moves to the side so I can step in.

"Can I head up to my room?" I ask, tugging on the straps of my backpack.

Granny sighs, resigned. "I am going to pretend you're not here."

I grin before climbing the creaky wooden staircase to the guest room I inhabit whenever I'm here. There's a new decoration on the door: a golden cross that seems far too gaudy for the old woman. I wonder if it was a gift from a concerned neighbour? I know vaguely that humans put these up to ward off demons. I trace the metal with my index finger. Not even real gold. Maybe I'll get her a better one as a parting gift.

Inside the room is just an empty shell; I don't see a single trace of myself unless I really look. But I'm here in the way the dust coats every surface, as if Granny can't bring herself to use the room even when I'm gone. I'm here in the nail marks I've pressed into the awful foamy wallpaper and the spot of red lipstick she can't seem to wash out of the curtains.

I upend my backpack on the bed, the contents spilling out over the floral duvet cover, and inspect my haul. Along with old nick-knacks from previous years, I've got a variety of new clothes. The old ones were probably a fine fit but every year the humans have new fashions and I like to blend in. Oversized checked shirts, crop tops and overalls were hanging on most washing lines on my walk here so I grabbed a few of each. Maybe the owners will think they blew away.

Once I've put away my small bundle of possessions, I'm left with the glaring stretch of days and weeks ahead of me. *One more summer,* I remind myself. *I can do this.*

The sun is filtering through the blinds so I head outside to see what has changed in the village since last year. The answer is most likely nothing. Nothing ever changes.

It must be the end of the workday because there are a few more neighbours milling around now. "Hello Mr Fleming," I say when I spot the postman doing his rounds. He snaps his gaze to mine at the sound of his name and then turns in the other direction, rushing back up the street he'd just come down.

I get mostly the same reaction wherever I go. Mrs Davidson at the tearoom touches her head and shoulders in a strange ritual that I know has something to do with the cross back at the cottage. Wee Davie McKenzie actually spits at the ground when I walk by, which I think is rude but also quite brave. Good for him. I distinctly remember he peed his cargo shorts last year.

The thing is, the villagers are used to me. My presence is always a shock at first, but then they just get on with their lives and ignore me. The children have been warned to stay away. I am permitted to buy cakes but not to sit in the cafe. No one exchanges pleasantries but they also don't scream or, thank goodness, chase me down the street with pitchforks. I blend in enough that I am tolerated.

I make my way back to the cottage when I've done a lap of the village. Granny is in the kitchen making something with far too much cinnamon in it. I lean against the doorway, breathing in the smoke from the cigarette she has hanging from her lips.

"I'm hungry," I say, enjoying the way she jumps.

"Go to Hell." She raises a shaking, batter-covered hand to her face, taking the cigarette and smashing it into a carved glass ashtray beside her.

"That's bad for you, you know," I say, nodding at it. "You're not getting any younger."

She snorts wetly and I wonder what the insides of her lungs look like. "If I feed you, will you go away?"

"Until the next time." I smile with all of my dull, human-like teeth, but Granny shivers all the same, as if imagining what's beneath the illusion. She nods to the old, pistachio-coloured fridge and I go to inspect it. Inside are a couple of whole haddocks, their scales shining in the static light. I pull one out and leave her to her baking, throwing a *thanks* over my shoulder because Mum said to be polite. The moon is out along with the sun when I sink down onto the porch step to eat my dinner.

I tear into it, the flesh briny and tasting of summer. The fish back home don't swim in saltwater, after all. I'm almost down to the spine when a noise floats up the road, stopping me.

It's tinny and jangly but the song is vaguely familiar. It takes me a second, but when it loops back, I think I remember some words. *If you go down to the woods today, you're sure of a big surprise.* Well, I can think of a lot of surprises in the woods, but none I'd like to sing about. There are monsters far worse than me. I hum along anyway because the noise is getting louder and I want to see what it is. While I wait, I notice the villagers are acting strangely.

First, Mrs Brown from across the road runs out of her cottage with wild eyes. She shouts the name of her son, clutching at her hair like she's about to rip it out. When he appears from the other end of the garden, she snatches him up and runs inside, leaving his toys discarded on the grass.

Other children run down the street, stampeding over the cobblestones and into their houses. They are greeted with relieved hugs from their parents before the doors are slammed shut.

Up and down the road, the humans retreat inside, drawing the curtains across the windows. It all takes a matter of seconds but then the place is quiet, save for the cheery song getting closer and closer.

Granny appears behind me in the doorway. "I need to shut this door," she says. "In or out."

I lower what is left of my fish to the concrete step beside me. "What's going on?"

"The ice cream van." She casts a furtive glance down the street. "It's not safe."

"Ice cream?" I ask, perking up. It must be new. There hasn't been an ice cream van in all the other years I've been here. "Can I have some money?"

Granny curls her lip. "You're not the only monster in town now." Then she nudges me with the side of her leg until I lean forward, closing the door behind me with a thud.

I blink in shock, both from her touch and her words. *Another monster? Someone like me?*

These people have had me in their village every summer since I was eight and I've never had this reaction from them. I think back to earlier, when the postie saw me and power-walked away. Power-walked, not sprinted, screaming, not finding the nearest house to barricade himself inside.

It is with this thought that I unfold myself from the step. This is my town. I'm the only one who gets to scare them.

I stomp forward, unlatching and relatching the gate as I step through it. I can see the ice cream van now, chugging merrily along its route. It's white with a blue trim and there are badly painted cartoon characters on the sides. Their beady black eyes watch me as the van pulls up and stops.

Above the window, a sign proclaims the van sells ice cream. Except it's spelled wrong. The pink curling letters instead say *'I Scream'*.

I get a glimpse of glass bottles and sweetie tubs as the hand brake is pulled on, shaking the vehicle and dislodging a few pre-made packets of dolly mixtures with the force. Then a woman with a halo of curling blonde hair appears at the window and my rage ratchets up a notch.

Her voice is lilting and melodic, and she fixes a friendly smile on her face. "What can I get yo—"

"You're about as subtle as a brick wall," I cut her off, seething. "I mean, look at you."

And I do look, pressing my hands to the side of the van so I can stand on my tiptoes and glare at her. Now that I'm closer, it's even more obvious that she is *other*. It's in the blink of an eye, just before my lids close. Her skin and hair turn the colour of sea glass for that split second and I find I'm fluttering my eyelashes, just to glimpse of her true face. Then I realise what I'm doing and try to stare at the tub of cola bottles behind her head instead.

"I'm new to the area," she says, staring down at me quizzically. "Do you want an eighty-nine?"

"It's a *ninety-nine*." I make a noise somewhere between a snort and a growl. "I want you to go back to where you came from. This is my town."

"I haven't seen you around," she says, her smile faltering.

"I just got here but I come every summer." I curl my lip. "What's your name?"

"Hazel."

"You couldn't have picked something more modern? And look at your clothes. No one wears shoulder pads anymore."

Hazel squirms under my gaze, biting her lip. "No one told me."

I let out a sigh. Perhaps I've been too mean. "No wonder you haven't fooled anyone. These people know the old stories. They probably spotted you the second you washed up."

"Do they know about you...?" she trails off, leaving the space for my name.

"Fern," I supply, grudgingly.

"Isn't that a plant?"

My lip curls up. "It's a lot cooler than Hazel, which I believe is also a plant. Yes, they know about me but only because I've been coming here since before I learned to assimilate." Not that anyone here would even use that word. "But if a tourist came to town, I'm sure they wouldn't know what I am."

"Tourists?" Hazel blinks her huge eyes and I'm reminded of an owl.

"Outsiders. They don't come by often. We're in the middle of nowhere."

A slow smile is curling around her lips. "Where would we find tourists?"

"Round the coast, probably. As soon as you start seeing big hotels, you'll find them."

"Hotels?"

I don't think I've ever been asked so many questions; she really is clueless. Suddenly, a vision of a fishing net and pitchforks flashes before me. I've heard what humans can do when they're scared and brave enough. If I leave Hazel to her own devices, she might not even have a chance to learn, to blend in. "You're ridiculous. Meet me back here tomorrow." But then I have an idea. "No, wait here."

"You're very bossy," Hazel says brightly.

I grit my teeth as I march back to the cottage, having to break the lock on the door with a flick of my wrist before I can throw it open. Granny is probably hiding in her bedroom. I'm thankful the old woman isn't around to ask questions. I collect my prize and head back out, glad to see Hazel hasn't driven off. Maybe she has some self-preservation after all.

"Here," I say, thrusting the second fish at her. "There's no way you'll catch a human so this will have to do."

"I can catch my own fish," she says haughtily, but she takes it all the same.

"Here, tomorrow, same time," I say. "Try to stay out of trouble between now and then, yeah?"

"Okay, thanks Fern."

I grumble, knotting my arms across my chest as she moves back to the cab and waves before pulling away. My eyes snag on the painting on the back of the van. *Watch yer wains*, it warns.

"It's not even the right spelling," I say with a grimace.

***

The next day I wear a path into the grass waiting for the horrible jangly music. It's warm, even though it's early evening, and the plastic bag I'm clutching has left ink on my bare legs. At one point, I look back at my cottage, spotting my granny in the window upstairs. She glares at me and pulls the curtains closed so forcefully I think she must have ripped the fabric.

There's a faint scream just before the ice cream van's tune starts again, still far away. I've learned the song is called *Teddy Bear's Picnic* and I somehow have more questions than answers. Like yesterday, the villagers scramble into their houses. I have the urge to walk down to meet Hazel as the van appears at the far end of the road but I'm not sure why.

Finally, the truck stops outside my gate and I bounce on my toes, expecting to spot her face at the window. But to my surprise, Hazel lets herself out the driver's door, keys jangling in her hand as she greets me.

"Hi Fern," she says. She's wearing a bright shift today. It makes her legs look much too long.

I thrust the plastic bag at her with a growl.

"What's this?" she asks, inspecting the contents.

"Clothes that won't make you look like you're in costume." I shove my hands in my pockets. "I had to go to the next village over to find something decent for you."

"Thank you," she says brightly. And then she pulls her dress over her head.

"Not here," I splutter. "You are *ridiculous.*" I try to shove her back into the van but she's so much taller than me. It takes her a moment to realise what I'm doing and then she opens the door, pulling me in after her.

"You can't just get undressed in the middle of the road." The words come out in a hiss that isn't even remotely human.

"Is it okay to do it in here?"

I sigh, running a hand through my hair and pulling on the ends. "Fine, but I'll have to block the window or everyone's going to get an eyeful."

I don't know why I'm so incensed. It's not even her real body, after all. Maybe the humans have rubbed off on me too much. Taking my place at the windows, I spread my arms to take up as much of the view as possible. There's a lot of rustling behind me and at one point Hazel falls into my back. There is far too much bare skin.

"Sorry, still not used to these legs."

I roll my eyes but my heart is beating too fast now.

After way too long, Hazel announces she's dressed and I turn to survey my handiwork. The cropped polo and tennis skirt aren't really my thing but they look good on her. She pushes a matching headband into her hair and I immediately wish I'd done it for her.

"Do you think I'll fit in now?" she asks, a faint blush colouring her cheeks.

"Not in this village," I say, clenching my hands at my sides. "It's too late for that."

"But you said there were other towns with hotels and tourists." She says the words reverently, like they're somehow magical and mysterious.

"Yes, and you'll probably get on better there."

She worries her lip between her teeth. "I don't really know where to go. Would you take me?"

The refusal is sour in my mouth, ready to be spoken. It's not that I don't want to leave, it's just that I had resigned myself to one last summer in this little fishing village. Yes, Granny had made a promise, but so had I. But, then again... I think back to the exact wording of that oath. Spend the summer with the humans. That had been my mother's only stipulation. Perhaps I'm not as trapped as I thought.

I blink a few times, watching Hazel's appearance flicker between the illusion and her true self. Both versions look terribly trusting. It's not a good quality to have but I suppose that's my problem now. "Fine, but I'll need to get my stuff." I won't be coming back. Just before I duck out the door, I turn back. "What exactly did you do to make the whole town so scared of you, anyway?"

Hazel looks sheepish. "I might have eaten a cat."

* * *

"You're leaving." It's not a question.

I look over my shoulder to where Granny looms in the doorway of my bedroom and snort. "You're free from your promise a little earlier than expected."

"And you won't be back?"

I shove my baseball cap into the bag. "Would you like me to come back for a visit? I could call you sometimes, if you want? Let you know how I'm getting on or how I'm spending my birthday money?" The old woman says nothing as I straighten and heft the bag on my shoulders. "I know you'll miss me, Granny, but I have to grow up at some point."

"Thank you for not killing me," she says stiffly.

"Thanks for the room and the fish."

Hazel is in the driver's seat when I head outside. It's getting dark now but the headlights are enough for me to find my way to the passenger's door.

"Ready to go?" Hazel asks as I climb in.

I give the cottage one last look before I nod. "Please don't play the jingle."

* * *

It turns out the van has a radio, which I turn up loud as we drive. The sickly sweet pop beats are only a tiny bit less annoying than Teddy Bear's Picnic but Hazel tries to sing along to words she's clearly never heard before and it makes me warm inside for some reason. We drive for hours down winding roads until she announces she needs to sleep. Hazel pulls the van into a passing place and we both push our chairs back, propping our legs on the dashboard so we're sprawled out. Her flip-flops knock into my tennis shoes and it all feels very domestic. She's unconscious almost immediately and I watch her skin turn green as if she can't keep up the illusion in her sleep.

Ridiculous, I think again as I slide into a dream that's just flashes of a beach and Hazel smiling and ice cream scoops.

The next day, I can tell we're getting close to civilization by the dozens of caravans we pass on the road. Humans, I know, love a caravan in theory. But where do they go when the reality isn't as fun?

"Hotels," I say, pointing at the buildings in the harbour town below. "It's where tourists go on their holidays."

The car parks are full when we arrive and it takes us around half an hour of searching before we spot someone pulling out so we can nab their space. There are a few eyes on us when we get out of the van and I worry I've made a mistake. Maybe the tourists are savvier than I gave them credit for. But then we start walking down the promenade and their eyes stay on the truck. Right, they just want ice cream.

"Where should we start?" I ask, watching the crowd part around us like a school of fish.

Hazel twirls a curl around her finger and then lets out a squeal of glee. "Come on," she says, grabbing my hand and pulling me towards some fluttering flags. I know my palms are clammy from the heat of the day but she doesn't let go, even as we near a ticket booth.

"Three pounds entry," says the spotty teen behind the counter.

I go to reach into my pocket for the little change I have but Hazel stops me with a squeeze of her hand. Her palm is a little sweaty but I find I don't mind.

"Wish for free entry," she says with a twinkle in her eye.

I don't know why I don't question it but I suddenly feel like I can't refuse her. "I wish for free entry."

There's a shimmer in the air and then the teen nods dismissively. "On you go."

"How?" I ask as we enter the gates.

"I can give away wishes. It doesn't work when I ask for it but if someone else does…" She shrugs. "Nothing too big, though."

It turns out we're at a funfair. I've only seen them on TV but the screaming of the humans invites me in and soon I find myself strapped into a cart with Hazel beside me. It starts to crank forward, pulling us up the hill with shuddering motions.

"I don't like this," I say, knuckles white against the bar. I'm smaller than Hazel and there's a lot more room for me to fall out.

She puts her arm around my shoulders, tucking me into her body. On a normal day, I'd scramble away, hissing, but I'm frozen in my seat. "It'll be fun," she says as we reach the crest.

Then we're falling and there's screaming and I try to look for the source and I realise it's me. The shout is ripped from me like a sacrifice and by the time we reach the bottom of the hill I feel I've lost more than the sound. Tears run down my cheeks. My stomach turns over, threatening to escape my body with my dignity. It's horrible. Until we rocket back up another incline and I turn to look at my companion.

Hazel's head is thrown back, the wind whipping her blonde hair up over her shoulders. I'm not sure if it's her laughter or the coaster that shakes her shoulders, but I know her squeals are those of delight. The pink in her cheeks leaks down to her neck. I follow the blush with my eyes until it disappears under the collar of her shirt. I wonder if it goes anywhere else.

"See," she cackles. "It's great, isn't it!"

I didn't realise smiles were contagious to humans. They must be, because I can't help when I return hers. They truly are strange creatures.

The rollercoaster slides and then jerks to a stop, back where we started. I sit for a moment, collecting my scrambled thoughts, until I feel Hazel's fingers wrap around my wrist.

"You can let go now."

I look down, realising my grip is still tight on the lap bar. I extract myself, hands shaking, and Hazel offers me another grin.

"Come on, there's loads more to do."

I find myself following her unquestionably. Perhaps she's using her magic, luring me to my doom. I find I don't care.

After the fair, we wander through the town, stopping at a fish and chip shop for dinner. I tell myself that it's just a first course, but then when the battered fish hits my tongue I order another. Or rather, I *wish* for another, the air shimmering with magic.

By the time the sun is sinking over the sea, I'm shattered. We walk back to the ice cream truck but Hazel stops before we reach it.

"I don't want to sleep there again. It hurts my neck." She pouts before gazing longingly at the hotel across the street.

"I wish for a hotel room," I say as soon as I realise what she wants. "Do you think that's too big?"

"We'll have to find out," she says. But there's a shimmer and I know it worked. She drags me across the road, dodging traffic as the cars honk their horns.

We don't just get a hotel room; we get the penthouse right at the top. The bed is huge and white and there's a bathtub big enough for two people. I order another fish supper through room service and we eat it together on the balcony.

"I think I like chippies better than humans," I concede.

Hazel licks the oil from her fingers and I can't tear my eyes away. "Me too," she says.

"And I like this town more than the village."

"Me too."

I take a deep breath. "And I like being with you."

Hazel shivers and lets her illusion drop. "I'm not too ridiculous?"

My human ears feel hot so I pull off the flesh, replacing it with my own. Her eyes soften as I kiss her hand, now covered in bright scales. "You still are, which is why you need me around to look after you."

"Whatever you say."

It doesn't take long for us to settle into a life. Hazel keeps her ice cream truck and gets more customers than she ever did before. Sometimes I help, sticking flakes into the vanilla and handing out extra bags of dolly mixtures to the kids. Other days I sell jewellery I've made from sea glass that reminds me of Hazel's skin.

It's nearing the end of the summer, when I'd normally head back to my mum. Hazel is painting her human toes a coral pink but she smiles at me when I come close and I realise I never want this to end.

"I'd like to wish we could stay here forever," I say.

Hazel leans over and cups my cheek, eyes bright. "What are you waiting for, then?"

The words stick for a moment but when they spill out they're said into Hazel's lips. There's a tell-tale shimmer in the air and our mouths curve into matching grins.

The summer is endless, even when the days turn cold and short. We stay in the tourist town, anonymous and unthreatening, greeted every day by sea and sand and scoops of ice cream. I send off postcards, most of them to Mum but I can't resist sending a few to my granny, just so she knows that I still think about her and that I'm happy.

Caroline Logan is a writer of Young Adult Fantasy. Her Scottish fantasy series, the Four Treasures, was published by Cranachan Books and is available online and in all good bookshops. Caroline is a high school biology teacher who lives in the Cairngorms National Park in Scotland, with her husband and dogs, Ranger and Scout. She graduated from The University of Glasgow with a bachelor's degree in Marine and Freshwater Biology. In her spare time she likes to ski, paddleboard and play Dungeons and Dragons, though she is happiest with a good book and a cup of tea.

What Big Geese You Have

Adie Hart

"What do you mean, you already *have* a District Witch?"

My words slapped against the yellow stone of the courtyard, ringing out even over the trickle of water and the chatter of people strolling through the shaded arches. I winced as the courtiers sitting by the fountain fell silent – the better to crane their necks at me – and tried not to shift from foot to foot under the weight of their curiosity.

Professional. Be professional.

The palace steward, a nervous little man sweating through a silken shirt, wrung his hands together. "I'm terribly sorry, Miss Rutherford, but I can't think of another way to say it. There's already a District Witch handling the king's... ahem, request."

This couldn't be happening. I'd barely even arrived and already my first solo case was going wrong. I bit the inside of my lip to forestall the tears I could feel threatening to form, and took a deep breath. It was fine. I just needed to get to the bottom of the problem, and everything would be fine.

"Mr Falzon" – always address your conversational opponent by name; it makes them feel you care – "there must be some mistake. Perhaps I could talk to a superior?"

The steward wrung his hands even harder. "Miss Rutherford, I don't—"

"Don't worry, Roberto," called one of the fountain courtiers, with more than a shade of laughter in her voice. "I'll take it from here. Why don't you go and cool off?" She disentangled herself from her companions and sauntered across the courtyard; the steward nodded several times and, excusing himself with a mutter, hurried off.

"There, that's better," smiled the woman. "He's a sweet man, but I don't know who thought he'd make a good steward. He's terrified of dealing with people. Come and talk to me instead." She looped her arm through mine as if we were old friends and steered me towards a low stone bench.

"And who might you be?" I said. I couldn't work out a way to extricate my arm without being rude.

She grinned. "I'm the witch they already have."

I stopped abruptly in the middle of the colonnade, pulling my arm from hers, and actually looked at her properly for the first time.

I'd taken her for a wealthy courtier in a low-cut Varenian-style gown, but now that I was paying attention, I could see she *was* wearing the District uniform, though she'd taken as much liberty as possible with it. Where my dress was neatly buttoned at collar and wrist, as it was supposed to be, her sleeves were rolled up to the elbows, and she'd undone two - no, three - buttons to expose a delicate collarbone and a scandalous amount of cleavage. I felt my cheeks heating and snapped my gaze up abruptly. Now was *not* the time to get distracted by a beautiful girl.

I should have introduced myself, and returned the conversation to a normal course, but what came out of my mouth instead was the very eloquent, "Where's your hat?"

"Oh, I never wear it," she said lightly. "I don't think I have a very hatty face, do you?" Seemingly oblivious to my blush, she tilted her head from side to side for my inspection, pursing her perfect lips and batting eyelashes so long I could almost feel their breeze against my cheek. Her hair was loose, sweeping down past her shoulders in luxurious dark waves, and her eyes were the deep green of a quiet pool in a forest, the kind that tempted you to dive in.

I resisted the urge, dragging my mind back to more practical matters. "But it's part of the uniform."

"Yeah, but who's looking, all the way out here?"

"*I'm* looking," I said indignantly.

"Indeed you are," she said with a wink. "Now, sit down and have a drink – you must be parched. Marza, would you be so kind?"

This last wasn't directed at me; a smiling servant girl appeared with a tray and poured us both glasses of pale Varenian lemonade, and I sat awkwardly as they made cheerful chit-chat. I briefly considered refusing the glass, but the thirsty part of me overrode the petty part. I'd known summers would be warm this far south, but I hadn't been expecting it to be this intense; even sitting in the shade in the late afternoon, the heat was punishing. I drained my glass in one gulp.

"So, you're here about the princess thing?" said the so-called witch in a casual tone that made me bristle. She wanted to discuss the case in the middle of a bustling courtyard? So much for District discretion.

I couldn't keep the ice out of my voice. "If you mean am I answering an official request from King Marco asking us to investigate an unusual situation with his bride, then yes. And you?"

"Yes, that, exactly," she said, with a wave of her hand. "I'm Vi, by the way. What's your name?"

"Wilhelmina Rutherford," I said. "Just... Vi?" It was hardly a name. More of a sound.

"Well, Violet officially, but my friends call me Vi." She smiled. "Pleased to meet you."

Before I could reply, the steward reappeared, looking sweatier than ever. "Ladies, the king requests the honour of your presence at his table tonight. He will explain the... situation."

Good. In investigations of any sort, it's important to get straight to the person at the heart of the matter; any other input just gets you sidetracked.

"Thank you, Mr Falzon. Has a room been readied for me? I'd like to freshen up." I was acutely aware of the sticky heat of my skin and the travel-dust clinging to my skirts, neither of which were appropriate for meeting royalty.

"Um, well..." Did this man do anything *but* wring his hands? He glanced nervously at Violet, who stood and clapped him on the shoulder.

"I'll show you," she said. "Come on, Wills."

"It's Wilhelmina," I said, but she was already halfway across the courtyard.

* * *

"This is *your* room," I said, looking at the chaos. A District Witch usually travels with only a single sturdy satchel containing her essential supplies, but Violet must have been particularly adept at shrinking spells, because it looked like she'd somehow brought every possession she'd ever owned. There were clothes on every surface. Books teetered on the table. Even as I looked, a green satin something slithered off a chair to the floor.

Violet smiled apologetically. "It's the room they allocated for the District Witch."

So not only was she on my case, she was also in my room? This wouldn't do. "In a palace this size, they must have a spare guest room—"

"But they're packed to the gills for the wedding," she said. "There isn't anything else. We'll just have to share. I'll, uh, make some space." She shoved a pile of clothes off the bed. The singular bed.

I blinked in disbelief. "This is ridiculous. I'm not sharing a bed with you."

"What, you've never bunked up with a stranger on a case before?"

"No." I'd shared with my teacher on my journeywitch cases, but I'd known her for years. And she knew how to keep her things in decent order.

"You're lucky. Case before last I ended up in an inn in the middle of some huge festival – you've never seen so many people packed into one room! I'm still not sure if that farmer had six or seven daughters... Pretty sure all of them kicked, though."

"That sounds awful," I said, wincing as she hefted a clattering bag to the floor.

"You get used to it." She cocked her head. "So, I'm guessing you're a diplomatic specialist, if you're used to decent digs. Am I right?"

"Yes," I said. It wasn't strictly true – I hadn't yet decided on a specialty – but agreeing meant I didn't need to admit my inexperience, which it suddenly seemed imperative to keep to myself. If there was a mistake and the king only needed one witch, they were certainly going to prefer the one who wasn't fresh out of the Academy. "And you?" She seemed so determined to talk – so oblivious to whether or not *I* wanted to – that it seemed wise to keep the focus on her.

"Oh, hat-of-all-trades," she said. "One day removing gnome-blight from potatoes, the next prancing around a palace drinking lemonade. I like the variety."

"But you don't even wear your hat," I muttered, which startled a laugh out of her. I bit my lip; I hadn't meant her to hear that.

"True! But it's fun to be a walking contradiction. Ah, there." She shoved one last bag to the side of the room and dusted her hands on her skirt. "Ta-da! Your very own half of the bed." She sat down on the messy side and beamed up at me.

Her invitation set off a flutter in my chest which I forced myself to ignore. This wasn't going to work at all. "Listen, Violet. I appreciate that you're willing to share the room, but really, there's been some kind of mistake. I was assigned this case and I'm more than capable of handling it, so we don't need to share, because you don't need to be here."

"Oh, it's no trouble," she said breezily. "It's nice to partner up every so often. I haven't had a chance to work with another witch for years - probably since I was at the Academy. I won't tell if you won't."

And of course, I could hardly argue with that without sounding rude - or without explaining why it was so important to me to do this alone.

"I need to get ready for dinner," I said. Perhaps I could convince the king to send her away.

* * *

It wasn't my first time meeting royalty, of course - there were two minor royals in my year alone - but part of me was wishing that my first case had been something a little less grand. It was very gratifying to be assigned something so prestigious straight out of the gate, but a king with a princess problem was nerve-wracking in a way that a farmer with a kobold infestation probably wouldn't have been.

As we waited for our hosts to appear, I tried to calm myself by running through the case details in my head. King Marco of Varenia was to marry Princess Aurelia of Leorn at the summer solstice. He had requested a discreet investigation due to an "issue" with the arrangement, but hadn't provided specifics.

Perhaps the princess had turned up and refused him. Perhaps he'd changed his mind about allying himself with Leorn, but the two countries shared a long border and a longer history, so that would certainly be awkward to negotiate.

I tried to recall what I'd learned of Leorn: it was a coastal kingdom, wealthy thanks to its location on a major trade route. It had a number of unusual native plants and animals, and the royal family was known for its conservation efforts – their flag even featured a griffin, calling back to the old story that the current king's great-great-grandmother had once—

My thoughts were interrupted by a sharp jab in my side.

"Did you just *poke* me?" I asked Violet incredulously.

"They're here. Stop daydreaming," she whispered.

"I wasn't," I hissed back as I rose to greet the king.

"Welcome, welcome," said the king, taking his seat. He was relatively young, and handsome in a clean-cut, regal way. Suddenly it made sense why the other journeywitches had sighed and giggled when I'd been assigned the case, though I didn't see the appeal personally.

"Your Majesty," I murmured, dipping to the perfect degree and resisting the urge to glance at Violet to check if she was doing the same.

"And this is the Leorn princess." He indicated the young woman at his side, whose appeal I definitely did see: she was plump and beautiful, with tightly curled black hair. They were well-matched in looks, certainly, so I doubted it was a case where either wanted to cry off the marriage in revulsion, but the king's words seemed like a strangely aloof way to introduce one's betrothed, even for an arranged marriage. Clearly something was amiss.

"Honoured to meet you, Princess Aurelia," I said.

The princess gave a small laugh. "Actually, I'm Cecilia."

Panic flashed through me. How could I have got such a

simple thing wrong? I'd thought I'd memorised all the details so carefully, but obviously not carefully enough. "I am so terribly sorry, Your Royal Highness, I - my files - I must have misread—"

She held up a hand to stop me, but I didn't think people who were about to have you beheaded smiled so kindly, so I forced myself to breathe.

"Please don't worry," she said. "You're right to expect Aurelia, but I'm afraid my sister is the reason we called you here." Her sister. Of course. I wasn't wrong.

The king nodded. "Allow me to explain. My wedding to Princess Aurelia is supposed to take place in four days. However, the princess..." He rubbed a hand over his chin. "The princess has disappeared."

Well, that wasn't what I'd been expecting to hear.

"Disappeared?" asked Violet. "When?"

It was Princess Cecilia who answered. "The night we arrived in the city. We made poor time and arrived late, so we were only briefly introduced to His Majesty, then shown straight to our suite. When I woke up the next morning, she was gone."

"Was there any sign of a struggle?" I asked.
"None. The doors were locked, and no one saw her leaving."

"We searched the palace, of course, and I've been making discreet inquiries," said the king, "but this is a delicate matter, and I thought it better not to make it widely known that the princess was missing."

"Which is where I come in," said Princess Cecilia. "I've been pretending to be Aurelia at official functions."

"Oh, that's clever," grinned Violet, and the princess grinned back. "Of course, you're both strangers to the court, so who could tell?"

I glared at her. "It's not going to work in the long-term, though. You can hardly *marry* the wrong princess and hope people don't notice."

"No, indeed," laughed Princess Cecilia. "My apologies, Your Majesty - but I don't want to pretend to be Aurelia forever."

"Of course not," said the king, with a wry smile of his own. "I won't pretend there's anything more than politics between Aurelia and me, but even without a love match, princesses are not interchangeable."

"I'm not sure my mother would agree," said the princess dryly. "But that's the least of my worries. I just want to find my sister."

"Of course," I said. "I'll do everything I can to locate her."

"As will I," said Violet, smiling sweetly at my glare.

The rest of dinner was a flurry of questions. How did Princess Aurelia feel about the wedding? Did she know anyone in the area? Did she have any enemies? Unfortunately, the king seemed to know as little about his new bride as he might about blacksmithing, and Princess Cecilia seemed mostly confused by her sister's disappearance, telling us that Aurelia had been willing to do her duty, and (she blushed) was not immediately repulsed by her future husband. Neither royal could offer any ideas as to who might wish Aurelia harm or hope to prevent the wedding. It truly seemed as though the princess had just vanished into thin air.

I barely tasted a single bite, but eventually the final course was whisked away and a tiny glass of amber liquid was placed in front of each of us. I eyed it suspiciously; Violet took an appreciative sip, eyes fluttering closed in pleasure.

"Beautiful," she said softly. She was, I caught myself thinking. I'd clearly had enough to drink already.

"From my personal cellar," said the king. "Which reminds me, if there is anything you and your partner req—"

"She's *not* my partner," I muttered, then bit my lip, hard

enough to hurt. Now I was interrupting a king? I could not be messing this up any worse.

"My apologies if I used the wrong term. But now that you mention it, I'm not sure whether to be honoured or concerned that Aurelia's disappearance merits the attention of *two* District Witches."

Well, I wasn't going to get a better opening than that. I took a deep breath – more of a gasp – and spat it out. "Your Majesty, I don't believe it does require two of us," I said, ignoring the wide-eyed look Violet shot at me. "There was a failure of communication somewhere; we were both unaware of the other's presence until we arrived. Given the demands of the summer season, with all the festivals and the... agricultural needs, it may be better if only one of us stays to direct the investigation."

The king seemed taken aback, but nodded graciously. "Of course. I understand how busy you are, and if one of you must return to attend another issue, then I will take no offence."

"I'm more than happy to stay," Violet said, with that charming smile firmly in place. "I wouldn't dream of leaving you in your time of need." When she turned the smile on me, the sweetness turned to challenge. The arch of her eyebrow said, *your move.*

I weighed up my options. Violet wasn't going to back down and leave, so really, I should return to the Academy and request reassignment; at the very least, I should ask for clarification. But with a princess missing, time was of the essence, and by the time a messenger had made it to the Academy and back, it might be too late. I didn't trust Violet to carry out a proper investigation, if her lack of respect for the uniform and her casual demeanour were anything to go by. And besides, wasn't I supposed to be able to handle anything now? I didn't relish the thought of slinking back to the Academy with my first ever case unsolved; I'd never get another decent case if they thought I needed to have my hand held through every decision. Thinking about it that way, there was only one thing to do.

"I'll stay," I said, before I could overthink it. "But I'm in charge."

* * *

The next morning, I stood on the palace steps and squinted into the sunlight as the city awoke below me. Kadina, Varenia's capital, was beautiful, with wide streets flowing out from the palace into open squares lined with tall sandstone buildings. It practically glowed in the early morning light. I rolled my shoulders, stiff from a night spent with only my bedroll between me and the floor. A good District Witch is always prepared to camp, but natural ground is a cosier mattress than marble, and I was regretting not arguing for more pillows. It was hardly even fair I'd been forced onto the floor at all, but since Violet still seemed insistent that sharing didn't bother her, it had been the only way to preserve my dignity.

Third bell clanged from the palace tower; time for the markets to open, and well past time for the investigation to get underway. No doubt Violet was still lounging in bed. I'd shaken her awake just after dawn, but she'd insisted, from the depths of her pillow, that she could get plenty more sleep and still be ready to meet me at "a reasonable hour". How much longer did I need to wait before I could assume that she wasn't coming at all? At least if she didn't come, I supposed, I could run the investigation myself; although then she might decide to make enquiries without my supervision, which could be disastrous.

I was saved from having to make a decision by the sound of footsteps behind me. Unfortunately, if I'd had any hope Violet might look smarter once the case was officially underway, the sight of her unbuttoned collar dashed it.

"Sorry, Mimi," she said. "I was just too comfy." The apology was rather undercut by her grin.

"Nice problem to have," I said, with not a little sarcasm. "And it's Wilhelmina. Come on. We're off to the guardhouse." I started down the steps without waiting for her response. I'd done enough waiting already.

"What for?" Violet said, falling into step with me easily.

"What do you mean, what for? The authorities should be the first port of call in an investigation, you know that. They're the ones best placed to see any suspicious activity."

"They're also the ones reporting directly to the king. If they'd seen anything, the king would never have needed us."

"Needed *me*."

"Needed either of us," she said brightly.

I sighed. "Well, what do *you* suggest then?"

"Let's check the markets. Traders always gossip, and whether the princess was snatched or ran away, if she's still in the city she's got to be getting supplies somewhere."

I didn't want to admit it, but she had a point. And investigating the locals was the second task on my list, so we were really only skipping ahead a little. "Fine."

"Great," said Violet, linking her arm through mine and tugging me down a side street. "Besides, then we can get some breakfast."

* * *

By lunchtime, I had to admit that Violet had a knack for getting people to open up to her. Unfortunately, that meant we spent a lot of time listening to stories about precocious grandchildren and fixing everything from broken jewellery to minor cuts. The Varenians were certainly willing to talk, but we weren't getting anything useful, and with every hour that passed it got hotter. I managed to convince Violet to move to the more genteel shopping district, and pretended it wasn't partly to be able to sit in the shade while we wasted our time.

But whether we were standing at a stall or perched at a

marble counter, most people seemed more interested in the solstice celebrations than in the wedding itself, though a few women sighed laughingly that it was a shame they'd missed their chance to catch the king's eye. There was nothing malicious in their daydreams – it was unlikely any shopkeeper's girl would kidnap a princess just because the king had a nice face – so I tried to move the conversations on, but Violet seized any opportunity to flirt and flatter them and talk about nothing until I was tapping my feet with impatience. I'd been willing to give her a chance, but it was like she had no concept of investigation protocols.

Eventually, fed up with yet another conversation that went nowhere, I grabbed Violet's elbow, muttered something about District business, and dragged her out of the bakery we'd been loitering in, setting off towards the palace at a swift pace. We both winced as the heat pounded down on us, and I used my free hand to cast a quick breeze spell. It didn't help much.

"You'd be cooler without the hat, Ellie," Violet quipped around a mouthful of pastry.

I rounded on her. "For the last time, it's *Wilhelmina*. And I'm fed up with this. You're wasting time. We should be out here doing truth spells and interrogating suspicious characters, not sampling delicacies and flirting with shopkeepers!"

"And there was me thinking we were on a lovely day out," Violet sighed. "It would help if you didn't lurk behind me looking menacing."

"I do not look menacing."

"You do! Well, perhaps you're a little short to quite achieve it" – she ignored my squeak – "but you remind them that we're asking questions in an official capacity."

"We *are* asking questions in an official capacity."

"But they don't need to know that! If we're just friendly, they're more likely to let things slip that might be helpful. Goodness, it's like you've never done this before." She stopped in her tracks, then suddenly laughed. "Wait. You *haven't* done this before, have you? This is your first case."

I wheeled around, panicked. "I fail to see how that—"

"Oh my goodness, it is. It's your first case." She sounded so delighted, I almost expected her to clap.

"Whether or not it is my first case, might I remind you that *I* am the senior witch in this investigation? I am the authority here and I direct our investigation." I folded my arms and hoped she couldn't see me biting the inside of my lip.

"Oh, you're so cute! The authority." She snorted. "What are you, twenty?"

"Twenty-one." I aimed for matter-of-fact, but I've long since learned it's impossible to correct someone on your age without sounding defensive. Violet looked as if she wanted to pat me on the head.

"Ah yes," she said, suppressing a smile. "That year makes all the difference."

"It *makes* me a fully-qualified District Witch," I said with as much ice as I could muster. "I graduated from the Academy with the highest marks in my year."

"And I've actually been *doing* the job for three years, sweetheart, so I'm pretty sure I'll be fine. I can tell you right away that sometimes you just have to be a little flexible to get things done. Who cares if I don't wear my hat? Or if I don't fill in every form?"

"But those are the rules. That's just how it works."

She let out a wordless groan of frustration. "The rules are only helpful when they're helpful!"

"The rules stop things from going wrong!" I shouted. Immediately I wished I could take the words back. Violet flinched, and I dug my teeth harder into my lip to anchor it closed. I was pretty sure there was probably a rule about yelling at a fellow District Witch in public. Or maybe there wasn't, because real District Witches didn't need to be told how to behave like adults.

Violet's eyes were soft as she said quietly, "Wilhelmina. Did something go wrong?"

Hearing her say my name properly, in that gentle voice, was what undid me. Before I could even think clearly, I told her everything.

"My first year at the Academy was a disaster. Everything I did went wrong – I exploded potions, I accidentally insulted dignitaries, I broke *four* broomsticks. In the first year exams I was so nervous I turned myself invisible and they thought I hadn't turned up. They threatened to send me home, said I had all the raw talent required but none of the instinct." I sniffed.

"But they gave you another chance?" said Violet.

I nodded. "So I worked harder. I learned it all. By heart. I sat up every night with my books until I'd taught myself everything, not just what they told us." I laughed bitterly. "Every spell, every investigation technique, every *rule*. I just... learned it."

"Wow," said Violet. "That's impressive."

"Those same witches that threatened to kick me out applauded as I graduated top of the class. So I made it work. If I do everything the way it is in the books, I can't fail again." I swiped the tears from my cheeks with my sleeve.

Violet gave me a sad smile. "But they failed *you*, didn't they?"

"What do you mean? I'm fine."

"You're amazing, frankly, if you learned all that, but your teachers were *terrible*. They could have helped you develop that instinct – you think anyone's born just knowing what to do? Instinct is a skill you train like any other. They could have taught you how. They *should* have taught you how." She grabbed my hand; I was too stunned to pull away. "Real life doesn't always play by the rules, so we can't either. Sometimes you just have to improvise, but if it works, if it helps someone who needs it, why *wouldn't* you?"

Her cheeks were flushed and her eyes sparkled. I couldn't look away from her, couldn't force my mouth to make words.

"And when you're helping people, sometimes you might get messy." She cocked her head, considering me with those bright eyes. The air crackled between us like lightning. She leaned in and my heart did a treacherous little swoop, but she only whispered, "I think you could use a little mess."

Quicker than I could react, she snatched my hat and ruffled my hair.

"Hey!" I cried, but she was already dancing away to the other side of the street.

Before I could reach her, a little boy, no more than six or seven, flew out from a side street and nearly collided with Violet. I took advantage of her surprise to snatch my hat back and jam it on my head where it belonged.

"Miss Witch, come quick," panted the boy, tugging at Violet's arm. "You gotta stop the goose!"

"What's wrong with your goose?" she asked.

"S'not *my* goose, miss. It's *hers*. You gotta come stop it." The boy started pulling even harder at Violet's arm. She shrugged at me and let herself be half-led, half-dragged with him.

"Who's *her*?" I asked, jogging to catch up with them.

"The new girl. She showed up last week and so did the big mean goose."

I caught Violet's eye. No one had mentioned a new goose girl to us when we'd asked about newcomers.

"What's your name, kid?" said Violet.

"Conrad, miss. My mama's the henwife."

"Don't worry, Conrad," I said. "What's the goose doing?"

"It's got my mama," he said. "She was just collecting the eggs and it trapped her in. I'm scared, miss. Geese's mean all the time, but this one's big, too."

Right. We were preparing for a fight, then.

The boy led us down a series of back streets at a run, until the elegant squares of townhouses gave way to open streets, with larger buildings that looked like they saw more work.

"You came a long way to get help, Conrad," I puffed. I could feel the sweat dripping down my back.

"Mama said the witches'd know what to do, so I kept asking until I found you," he said. "Here, this way!"

We didn't need telling twice. The air was a cacophony of honks and hisses. As we skidded into the poultry yard, it took me a moment to resolve the churning mass of feathers into individual geese and chickens. The birds were all screaming their fury at one enormous goose, at least twice the size of the others, that was giving as good as it got. It stood on the steps of a large henhouse, wings raised, hissing.

"Conrad, is your mama in there?" asked Violet.

"Yes, miss," he said. "The goose won't let her out."

She crouched down next to him. "Okay. We're going to fix that. Can you do an important job for me? Can you calm down the other birds so we can get to the mean goose?" Her voice was firm but reassuring. That didn't stop me flashing her a look of alarm – I didn't want to get anywhere near that thing – but she winked at me.

"Maybe the chickens? Sometimes they listen when I use my whistle." Conrad didn't sound sure, but he nodded decisively at the end, like he wanted Violet to believe in him.

"Great. You get that magic chicken-whispering whistle, and Wilhelmina and I are gonna help your mama." As he ran off, she stood up and said quietly to me, "Don't you worry either. We only have to get within aiming range, not right up to it. I just wanted him to have something to focus on."

"You're good at this," I said, before I'd realised my mouth was even open. "The people part." I hoped she thought I meant with Conrad, but her practical manner had steadied me too.

She smiled. "It comes with practice. Let's hope we're both good at the goose-subduing part."

I tried to force myself to match her smile, but I'm not sure I managed it. "I never learned anything about geese..."

"Well, here's your crash course in making it up as you go along," she said. "First we need to get a bit closer, so... got anything in the way of crowd control?"

I scanned the yard, desperate for ideas. Conrad's whistle sounded, and some of the flapping and squawking subsided. Violet and I were able to take several steps towards the henhouse.

"That's great, Conrad," called Violet. "Keep it up!"

"Food!" I said, pointing at a bin propped against the henhouse, then jumped back as several geese rounded on me. "Will they stop if we feed them?"

"Now your cauldron's bubbling!" Violet waved her hand, and a stream of what looked like corn flew out of the bin and rained down over the yard. A piece bounced off Violet's nose, making her squeal. "Okay," she said, laughing. "I'll concede the hat has some uses."

Soon the flood of fowl was completely distracted and the only noise left was their contented pecking. The largest goose, however, completely ignored the whole affair. No longer needing to hold its ground against the other birds, it turned to jab its long neck inside the henhouse, hissing, and I heard Conrad's mother yell.

"Oh no you don't." I aimed a holding spell at the goose – the standard kind, where you trace the outline of your target and invisible ropes wrap around it – but it seemed to slide off, and the goose's wings kept flapping. I'd never seen that happen before. I'd taken down full-grown men with that spell in tests. Perhaps I'd simply missed? Or maybe the flapping was interfering with the spell finding somewhere to take?

"Net?" asked Vi. Of course. There was another form of the rope spell, one that allowed witches to weave their spells together into a net that could be dropped on a larger area to trap multiple targets – or in this case, one extremely angry goose. I grabbed her hand and as we spoke the words in unison, I felt the net weave together in the air above the goose.

"Now," I said, and we both let go of the spell. The net dropped. The goose hissed in rage, but found itself pinned to the ground.

The henwife peered out of the doorway. "Is it safe?" She stepped carefully around the goose and braced for Conrad, who flew into her with an audible thud. "There, love, it's all well, now. I told you the witches would know what to do, didn't I?" To us, she said, "Thank you. Good thing I saw you going round the market this morning, or I wouldn't have known who to ask. I know I must seem a fool to need help with a goose, but there's something odd about that one. Been scaring my chickens all week, then today it flew out of nowhere when I started looking for the eggs."

"Geese's mean," mumbled Conrad into his mother's side.

"You were very brave," said Violet to the little boy. "Honestly, we couldn't have done it without you."

Conrad beamed at the praise and began to regale his mother with a dramatic retelling of his part in the rescue. He was adorable, but we couldn't afford to get distracted; I wasn't sure that spell was going to hold the giant goose for long. While Violet laughed, I slipped past her and went to check on the net.

"What are you *doing*?" came a woman's voice, full of horror. "Get away from her." She rushed across the yard and crouched by the thrashing goose.

"I assume you're the new goose girl?" I asked.

"Yes," she bit out. "Take that spell off right *now*."

"But the goose—"

"She won't attack you. She's just frightened."

Oh, that was rich. "Frightened? Not half as frightened as that poor henwife and her child," I said coldly.

Violet came up behind me and put her hand on my shoulder. "Still, no harm done," she said brightly. "How about we take the spell off, and then perhaps we could trouble you for a drink. Hot, isn't it?" I glanced at her, but she widened her eyes at me in a way that I assumed meant, *follow my lead.*

The goose girl's eyes narrowed, but she nodded briskly. "Fine. Just let her up, please."

We released the spell and the goose scrambled to its feet. The goose girl waved us after it as it waddled offendedly towards the larger building, which proved to be the poultry workers' lodgings. We stepped into a comfortable common room – or at least, it would have been comfortable had it not been oppressively stuffy. In fact, it seemed even hotter inside than out. The goose disappeared through a doorway at the back of the room with a honk, leaving the three of us standing awkwardly together.

Back straight and chin high, the goose girl fetched a jug and poured us both a glass of the lemonade that was ubiquitous in Kadina. I sipped it, leaving Violet to open the conversation she so clearly wanted to have.

"So," she said, in the chatty tone that had been charming shopkeepers all morning. "What do you *feed* that goose? It's enormous!"

The goose girl's smile was polite, but it didn't quite reach her eyes. "She's a special kind. Montian. They breed them for size over there."

"I had no idea. I wonder why – I always thought geese were quite big enough!" laughed Violet, gaining another tight smile but no reply.

I thought I'd better attempt to make conversation, in case I was accused of lurking again. "Are you from Montia originally, then?"

"No." She folded her arms, and it was clear no elaboration would be made. I bit my lip; maybe lurking was more my style after all.

Violet pressed on gracefully. "Conrad said you brought her with you when you started working here? Isn't that pretty unusual?"

"She's... something of a pet." An edge came into the goose girl's voice. "Why, is that against some rule? I asked the head poulterer and I pay for her food myself. What happened today was... it's not like her. I assure you it won't happen again."

"Oh, not at all. I'm just interested in birds. My grandmother keeps ducks." Violet started towards the doorway at the back of the room, still chatting away. "In fact, she's thinking of branching out to geese and she *loves* unusual breeds. I'd love to take a closer look at your giant—"

"No!" said the goose girl sharply, before recovering her poise. "I mean, please don't. She needs to rest and I don't think seeing witches again will help." She took my glass and held her hand out for Violet's, giving her no option but to come back, then turned a brilliant, cold smile on us both. "Now, I believe you've finished your drinks, and I wouldn't want to keep you from your important business. I promise I'll apologise to Berta and I'll keep the goose under better control. Was there anything else I could help you with?"

"You've been very helpful, thank you," said Violet as the goose girl herded us to the door. Then she stopped, putting a hand up to her chest in mock surprise. "Oh, where are my manners! I forgot to ask your name."

"Auri." Was it my imagination, or did she hesitate?

"Oh, that's pretty. I'm Vi, and this is Mina."

"It's *Wilhelmina*," I muttered.

"She always says that," chuckled Violet, meeting my glare with a wink. "It's full names or nothing for Miss Wilhelmina here. I'm guessing yours is short for Aurelia? Oh, like the foreign princess!"

Something flashed in the goose girl's eyes. "So what? It's a perfectly common name for girls my age. There are probably a hundred Aurelias just in this quarter of the city."

"Oh, I'm sure," said Violet placatingly. "Sorry, you must get that all the time. It's a nice name, anyway."

"Thank you," said the goose girl, with a tight little smile. "I hope you have a lovely day."

In the face of such perfectly-deployed politeness, there was little we could do but leave. As we stepped out into the sunshine, I braced for the heat to slap into me, but to my surprise, it didn't feel much warmer than it had inside. Perhaps I was finally adjusting to the Varenian weather.

"Well, there's our missing princess," I said.

Violet laughed. "I think you're right. Pretty sure they don't teach goose girls that kind of weaponised politeness." She linked her arm through mine. I briefly considered trying to shrug her off, but it was easier just to start walking. "Told you there was more to witching than following the rules."

I hated to admit it, but she was right. If Conrad's mother hadn't seen us at the market, or if we'd refused to help him because we were busy, we never would have been in that yard to stumble across the princess. And I *was* glad we'd been able to help. The look on that little boy's face as he hugged his mama... that was exactly why I'd wanted to do this job in the first place. "Fine," I said. "I'll concede your methods aren't entirely a waste of time."

"Attagirl," she said, bumping me with her shoulder. "Now we just need to work on your conversation, stop you unwittingly menacing the populace. You're too cute to be this grumpy."

"Thanks, I think." I was surprised to realise that I didn't hate the idea of her teaching me how to be charming. Purely because it was useful, of course; not because I wanted to spend any more time with her than necessary. "But we can work on my flaws later. For now we should head back to the palace and tell the king."

"Whoa, whoa, whoa," said Vi, dragging me to a halt. "I want to do a little more investigating first."

I gaped at her. "What? We're here to find the princess, we found the princess, let's go."

"But don't you want to know what she's hiding? It makes no sense. Why would she run away from her wedding, but stick around in the same city? Why pick such a hard, dirty job when she's almost certainly got more noble accomplishments to trade on? And there's definitely something weird about that goose. The other princess didn't mention anything about it, so it's new – and it's bothering me."

I wanted to tell Violet that it wasn't any of our business, that I was *this* close to finishing the case perfectly. Princess located, returned, and married; well done, Wilhelmina, full marks again. But my conscience pricked at me. Princess Aurelia wasn't a lost necklace or a sheep that had wandered off. Maybe we did need to know her side of things before we acted – and besides, I *was* curious.

"So what do you suggest? That we lie to the king and come back again tomorrow?" I asked sarcastically.

"Of course not. We'll be *circumspect* with the king, and come back again tonight."

* * *

Dinner was excruciating. The king didn't question our vague update, but my chest tightened every time I spoke. The only consolation was that he seemed too preoccupied with Princess Cecilia's witty conversation to notice my stewing. It was a relief when we were finally able to flee to our room.

I didn't mean to fall asleep, but I woke to Violet's hand on my shoulder.

"Let's go," she said. "The guards passed five minutes ago, so we've got a clear path."

I crept after her into the darkened corridor, feeling faintly ridiculous. District Witches didn't sneak out; they might need to disguise themselves for an investigation, but this felt unnecessarily dramatic. Violet was probably enjoying herself greatly.

We made our way down the servants' staircase and into a warren of corridors that smelled as though they were near the kitchen. I followed Violet through a little door out into the night air, and we picked our way through a small herb garden until she suddenly stiffened. Footsteps. Heavy ones. Coming our way.

"Damn," whispered Violet, and pushed me against the wall, pressing her hand over my mouth and her entire body into mine until we were buried in the castle's shadow.

"Mm-ff," I said, trying to ignore the sudden flare of heat rising through me at her closeness.

"Sorry." She dropped her hand. "Listen, you know what I said this afternoon, that sometimes we have to improvise?"

"Ye-es," I said warily. The footsteps sounded closer.

"Okay, good. Sorry about this."

I opened my mouth to ask what exactly she was apologising for, but the words never made it past my lips, because there was a Violet in the way.

Violet was kissing me. Violet. It took me a second to realise what was even happening, because it just didn't make any sense. She was so perfect; why would she be kissing me? She'd probably made a mistake, probably tripped and hit my lips accidentally and she was probably going to stop any moment now—

She stopped.

I tried not to feel my heart sink at being proved right.

She rested her forehead on mine and chuckled softly. "Stop thinking so hard, Willa. I can practically hear you making a list of pros and cons."

Of all the irritating—

I surged forwards and kissed her fiercely. She made a smug little noise of triumph that made me half want to strangle her, but instead I tangled my hands in her beautiful hair like I'd been imagining all afternoon. It's not that I was a stranger to kissing - I'd had girlfriends before - but kissing Violet felt like something else entirely, like drinking slightly too much wine, like running down a hill, like the first upwards swoop of a broomstick flight.

It felt like the moment a spell finally sparks.

I forgot all about princesses and geese and even about the overwhelming heat, until, still laughing a little, she broke the kiss.

"Well," she whispered. "I think that worked."

"Bu... Vi... I..." I raised a hand to my lips and tried not to notice it was shaking.

"Ha, is that all it takes to get you to call me Vi?" Her eyes were sparkling. "If I'd known that I'd have done it long before now."

I spluttered, but she had a point. Me ignoring her nickname was just as rude as her pressing unwanted nicknames on me. "Sorry. I'll call you Vi."

"Oh, please don't," she grinned. "The way you say *Violet* in that disapproving voice has kind of grown on me."

"Well, maybe I didn't hate you calling me Willa." All of a sudden the air felt heavy between us again. I shook my head to clear it. "We need to get going."

"Yes." Neither of us moved for a moment.

"No, come on," I said, wriggling free of her. "Before whoever that was comes back."

"I should think they'll steer clear for a while. Privacy, you know," she said wryly. "It's why it's such a good way to hide. No one questions why two lovers might be sneaking around."

Something in my stomach flipped. Of course. The kiss had just been part of this whole stealth nonsense. Of course it wasn't real. "But why did we need to hide in the first place?" I asked. "We could have just told them we were on official business. It's literally our job to be sneaking around."

Violet blinked. "Oh. Yes. Well, maybe I just wanted an excuse to kiss you."

"You, uh, what?" I said intelligently.

"Was I wrong?" she said, motioning back and forth between us. "There's been something fizzing between us since the moment we met."

"Annoyance! That's annoyance!" But even as I said it, I was smiling. Maybe there had been just a little bit of something more. "Oh, come on. We have a princess to spy on." I grabbed her hand and dragged her out of the garden.

* * *

I'd expected the poultry yard to be quiet, but it seemed geese weren't much for silent slumber; there was a constant exchange of sleepy honks from the gooseshed as we approached the workers' lodgings. Violet murmured a spell and the lock snicked open.

"We're breaking and entering now?" I whispered.

"Unless you can see through walls," came her reply from inside. "Hurry up."

Stepping through the door was like stepping into a furnace. It had been hot as we'd walked through the city, but I'd assumed it was just the stones releasing the day's heat into the night. Now that I thought about it, it had become even hotter the longer we walked. In here, it was almost intolerable.

At the back of the room, where we'd seen the enormous goose disappear that afternoon, the edges of the doorway glowed with a vibrant golden light. Surely no one would have a fire burning in this weather?

"Gotcha," muttered Violet. She strode across the room, barely pausing to whisper the unlocking spell once more. When the door clicked open, she entered the room, but stopped abruptly before I could follow.

"Oh," she said. "That's unexpected."

"What?" I whispered nervously. She didn't reply, just moved slightly so I could squeeze next to her and look for myself.

"Oh," I said.

It was an egg. A very large egg, as tall as my knee and sitting in a nest of twigs and fabric that took up half the storage room. Oh, and it was golden. Not just the light it radiated, which was bright and butter-yellow, but the egg itself looked like it had been wrought from delicate, shining gold.

"I don't think that came out of a goose," said Violet with a shaky little laugh.

"No." My voice wavered too. Even the giant goose we'd been looking for would have struggled to lay an egg that big.

"Do you think it's really gold?" Violet knelt down next to the nest and stretched out a hand. I took a step closer too, fascinated by the egg's glow, but before either of us could touch it, a large white shape shot out of the shadows, hissing in rage.

We leapt back from the nest and took up defensive stances. The goose was a storm of white-feathered fury, jabbing at us until it had pushed us right back against the wall.

"Shh, shh, we were just looking," said Violet in a whisper she probably intended to be soothing, but which set the goose hissing again. To me, she said, "Does it seem bigger to you?"

"Closer up," I gasped as the goose bit my arm.

"No, I mean, does it seem bigger than it is? Like it's taking up more space than it should? Ow, you feathery bas—" She clutched her leg. "There! Did you see its wing hit me? Because I didn't."

She was right. What we could see of the goose's body didn't match its reach. My holding spell had failed earlier too; I'd thought I'd missed, but what if I hadn't, if I'd just miscalculated where its edges were?

"An illusion," I said, racking my brains for a nullifying spell. "Can you hold it off me for a—"

"On it," grinned Violet, stepping towards the nest and swearing colourfully as the goose wheeled on her. The spell poured from my lips in a desperate torrent as the goose's foot came up and left a set of crimson slashes on Violet's forearm. Her yelp made my blood turn cold.

For a moment, nothing happened, and I began to think the spell hadn't taken, that I'd failed again. That Vi had put herself in harm's way for nothing. I shot a panicked freeze spell at the goose and rushed forwards to pull Vi away. We crashed into the wall together, and I buried my face in her shoulder, bracing for the next attack – which didn't come. The goose gave a frustrated growl.

A growl?

I looked up. The goose struggled to lift its feet, snapping its beak at us. The freeze spell had taken; as I watched, it became clear both spells had. The goose began to blur at the edges. Slowly, its feathers darkened to a lustrous amber. Its rounded beak gave way to a wickedly curved one, and its body expanded, webbed feet fading until four heavy, furred paws stood in their place.

"I knew it! It's not a goose!" said Violet.

"No," I breathed. It was definitely not a goose. It was something much, much rarer.

"It's a... Actually, what *is* that?"

"She's a griffin," came a quiet voice from the doorway. The goose girl – the princess – rushed to the beast and knelt in front of it, stroking its tawny head until it stopped growling and nuzzled into her hand. "Hush, Iridia, hush. It's all right, I'm here. I won't let them take your egg."

"We don't want your egg," said Violet indignantly. "We were just looking."

I expected the princess to snap back, but instead she sighed. "Looking for me."

"Yes, Your Highness. Your sister is very worried about you." She didn't deny the title, but I thought it was probably better not to mention the king until we'd worked out what her motivations were. Violet's circumspection was rubbing off on me.

"Oh, poor Ceci," said the princess. "She must be so confused – but I couldn't stay, not when Iridia needed me." She stroked the griffin's head again, and I quietly undid the freeze spell. It didn't seem like we were in any more danger.

"Because of the egg?" Violet looked pale; she was still clutching her arm where the griffin had swiped it.

"Yes." Aurelia sighed. "I should start at the beginning. The Leorn royal family has been raising griffins for centuries. I've always felt a particular bond with them, and I was there the day Iridia hatched twelve years ago. She's my truest friend, and I would never have left the country if I'd known she was laying – alliance or no alliance! I should never have left anyway, should I, my sweet?" She kissed the griffin's forehead. "I should have told that silly old king I was staying with you."

I frowned. "Then why didn't you leave a note?"

"I didn't have time. When Iridia tapped at my window, I was just so happy to see her. I climbed out before I knew it. I thought I'd spend the night with her, then talk to my sister in the morning, but then – well." She gestured at the egg. "Poor girl didn't want to lay without me. She must have flown all that way to find me."

Violet chuckled. "I'm assuming a griffin hatching is not an everyday occurrence."

"No," Aurelia said. "More like... the birth of a royal baby, perhaps. They need to go back to Leorn to be looked after properly, but I had to hide them until they could travel again. I bought an illusion spell in the market and disguised Iridia as a goose, then begged for work until I found this place. Now we're just waiting for the egg to hatch, but it's taking so long. I think something's wrong."

"What do you mean?" I asked. The egg was still casting a sunny glow over us; it certainly looked full of life.

"I've never seen an egg take more than three days to hatch. And they get hot, normally, but not this hot."

"I *thought* it was unusually hot, even for a Varenian summer," said Violet. "Actually, if you don't mind, I'll sit down." She crumpled more than sat, all her usual grace gone.

I dropped to her side instantly, peeling her fingers from her arm and trying not to wince at the blood. "Vi, this is deep. Why didn't you say something sooner?"

"I was interested in the story," she said, with a smile that wasn't quite strong enough to reassure me. "Ooh, can you tear off a bit of your skirt to bandage me up?"

"No, you idiot, I'm going to use an actual bandage." I rummaged in my satchel and held one up. "Honestly. That's so unhygienic."

"S'more romantic." She winked at me, and I was relieved to see some of the colour coming back into her face. "This is pretty good, though."

I was saved from having to respond to that by a cry from the princess.

"The egg!"

I leapt up. The egg was wobbling back and forth erratically. Iridia stepped into the nest and curled around it, holding it steady. We all held our breath as a crack appeared in the top, then another, then... nothing. The egg lay there, glowing but perfectly still.

"Why did it stop?" cried Aurelia. "Iridia, is it all right?"

The griffin nudged it with her beak, then cooed, a softer noise than I'd heard her make yet.

The princess wheeled on me. "What did you do? Why did it only start to hatch now? Whatever you did, you need to do it again."

"We weren't doing anything," said Violet defensively.

"Wait – the blood," I said. It had started to hatch when Violet had stopped holding her arm.

"It needs blood to hatch?" Vi gasped. "That's kind of horrifying."

"Certainly not," said Aurelia. "I've attended several hatchings. There's nothing so violent."

"No." I screwed up my eyes, trying to think. I knew this. My bestiary was a large green book – griffins had been about halfway through, on the left-hand page – diet, territory, breeding... "Salt," I said. "It needs salt."

"Again," said Aurelia, "I've never seen the keepers use salt, or anything for that matter."

"They wouldn't need to. Your castle's at the coast, right?" I waited until she nodded. "So the salt is already in the air. Not like Kadina."

Aurelia's eyes snapped wide with understanding. She rushed out of the room.

"I'll concede your methods aren't entirely a waste of time," said Violet in a prim voice.

"If that's meant to be an impression of me, it's terrible," I said, but I let her slip her arm around my waist. She probably needed to be propped up, anyway.

Aurelia came back with the salt jar and we all took turns sprinkling the nest with salt, making Iridia sneeze. Almost immediately the egg's glow grew so strong I had to shield my eyes, and it began to rock once more.

"It's working!" Aurelia threw her arms around Iridia's neck in joy as the first shard of golden eggshell fell, then the next. The last part fell, the golden light faded, and the little griffin stumbled out on clumsy paws, egg-wet and blinking up at its mother. Already, the room felt cooler.

It was several minutes before any of us spoke, too enthralled by the tiny creature to spoil the moment, but eventually Aurelia cleared her throat. "Thank you," she said, with her eyes full of tears. "I would never have thought to try that."

"I'm glad we were here," I said.

"What will you do now?" asked Violet.

"I need to wait for the little one to be strong enough to travel back to Leorn – oh, but I can't stay here," Aurelia said. "The spell's gone. Unless you can put it back on?"

"I don't think that will be necessary," said a deep voice, and we all turned in shock to see King Marco step into the room. He laughed softly. "My apologies. I didn't mean to startle you.

Princess Aurelia, I am delighted to find you safe, as is your sister."

"Auri!" There was a rush of movement and suddenly Princess Cecilia was hugging her sister. "I was so worried!"

"Ceci, I'm so sorry. I had to—"

"Yes, I can see that! Hello, Iridia, nice chick," said the princess conversationally to the griffin, who acknowledged her with a long blink.

"But how did you find me?"

The king smiled. "Ah, for that you'll need to thank these two."

"But we didn't tell anyone where we were going," I said.

"No, but a guard informed me she saw you..." He quirked his lips. "Acting strangely, shall we say. She alerted me that you were attempting to leave the palace in some secrecy, so I decided to follow you. Might I suggest that if you're going to try to hide your identities in future, you don't wear your uniforms?"

I felt my cheeks heat.

Vi just laughed, and whispered in my ear, "I can't believe I got told off for wearing *too much* uniform," which made me bite my lip even harder.

"As I was saying," said the king to Aurelia. "There's no need for you to hide away here. I'm sure we can accommodate your companions at the palace until they're strong enough to return home."

Aurelia took a deep breath. "That's very generous of you, Your Majesty, but I've realised I can't marry you. I am deeply sorry, but I can't - I can't do it, I can't live away from the griffins. It's not just Iridia, it's all of them. They're my whole life. I have to return to Leorn."

"I see." Was it my imagination, or was the king repressing a smile?

"Oh, Auri, I was hoping you'd say that!" beamed Princess Cecilia.

"You... were?" Aurelia looked as confused as I felt.

"Yes. I know you were prepared to do your duty, but you'd be so miserable if you had to live here, even if Iridia stayed too. And, well, you've been gone a week and I've been spending a lot of time with the king pretending to be you..." She glanced at the king and swallowed hard. "And I would be happy to take your place."

"I thought you said princesses *weren't* interchangeable?" Violet asked the king saucily.

"Indeed they aren't," he agreed. "Which is why I believe Cecilia and I will suit quite nicely."

"Is that a blush I spy, Your Majesty?" said Violet, before I elbowed her.

"Perhaps," he said gravely, but his eyes betrayed his amusement. "Now, Princess Aurelia, if that arrangement works for you, might I suggest we all return to the palace and get some sleep? Some of us are getting married in a few days and need to look our best."

* * *

We made a strange procession on the way back to the palace: three royals, two griffins, and a pair of District Witches bringing up the rear. The streets were much cooler already, and there was a whisper of a breeze in the air that I had not felt in days.

Violet's arm being linked through mine was starting to feel worryingly natural. I told myself again it was just to keep her steady, though she'd recovered all her colour. But it was nice to feel her hip bump mine as we walked.

"We make a good team, huh?" she asked quietly, once we were alone, climbing the stairs to our room. "Not just one, but two happy princesses. And I never thought I'd see a griffin hatching."

I smiled. "If I had to work with someone, I suppose you weren't the worst."

"Oh, I'm going to show up to all your cases from now on," she said wickedly. "Just try and stop me."

"You are *not*," I said. "I'm going to have to write this one up as partnered as it is. You owe me a solo case."

"Fine. You can do the next one solo."

"Very generous of you," I said.

"I'll just lurk behind you with my arms folded, not helping."

At that I had to laugh. We reached the top of the stairs, and I stopped to look at her.

"Would you really want to work with me again?" Surely she was kidding.

She smiled softly. "Willa, why wouldn't I? You're smart, you're obviously talented, you're quick in a crisis, and you're adorable. You just need to loosen up a little, and you'll be almost as good a witch as me."

"*Almost?*" I squeaked. "May I remind you I was the top witch—"

She silenced me with a quick kiss. "See, we'll just have to work together again to decide who's better. But first, we need to get some sleep. And you're *not* wearing the hat to bed." She snatched the offending item from my head and ran down the corridor.

I only waited a moment before I gave chase.

Adie Hart is a lover of stories and the words behind them. With a background in the history and literature of the Ancient World, and an abiding love of classic fairy tales, she writes everything from fun fantasy adventures to dark mythological retellings.

When she's not writing, she can usually be found reading, gardening, or trapped under her large cat!

The Forest at the End of the World

Josie Jaffrey

In the middle of the forest at the end of the world, there's a boneyard where old things go to die. Creatures collect under its trees in piles of bone and sinew, each one the last of its kind. They walk their final steps into the shade to lay themselves down amongst skeletons of animals so odd and forgotten that nothing now living would recognise their form. They're relics, memorials, repositories of the past waiting to be rediscovered. That is the fate of all living things. When we are distilled beyond the point of worthlessness, rendered obsolete, the forest will be waiting for us too, bony arms outstretched.

But that isn't the folklore Zuri knows. The story her father tells goes like this:

In the beginning, there was a fire in the forest at the end of the world. Before the fire, the forest was empty. There were trees, and plants, and rain, and earth, but nothing with a heartbeat or a conscience or a soul. When the fire came, it burned itself into the world and left seeds of itself behind, little sparks of consciousness that woke and grew and spun themselves into something new.

That's where we come from, Zuri, he would say. We all came from the fire, and one day we'll go back to it too and be reborn.

Zuri knows this is true, because it's happening now.

* * *

In the middle of the great continent, fire is falling from the sky. From the ground, it seems almost as though the clouds are combusting and breaking away from each other, like flaming chunks of cotton wool igniting in the hot air. They fall hard and far, not stopping when they reach the ground but instead burning straight through the earth and into the rock beneath, on and on, turning underground rivers into steam as they blaze their way toward the mantle, seeking common heat. If you could get close enough to them, you'd see the spots where the fire falls become craters filled with lava that bubbles up from under the surface. But nothing can get that close; the falling flames are so hot that they eat the air for miles around as they descend, ripping moisture and oxygen from it as they strip all vegetation from the landscape. Any creature that sees the impact is conscious of little more than a distant brightness before the searing wave takes them.

From beyond the next valley, so far away that the view is lost over the horizon, Kade watches the smoke and steam rise. He sought this vantage point in the hope of running, but in what direction? He can look to all four points of the compass and see something that worries him. To the north, east and west, smoke turns the skies dark. To the distant south, past the rolling hills and valleys, the salt pans reflect so much sunlight that it threatens to blind him, and beyond them the desert waits. Surrounded by so much heat, there is no good option.

"South," says Ama, his wife and the mother of their child. Zuri is just three years old and too small to climb up here on her own; for the moment, she has been left behind in the care of their township in the valley below. Her parents don't want her to see their worry and despair, though she will see far worse before this is through. With forty residents in the township and food enough for only a week more, she has seen worse already as they have been forced to cut and cut. They were once more than two hundred.

Kade knows they must move now, even if he cannot see what lies beyond the smoke. He doesn't want to. He is attached to his home, though it is not what it once was. The river has dried to a trickle, the crops turned yellow and brittle, and the animals so emaciated that they have long since been butchered for their meat. But there are other colours in the township beyond the sepia tones of endless summer, like the walls of the house he whitewashed with his brother and the blue glass monument that marks his father's grave, the spot where they burned his body to ashes and turned them in the earth. The trees might be dying and the ground reduced to nothing but baked clay, but he loves it still, loves it so much that he has never imagined he might end up be elsewhere. The thought of leaving it behind cuts deep, as though he's excising a piece of his soul to cut the bond between himself and his past. To him, they are the same thing. He might as well cut himself in two.

And yet.

The animals have been moving south for days, fleeing through the valley on their way to a promised land that may not exist. The animals move because there is nothing left to eat where they are, because the ground is cracked and empty, not because they think there will be more elsewhere. Kade knows this and takes no comfort from it. Why move at all if there is nothing better over the horizon? Why not stay in their homes and die in their own lands?

He doesn't have to put these questions to Ama, because he has done so enough times over the past two days that a look is all it takes for her to know his mind. She is more practical than he is, more resolute, more energetic. She will keep walking until she can only crawl, then crawl until she can only pull herself along the ground, will only stop moving when she is dead if that is what it takes to win even the chance of a future for their daughter. Kade is not like Ama. After years of praying and striving, only for the land that he lavished with attention to fail him, he is tired. He would lie down right here and wait for the end if only she would let him.

"South," she says again, and that is the end of the discussion.

The township packs up quickly; there isn't much left to take away. Each family carries their own ration to spread the load and the risk of loss. They each carry their share of grief too: the loss of their homes, the futures they had hoped for, and the family members that have been left behind. Not everyone is fit enough to make the trip. Ama's mother is amongst that number, a woman as determined and merciless as Ama herself. With few years left ahead of her, she insists that she will slow them down, and she isn't wrong. She walks with a stick when she walks at all, which is rarely these days. They leave her in their house with a small store of food, a stack of books, their love and their memories. Ama cries, but only until Zuri comes to say her own goodbyes. Then her tears are wiped away to reveal a smile so genuine that it is hard to spot the force behind it. Kade does, though. He always can with his wife. This is how he knows her strength, by the way she smiles through her pain for the sake of their daughter.

"I'll see you soon," Zuri's grandmother promises, showering the little girl with kisses. "After your trip, we'll be together again."

The words might hold more truth than the old matriarch would wish.

The rain starts the moment they reach the top of the fell overlooking the valley, and it feels like an omen.

* * *

It rains through the night. The caravan planned to travel in darkness so they could sleep through the scorching days in whatever shade they could find, but the downpour makes the ground sticky and slippery at first, then turns well-worn hill paths into torrents that force them into the spiky undergrowth crowding on either side. It's impossible to navigate, impossible to find a footing as the moon hides behind the storm clouds, so they shelter under the drought-stripped trees as best they can and try to sleep. When they wake in the morning, all trace of the rain is gone, but so are two of their number, along with their packs. Whether they continued in the night without stopping – either unwilling to stick with the others or unconscious of their decision – or whether they were carried away by the storm, no one knows. The wandering township now numbers only thirty-two.

Worse, despite the heavy rain, there is no water to be found. The lakes they pass on their way to the salt pans remain stagnant and almost empty, the streams still dry, and not a single puddle remains on the ground. The cracks in the earth start to steam as the sun hits them, burning and softening the feet of those without shoes until they are forced to stop and fashion some from their clothing or risk laming themselves with blisters. The rest of the caravan waits for them this time, but they know that sooner or later they will leave more people behind. When the group finally moves off, the smoke coming from the north chases them on their way.

Despite the rain, the fires still rage behind them. That scares Kade; there must be something supernatural about a fire that can't be quenched by a storm so strong.

"Tell me a story," Zuri says as he carries the shoeless girl on his shoulders.

"I can't think of any." After a sleepless night and a meagre breakfast of dried meat and fruit, Kade feels barely strong enough to keep the child aloft. He wishes he could pass her to her mother, just for a little while, but Ama is at the front of the line directing their route.

"So tell me an old story."

He thinks of the burning at the end of the world, then, and wonders if this is it. But that won't do at all. He scrambles for a different tale.

"Tell me the one about the founding," Zuri suggests.

She is asking him to break his heart open. Since leaving the valley, he has gathered the memories of his home in close and locked them away for a day when they are less raw, less urgent. He spent the night trying not to imagine the deluge bringing the roof of the house he built down onto his mother-in-law's head, trying not to picture his last stringy crops washed away with the bones of their last goat, his father's glass grave marker toppled in the mud.

He pulls it all inside and seals it shut.

"Why don't you tell me a story instead?"

The little girl hums in thought, then jumps as the air cracks with thunder. The wanderers look up, hunching their shoulders to keep their heads low. Dark storm clouds are gathered above them, but there is no more rain. It feels too hot for it, as though the water would evaporate before reaching the ground. Kade slides Zuri down from his shoulders just as the first lightning bolt forks across the sky and grounds itself on a withered tree to their right.

Like all the vegetation around them, it isn't a large tree. Not big at all. Not much taller than the height of his little girl on his shoulders.

That's when Ama calls another halt. They have no choice but to crouch in the scant cover of the brush and wait for the lightning to pass.

* * *

The storm goes on too long, for days. Summer storms in the township are usually brief affairs, cathartic breaks in the sky that douse the land with water and quench the heat. This one is different, and they can all feel it. It's not natural for weather to hang in one place for so long, cracking above their heads, strobing light across the cloud-shaded landscape, circling them like a starving dog circles a lame deer.

When the rain finally comes, it does so meanly, in short showers of miserly drops that barely wash the dust from their skin. Hours of frantic labour with bowls and oilskins net them four litres of water. It's only a fraction of what the delay has cost them from their stores, and even the most optimistic amongst their number knows it won't be enough to get them all safely down the hills to the border township that waits on the edge of the desert. There are wells there. Those sunken stores have been the hope that burned in all their chests as they made this hopeless march out of their valley, that have sustained them through the blazing days and torrential nights. The rain might not settle in this cracked-clay, hilly region that was once their forested paradise, but all that water has to collect somewhere, doesn't it?

Kade is starting to question even that. The land and skies he once knew have turned on him, and their trust is broken. It bewilders him to see the familiar turned foreign, the reliable turned unpredictable. He is used to the gentle vagaries of nature, but this? Fire falling from the skies while rain steams up from the ground? There is nothing natural about this.

Ama leaves the group of matriarchs and seeks him out. She has been doing this sometimes, rarely, when she needs comfort more than advice. To Kade, it's just another sign that things are terribly, terribly wrong. He knows this before she speaks a word, by the silence in which they sit side by side, watching their daughter pick through the spongy dirt to find treasures of glass and wire. Usually Ama would stop her, afraid she might break her skin on the sharp points, but now they simply watch as lightning reflects off dangerous remnants of the world that came before them.

The reminder is bleak.

Ama's words, when they finally come, are bleaker still.

"Only half of us will make it to the desert. At best."

"At best?" Kade glances at Zuri as he speaks, but their voices are low and the girl is absorbed in her digging. She hasn't heard, he is sure.

"At worst, maybe ten of us. Maybe five. Maybe none. Either we brave the storm or we huddle here and die of thirst."

Kade looks out at the path. It winds down and then up again, down and up, tracing the undulations of the diminishing valleys on the way to the salt pans. He expected that portion of the journey to be the difficult one, the dry march into the desert, not this faded green portion so close to home. It's only now that he can see the danger. As the height of the hills decreases, so does the height of the vegetation. The wanderers might be safe to walk for the moment, if they crouch, but very soon they'll be too exposed to hope that anything more than prayers might save them from the lightning. There are already fires burning around them from the strikes, and all the while more and more smoke drifts down from the north.

"We're moving, then?" He tries to keep the tremor from his voice.

"Some of us."

They put it to a vote in the end, those who wished to press on to the border township against those who would rather wait here for the storm to pass. At least, those were the choices presented, though it was clear to everyone that the latter was a death sentence.

The vote was not truly calling for opinions. It was calling for volunteers.

Those left behind knew this when they raised their hands. They knew this when they surveyed their wrecked feet, their stiffening joints, or their tired lungs. They knew this when they paired their farewells with bundles of food and water, promising they had plenty for themselves while leaving their own packs empty. The spirit of the township they had built together was strong. They wouldn't see it die with them.

Kade feels the weight of their trust as he walks away with just ten others, hand in hand with his daughter.

His feet are cracked and blistered. His joints are agony. His lungs rattle wetly with every breath.

He keeps walking not because he is strong, but because he is too weak to admit that, sooner or later, he will slow the others down.

* * *

Through the morning haze, with the desert behind it, the border township looks like a mirage. It's circled with high mud walls, but the many buildings inside poke above the edge, promising the kind of comfort the travellers haven't experienced since abandoning their homes weeks ago. The sight and smell of cooking fires draws them on.

They've left the storm behind them, but it has not been an easy journey. Their backs feel permanently damaged from holding their bodies bent below the height of their surroundings. Kade has been shaking so much that he couldn't carry Zuri, did not even dare to hold her hand in case he was struck and passed the charge into her tiny frame, so the days have been filled with her cries and complaints. She's too small to understand that he loves her too much to hold her close.

She's quiet now, though. They all have been since they lost their leaders.

The two women were walking at the front of the line, blazing the trail through the increasingly featureless landscape – no trees, no bushes, just salt beneath their feet – when the lightning struck. It had been striking all morning, a mile away, two miles away, but this time it zeroed in on the women's heads as though it had been directed there. They were dead before they hit the ground.

Ama, previously only a member of the council, now leads

the ragged remains of their township: their family of three, two teenaged brothers, a young couple, a middle-aged man and one last matriarch. Nine altogether.

They would have fallen to pieces without her. She was the one who knelt before the singed bodies and tried to revive them, who pulled their cloaks over their faces and stripped the ceremonial beads from their hair. Metal. Perhaps they should have thought about those earlier, the clicking relics of the past that marked their office, but also drew the lightning to them. That's what Ama said when the brothers began babbling about fate and god and the hopelessness of continuing. She offered them science, kept them walking, kept them focussed, and stopped them from panicking.

Even now, approaching the border township beyond the salt pans without knowing what might lie within, she has a calm about her that Kade can't replicate. He's tried it before while soothing Zuri, but he just can't lull her the same way. It's magical, the way Ama channels her serenity out to others and takes their anxiety into herself. Kade is the only one who sees beneath the surface, sees her own insecurity and pain. She makes sure of that. To everyone else, Ama is invincible.

Even now, as the arrows fall.

They are unfletched, unworked, just dry twigs tipped with sharp things dug from the ground. They don't fly true, so it's more by volume than by skill that they hit their marks.

"Back," Ama orders, her voice loud but flat.

It's too late for the matriarch and the young couple. They lie in a field of arrow shafts, unmoving. To Zuri, it looks as though their bodies have sprouted growth, as though they are turning into trees in front of her eyes and might lift their branches from the ground at any moment to send out shining bright leaves. Her father has told her stories about the cycle of life, about green things springing from the earth, about the verdant forests of his youth. She wants to see the magic for herself, but he holds her back.

One of the boys has a cut on his leg. It's bleeding, but it doesn't look deep. A graze, nothing more. The flies will find it soon though, even as quickly as the blood will dry in this heat, so he wraps it tight.

Kade is the only one who realises there has been another injury. His eyes always go to Ama when things go wrong, as though the mere sight of her face will soothe him, so he saw the slight jerk, the falter in her step as she backed away from the border township. She keeps watching its walls now, putting herself between them and her family like a shield. Kade can see her elbows working as she worries at something by her hip. A drop of blood spatters to the ground, then a twig broken into several pieces follows it. Throughout it all, she keeps her back turned to her people.

Six now.

They are too distracted to notice, but Kade has seen and can't pretend otherwise. When Ama finally turns, their eyes lock for a second before his gaze drops to the blood on her hands. With fierce eyes and a tiny shake of the head she makes her will known: he will say nothing.

Nothing at all.

* * *

The stragglers sleep on the salt through the heat of the day in whatever shade they can create, then at nightfall they return to the border township. Ama directs their path, leading them in a route that is beyond bow range. They never get close enough to find out whether there's water in the wells or food within the walls. The bodies of their fellows are gone though, which feels like answer enough to the second question.

They move on: Ama, Zuri, the brothers and Kade. The other man wandered away while they slept, leaving his pack behind. Those remaining didn't bother looking for him – if he had been within two miles of them, they would have been able to see him on the shining plain that surrounded their campsite.

Sending out searches would have been a waste of time and resources, so instead they took his supplies for themselves and followed Ama into the unknown.

And to them, the desert really is unknown. They don't know anything of this place. It's only now that they are discovering that it's not really a desert at all; the ground looks like sand but feels like rock. Occasionally, back in Kade's younger days, someone from their township might have ventured as far as the border looking for trade or adventure. That hasn't happened for decades now. People stopped coming back from those trips, and Kade suspects their recent encounter might explain why. Zuri keeps asking him where they're going, but he has no answers for her. He's too scared to ask Ama what waypoint she's fixing on in the distance, because in this clouded moonlight he can't imagine that she would have an answer for him either. There seems to be nothing ahead of them except the dark, the rustle of the dirt and the steely conviction of their leader.

They don't stop for comfort breaks because they can't afford the time. Instead, those who need to empty their bladders – a rare enough occurrence when they are all so dehydrated – simply step off the path and catch up afterwards. Zuri needs breaks more often than the rest. It's not just that she's small and doesn't have their endurance, it's also that Kade has been giving her more than her ration by sacrificing his own. He's so thirsty that he's dizzy with it. In these circumstances, it was perhaps inevitable that they would get separated from the others.

Kade doesn't understand it.

He had his eyes on Ama and the brothers. They were walking all together when he split off with Zuri, clumped together as though for safety, too tired for conversation and too scared for songs. One moment he'd been watching Ama's back, her pale hair cascading down her shoulders and clearly visibly despite the darkness, and the next she seemed to blink out of existence, as though she'd never been there in the first place.

Kade gathers Zuri into his arms and runs around frantically, unable to remember in which direction the travellers had been moving. He squints into the dark, scans the ground for tracks, even appeals to Zuri's younger eyes, but there is no trace of the rest of their party and, worse, he has let himself become disorientated in his panic.

He breathes. He must calm himself. He must put them back on the right path.

"It's okay, Zu," he murmurs softly into her ear. "I'll work out which way they went and we'll catch up in no time."

Unfortunately, that's easier said than done. He thinks of the fires, the only feature by which he might navigate in the clouded night, but to no avail. Up until now they have managed to keep the smoke at their backs, but suddenly it seems to surround them. It's so pervasive that every direction in which he turns could be north. He wastes his energy walking and sniffing, running and scanning, straining his ears for the slightest noise.

Nothing moves. No one calls for them and his own calls go unanswered.

Kade has no choice but to wrap his daughter in his arms and wait until morning.

The smoke makes sense, then. Kade can no longer see the border township. Instead, there is smoke engulfing the horizon where it once stood. It's so thick even here, miles from the place, that the sunlight is hazy and the ash burns his eyes. The phlegm he coughs up is black and red. Using a small measure of their precious water, he wets a rag and ties it over Zuri's mouth and nose. The moisture will bake away quickly, but hopefully not more quickly than he can get them out of the worst of it.

Putting the sun on his left, he cradles the girl to his chest and runs.

* * *

The conditions get better over the next week, but not by much. Less smoky, more desperate.

And still there is no sign of the others.

Their supplies are low, very low, and Kade is fading faster than he realises. The walking feels easier because the weight on his back is lighter, but that's only because they have so little left. They got lucky after the separation, stumbling across a large pack that someone had dropped in the middle of nowhere, filled with water and food. There was a marker flag in the ground next to it, a red bandanna tied to a stick, so Kade assumes it was a stash for someone who never made it this far. Their loss was Zuri's gain.

But water doesn't last long out here and Kade knows they'll never get so lucky again. He's long since given up on any hope of wells or springs; the ground is dry and unyielding beneath their feet. The clumps of grass they see now are more bone-coloured than yellow, as though the pigment has been leeched and bleached from them, leaving just husks in their wake. Kade feels the same way, though he is far from pale: his skin is a mottled pattern of tan and red that peels and bleeds. It's all he can do to keep Zuri wrapped up and safe from the sun, so there's little fabric left to shield his own hide.

But he can handle the pain. It is more important that he is sparing with everything. He knows that what they have now is all they will ever get until the end, however that comes.

He wonders about that more and more. They came out here because they were running away from something, not towards something. They have no destination. As far as Kade knows, there is nothing waiting for them at the end of the plain. The only reason to carry on in this direction is that he believes his wife will be doing the same. If it were up to him, he would already have stopped. He would stop here right now, but what would he do with Zuri? He couldn't just sit and watch her die of thirst and starvation. The kindest thing would be to kill her and himself, but that would require positive action, and he isn't brave enough for that. He can't make that decision. It's too hard.

But he's so tired.

A desperate hope keeps him going: they will be reunited with Ama, she will have a plan, and she will save them all. Just like she always does.

In the end, they find her by following the carrion birds. It is less of a surprise than Kade expects. He knew she had been bleeding when he'd last seen her, trying to hide her limp. The only real surprise is that she made it this far.

"Mama?" Zuri says.

They're still fifty metres away, but Kade knows the bundle on the ground is his wife. He can see the teal of her skirt beneath the mud, the blonde of her hair beneath the blood, the curve of her cheek beneath the crow's claws.

Kade walks on, cradling the child in his ever-weakening arms.

"Is that Mama?"

"No," Kade says, and it doesn't feel like a lie.

Ama wasn't the body behind them. Ama was the spirit that is filling him now, pouring strength into his weak and lazy limbs. He will keep walking until he can only crawl, then crawl until he can only pull himself along the ground, will only stop moving when he is dead if that is what it takes to win even the chance of a future for their daughter.

Because that is what Ama would have done.

* * *

It takes three more days.

Kade has given up on a regular sleeping schedule. Instead, he walks when he can and sleeps when he can't. He carries Zuri constantly, because she is tired and he is desperate to rebuild her strength. She has to be able to walk on her own. Soon she will have no choice.

Eventually, he spots a feature ahead on the unbroken flat of the plain. That's the direction in which he crawls when he can no longer walk, with little Zuri riding on his back. By the time he can no longer crawl, the feature is clear enough that he can see, unbelievably, that it is a forest, not more than a mile away. He is so close.

It's come too late for him, he knows, but they are not the only ones heading for the trees. He can see movement in the distance, animals and maybe people too, all making their way towards sustenance and safety.

But not him.

"Do you remember the forest at the end of the world?" His voice breaks into croaks and whispers.

"No," Zuri says, but Kade knows she just wants to hear the story again, one last time, so he tells it as he ties their last supplies into a bundle and slips them over Zuri's shoulders.

"In the beginning, there was a fire in the forest at the end of the world. The fire made all the living creatures that exist, our flame from its flame. We're all born from the fire, and one day we'll all go back to it and be reborn."

"Is that the forest?" The little girl's eyes are opened wide and fixed on his.

"Maybe." He can feel his lips cracking as he smiles. "You could go and explore it. Find out whether it's true or not. Then, when you're older, you could come back and tell me. Okay?"

"You'll wait here?" she asks, uncertain.

"I'm not going anywhere. Promise."

Satisfied, she takes her pack and strides away with steps that are too big for her stature. Long after she has disappeared into the woods and out of sight, Kade feels the splash of raindrops on his skin. He turns onto his back and lets them fall into his mouth. His lips taste of blood.

In the distance, thunder rumbles. One second passes – he counts it – before lightning forks down onto the highest tree in the forest at the end of the world. It passes fire among the tinder-dry branches, engulfing everything in slow and painful minutes.

Lightning strikes again, hurrying the flames. In the negative that is burned onto the inside of his eyelids, Kade sees the phoenix in the shape of its fork. He sees the raised head, the feathered wings, the triumphant resurrection of bones from the ashes, and in the spread of its light he feels that this is not the end.

This is just the beginning, again.

Josie Jaffrey is a fantasy and historical fiction author who writes about lost worlds, dystopian societies and paranormal monsters (vampires are her favourite). She has ten novels published so far, along with lots of short stories. Most of those are set in the Silverse, an apocalyptic world filled with vampires and zombies. She's currently working on vampire murder mysteries (the Seekers series) and a YA series about the lost civilisations of the Mediterranean (the Deluge series). Researching the latter is the first time she's used her Classics degree since university.

Josie lives in Oxford with her husband and two cats (Sparky and Gussie), who graciously permit human cohabitation in return for regular feeding and cuddles. The resulting cat fluff makes it difficult for Josie to wear black, which is largely why she gave up being a goth. Although the cats are definitely worth it, she still misses her old wardrobe.

It is Written

S. Markem

"Bumbulum mauris"
— Marcus Aurelius Antoninus.

Once upon a time, in a world before speculative fiction, there lived a wizard called Blagre.

He was, without doubt, an archetypal wizard. So stereotypical, in fact, we can save a bit of time - and my word count - if you just ‹*insert favourite wizardly tropes here*›.

The only thing that set him apart from all the other wizards was his unshakeable belief he was a work of fiction - and therefore, so was everyone else. I know, ludicrous, right?

On a particularly ***summery*** day, right in the middle of ***summer,*** we find him in his solar, books strewn everywhere and a collection of enormous, hand-drawn maps pinned to the walls. His faithful friend and chief administrator, Bill the Gnome, joins him - let's begin the tale from there, shall we?

"I say, Blagre," said Bill, tugging at his long beard. "That's quite an impressive set of maps. What are they?"

The wizard cleared his throat and stroked his equally long greying beard. "They are maps outlining some of my earlier adventures. I am designing a computer game based on my experiences."

"Very interesting, although might I ask what a 'computer' is?"

"I'd love to tell you, Bill, but I don't know. They haven't been invented yet. However, it is the early bird that catches the worm – no harm in being prepared."

Bill shrugged. "Is this what you summoned me for? Maps and feeble jokes?"

"Oh no. No, no, no, no, no – deary me, no. I called you about something *much* more important altogether.

"I'm all ears," said Bill, stifling a yawn.

The wizard became quite animated and began pacing the room, occasionally hopping as the mood took him. "You see, Bill, I had a dream. A vision you might say. Very worrying stuff, what, what. And in that dream, our *author* spoke to me and..."

Bill, like everyone else, was used to humouring the wizard, but today he wasn't in the mood. "Oh, not this nonsense again. I have important paperwork to attend to and the plumbing won't sort itself out, so if you'll excuse..."

"I am *most* serious, Bill," said Blagre in his *most* super-super-serious voice. "This is an *existential* crisis, no less."

"Oh, very well, out with it then. Although, how come he is *our* author? Perhaps I have an author of my own? Have you ever considered that?"

"That *would* be ridiculous, Bill. You are clearly a supporting character. Now, stop interrupting me. I was telling you about my dream. I have been told we are soon to appear in an anthology. A collection of fairy tales. The theme is, 'Summer' – and yes, I know that's a pretty feeble premise, but I had no say in the matter. And it's not even the correct spelling of faerie, I might add."

"So?"

"So? *So?* Why, it will be an unmitigated disaster as far as I'm concerned. For one thing, summer is the off-season for adventures – I had a fishing trip planned. But what's worse is, I am fresh out of faerie tale material. There's nothing going on. I vanquished the Dark Lord (again) only recently, and I was already scraping the barrel with that one."

"Oh, I see."

"I don't think you do, Bill. I am facing either the existential threat of not making the editorial cut, or worse, I may end up in a boring story. It's an anthology, Bill! Goodness knows what other stories I may be slotted between. This could be the end of me, one way or the other."

Bill popped himself onto a nearby stool, smiled his most reassuring smile and took off his pointy red hat. "Now, now, don't take on so. I'm sure there must be something suitable for a bit of questing. What about Smug the Dragon? He's a royal pain-in-the-posterior by all accounts."

"Too late. He was bested by Sir Betonix only last week. His is now little more than an amusing house pet."

"All right then, what about the Nameless Ones? They're jolly evil and usually good for a bit of faerie tale nonsense."

"Alas, they have retreated to the nameless dimension from whence they came, and vowed never to return unless I let them win next time. They're the first ones I thought of."

Bill scratched his forehead. Then he chewed his lower lip. Then he said, "I know, what about the ancient evil that haunts the Dark Wood of Dundee? No one has dared to take it on yet, as far as I know. That'd make a great yarn – epic stuff."

Blagre threw his hands in the air, "Good grief, Bill, no, no, no, *no*. For one thing it's too far away – at least a dozen paragraphs – this is a *short* story. And it's also in Scotland – I'm not *that* desperate."

"I think you may be right then – literary suicide awaits. Shall I make some tea while we wait?"

Frustrated, Blagre kicked a nearby scroll in the direction of Bill. "You refuse to take this seriously, as usual. Well, we shall have to go and ask someone else. Someone with greater knowledge of these things than you or I. And we better be quick about it. We're nearly three pages in already!

***

One hop, skip and jump later...

"Alas, Master Blagre, I cannot help thee – I draweth only blanks."

Paltrow the Elf – beautiful-but-not-that-hot-for-an-elf, twirled her blonde hair around her finger and then stuck it in her mouth – her hair, that is, not her finger.

"But... but... but," exclaimed the wizard, "you're an elf for goodness' sake. You're over a thousand years old. You are from the race of beings first awakened on this earth. You are the composer of hundreds of epic poems about all sorts of fantastical this-and-that. You must have *some* ideas?"

"Sadly, no, dearest wizard. My poems – I simply madeth them up! The product of an over-active imagination. I spent nigh on nine hundred and ninety years stucketh at home. Thou might say, I hath led a sheltered existence. I am afraid thou art wasting thy time here – and thy word count."

The wizard looked forlorn. "Gak, if we can't even rely on elvish clichés, what *are* we to do Bill? Time is short, and this pointless diversion didn't even have a decent gag in it. I feel dark clouds gathering around me." The wizard fell to his knees, a tear forming in his eye.

"Well, whatever we do next, let's keep the melodrama to a minimum, shall we? Nobody enjoys over-acting."

"Perhaps thou might composeth an epic poem?" said Paltrow.

"What? And practically *guarantee* that no one will read it? I think not."

Bill thought for a moment, and then said, "Who is the most adventurous person we know? Because what we *really* need is a loveable rogue – the kind of chap for whom danger and adventure always comes their way. You know the type – it's been done to death, after all."

"Brilliant, yes! That's *exactly* what we need – and we know the very man, don't we?"

"Ahem, yes. Was I being too subtle?"

***

Later that afternoon...

"Oh, come on, Art, please?" The wizard was kneeling on the floor, literally begging.

"I'm sorry, Blagre," said the handsome figure, twiddling his bushy black moustache. "I'd love to help you but I'm on a break, you see. My innate good luck is at an all-time low, and everyone knows the best adventurers – or certainly those still alive - are defined by how lucky they are. I'd be no help to you."

Art L'Wart was not a man of great stature, but, as is so often then case, he made up for this with bags of charisma – and sarcasm – and a big moustache – but mostly charisma. He was an accomplished thief, a devil with a sword, and a seasoned adventuring pro – *exactly* what Blagre needed, in fact.

"But Art," the wizard continued, "you are *exactly* what I need. I suspect the narrative has already made that clear. Why, you only have to spend ten minutes in a pub and adventure falls into your lap. It is a rare gift! You are the very genesis of almost all great literature."

"That's as maybe, but *'no luck is bad luck'*, as we say. Until I feel lucky again, I'm sticking to familiar territory e.g., the pub. I'm on my way there now and you are most welcome to..."

"Wait, that's it," cried Blagre. "I *knew* you'd be an inspiration."

"Glad I could help," said Art, somewhat confused.

"Yes, yes, why didn't I think of it before? Familiar territory."

"I fail to understand?" said Bill.

"It's so obvious to me now. We are appearing in an anthology, are we not?"

"If you say so."

"And what is an anthology? I'll tell you: a collection of random stuff read by random people – and the only copies sold will be to family and friends."

"True, true, that is the destiny for most anthologies – that, or stocking fillers."

"Precisely," said Blagre, rubbing his hands together. "Which means, the chances of anyone having read anything I've been in *before* are infinitesimally small."

"Let's face facts," said Art, "they were pretty small anyway."

"Therefore," the wizard continued, ignoring Art's remark, "that means we don't have to find a *new* adventure at all! We can simply re-do an old one."

"What?" the others said, in unison, which is why I only wrote it once.

"Yes, we simply pick something exciting we've done before – and then we do it again. Not only will this provide ample entertainment, it will not rely on Art needing any good luck, because success is a forgone conclusion."

"Er... er... pardon me if I have misunderstood," said Bill, "but that sounds suspiciously like plagiarism."

"Don't be silly. You can't plagiarise *yourself*."

"Well, that's as may be," said Art, "but it sounds dicey – and I don't remember volunteering to come along."

"Nonsense," said the wizard, grinning from ear to ear, "you *must* come along. If we have to think of something you *hadn't* been involved in, we'd be back to square one. Come friends, I know the perfect thing. Let us pray the narrative takes a sudden leap, or we may run short of words! I feel like we're at the half way mark already. Oh, one more thing. Go and get a faerie, will you? Preferably in a bottle."

"What on earth for?"

"I will explain later."

"I have a bad feeling about this," said Bill, "and may the gods of literature forgive me such a gratuitous cliché."

***

A few days later ...

The wizard and his companions stood at the top of a small hillock and gazed up at a dark, twisting tower that rose up, up, up, up and even further up, into the clouds. An improbably long way, basically. A faerie tale sort of tower – you know what I mean.

"Gosh it's hot today," said Blagre.

"It's summer," said Art, "what did you expect?"

"I know, I know... just making sure it's clear we're staying 'on theme'. Did you remember to bring the faerie, Bill?"

"I did," he replied, shaking a large glass bottle.

"Ow, ow, ow!" came a faerie princess-like voice. "Mind how hard you shake that, you hairy oaf."

Princess Havfrue, a six-inch-high faerie with golden gossamer wings, skin as black as liquorice, beauty beyond compare and piecing blue eyes that hinted at an intelligence she didn't actually possess, dusted herself off. She was invisible, however, so you couldn't see any of that – just take my word for it.

"Oh, good grief," said Art, "is *she* the best you could do, Bill?"

"It was short notice."

"I am not exactly thrilled to be here either," said the princess. "I despise being reduced to a plot device – and what's with the bottle? I would have come voluntarily."

"You would?" said Blagre.

"Well, no, probably not if truth be told. You might have used a clean bottle though Bill, it stinks of beer in here – at least I hope it's beer. I didn't even have chance to dress for the occasion. All I have on is my house-dress."

"What does it matter?" said Bill. "You're invisible. Who'll know?"

"*I* will know, you half-witted crock-polisher. It's a good job this is only a short story."

"Enough chatter, my friends," said Blagre. "T'is time we got on with our business here."

Art looked up at the tower again. It was a real masterpiece of wizardly evil. It even smelled of evil – eggy. "Where are we exactly?"

"You don't remember?" said Blagre.

"Well... just humour me... and your – er – readers."

"Oh right, yes. Well, this is the tower of the Great Malevolent, Robaratomychum. At one time, my greatest enemy and all round bad, bad, bad wizard. We duffed him up, once and for all, about three years ago and imprisoned him in this tower for ninety percent of eternity. Remember now? He's the wizard with the gammy leg."

"Vaguely. Are you sure I was there?"

"Yes! Well – fairly sure. It doesn't matter. The point is we had a super-duper battle, a real page turner, so he's the obvious choice."

"How will he know we're here?" asked Bill. "I'd knock on the door, but there appears to be none."

"Fetch the Parleyhorn, t'is in the saddlebags on yon pony."

"The what?"

"It's a horn. Brass thing with a blue gemstone on it. Wizards rarely meet, and when we do, we sound the horn to signal we wish to discuss matters under a truce. T'is a time-honoured tradition, so – give it a hoot will you."

Bill scrabbled around in the saddlebags until he found the aforementioned horn. It was a tiny thing, no more than six inches long. He put it to his lips and blew. Although small, the sound that came forth was deafeningly loud and not entirely unlike flatulence.

"Is it meant to sound like that? Am I doing it right?"

Blagre giggled and nodded.

"Should I blow it again?"

Blagre, struggling to contain his laughter, nodded vigorously.

Bill placed the horn at his lips and once again, the sound of thunderous, unmistakable flatulence filled the air. This time Blagre couldn't contain himself and he roared with laughter. "Ahh, gets me every time," he said, at last.

"You really think that's funny, don't you. Good grief, how old are you, man?"

"Being a wizard is such a serious business that we have a real weakness for juvenile humour. And besides, it's the number one rule of comedy, Bill. There's nothing funnier than farting. The Greek classics are full of it."

Bill raised an eyebrow and looked up to the heavens. "What happens now then?"

"Now, we wait for a reply."

Moments later, the reply came. Another deafening, ripping sound that also sounded suspiciously like flatulence, but this time it was deeper and wetter – the kind of sound that is often followed by an unfortunate accident.

Blagre, tears streaming down his face, looked skyward. There, above them, peering over a ledge, was a face. The face belonged to a man: gaunt, moody, chiselled, evil - presumably the Great Malevolent, Robaratomychum himself. The face looking down seemed to be chuckling.

"Hello there, Bob. How's things with you?" Blagre shouted.

"Oh fine, thank you. Plenty of time on my hands what with eternal confinement and everything. I've taken up baking you know - you should taste my chocolate soufflé sometime."

"Oh, really?"

"No, of course not you fictional moron. I've been locked up here for years with nothing to do but brood over my unfortunate situation and plan the myriad sick and twisted - and thoroughly evil - misfortunes I will one day visit upon *you*. How have you been? How's business?"

"Oh - er - not so bad really. Not much to tell... Anyway, listen Bob, I have come here with a proposal but time is short, so let me give you the background in the space before the next paragraph."

***

We pick things up next when ...

The two wizards stood facing each other atop Dragon's Nest Plateau. The wind howled and tore at their clothing, the rain lashed their bearded faces and the thunder and lightning thundered and - er - lit(?) all around them.

Art took up his position behind a nearby rock, ready for what had originally been a surprise ambush. Bill and the princess-in-a-bottle sat on a nearby ledge to watch - they hadn't been in the original scuffle.

Blagre shouted, trying to make himself heard above the wind, "I don't remember the weather being this bad last time, Bob. It appears even fiction is not immune to climate change. It does add to the drama though."

The Great Malevolent smiled a malevolent sort of smile (that's where he got the nickname). "Let me just be *absolutely* sure of our bargain, Blagre. If I go through with this nonsense, you will reduce my sentence to only *half* of eternity in the tower, agreed? No tricks, no sub-clauses or anything of that nature?"

"Agreed. You just do like I told you – just like last time. But, before you attack me, I need to recite my epic line."

"Your what?"

"My line. Ahem," Blagre cleared his throat, "Now, foulest of foul," he cried, "I shall banish thee. Thou shalt not cross this plateau alive – you cannot pass."

"You did *not* say that last time."

"I did so."

"Did not."

"I did – well, I may have edited it a bit but..."

"And it sounds suspiciously familiar. Trust you to lack any originality. Shall we get on with it then?"

Blagre lowered his head. His eyes were as burning coals and all his wizardly wizardry was plain for all to see. He twirled his staff in his right hand, and in his left, blue flames struck up from his palm. He prepared to battle the Great Malevolent and once again claim his place in history (and the anthology).

"Wait, wait... hang on a moment," said the Great Malevolent, raising his hand.

"What is it? I got all worked up for that."

"Something is missing. Something is not right. Let me think... Last time, wasn't I wielding the Staff of Eternal Banishment? Wasn't that the whole point? You were fighting me for it."

"Oh, yes... yes, I think you were," said Blagre, scratching his beard.

"We lack dramatic tension without it. You did say this was an anthology? You may have to stand out against some pretty stiff competition, you know. There's a lot of desperate authors out there. It's a competitive business, or so I'm told."

"Yes, good point. But, don't worry Bob, I happen to have the staff with me. We'll sort this out before you can say '*Deus Ex Machina*'. Bill, go and get that big staff with the green emerald on it will you. It's in the baggage somewhere."

And so, after a sentence-long interlude, the two wizards once again faced off against each other.

"Now, don't forget," said Blagre, "Art will come at you from your left – you took quite a tumble last time, but no sense in getting hurt this time around. Art thou ready?"

"Who me?" said Art.

"No, no I meant… oh, it doesn't matter. Let us begin." Blagre nodded toward his opponent.

The Great Malevolent once again smiled his namesake smile and then raised the Staff of Banishment on high. He said, "You are either epically stupid or barking mad, Blagre. How you bested me the first time still keeps me awake at night. It's downright embarrassing. But no matter. I sincerely hope you enjoy baking."

And with that, he struck the ground with the staff. There was a blinding flash, a funny sort of smell – a bit like socks that have been worn two days running – and then everything went black. Very, very black.

***

Three weeks later…

Blagre, Art, Bill and the princess (who was no longer in her bottle) sat around the kitchen table of the Great Malevolent's tower – their eternal prison – feeling sorry for themselves.

"Oh, of *course* he can be trusted, *you said*. We wizards have a code of ethics, *you said*. He'll be happy to be in the anthology, *you said*," moaned Art, pulling faces at Blagre.

"Oh, do stop it," said Blagre. "I feel bad enough as it is. Three weeks and I still have no idea how we're going to get out. And what is that smell?"

"Good grief," cried Bill, "the soufflé. I completely forgot."

The princess made herself visible (faerie princesses can do that). She stamped a bare foot and wagged a finger at Blagre. "You had better come up with something soon, Mr Wizard. This confinement is extremely disagreeable – Art snores, Bill can't bake to save his life and I have been in the same dress for *three weeks*! It won't do, it really won't."

"Can't you have a word with your author, or narrator, or whatever you call it?" said Art. "At this point, surely *anything* has to be worth a try."

"Sadly, it doesn't work like that," said Blagre. "If it did, I'd have asked him to make me taller years ago... and this bald patch really bothers me... but alas, we are alone in this predicament. Narratively speaking, we have fallen foul of a complicated plot error and I see no way out for us. We do not have enough words in this story left, and only a literary *genius* could come up with a conceivable way of escaping eternal banishment – and on that score it's pretty obvious we're out of luck."

"So, there is no hope?"

"None that I can see," said Blagre, "however, at least it's an original story now... small comfort, I know."

"I feel a bit odd saying this," said Bill, "you know, being a mere supporting character and everything, but I *think* I have an idea. Do we still have the Parleyhorn with us?"

***

An unspecified amount of time later...

The companions sat in the garden of the Green Pixie Tavern, drinking beer and generally making the sort of medieval merriment you'd expect at the end of a faerie tale. Oh, did I mention it was sunny out? July. Middle of **summer**, in fact.

They had escaped from the tower by the most implausible means imaginable. So improbable in fact, it would only sound more ridiculous if I put it into words.

Therefore...

Art banged his tankard on the table. "A toast," he cried. "To us and our daring escape!"

"To us," Blagre echoed, "and I think we squeaked in just under the word count."

Art drained the remains of his tankard, wiped his moustache with the back of his hand, and said, "You know I still can't quite believe we escaped and at the same time managed to put Bob back in his prison. That plan of yours Bill, it was... it was... hey, I'll be darned. Do you know, I can't actually remember how we did it. Not a thing. And I've only had three beers."

"Don't be silly," said Bill, "we got the er – and we did the er – hey nonny, I can't remember either. Not a sausage. What gives?"

Art peered at the wizard through half-closed, half-drunk eyes. "There's wizardly business afoot, or I'm not a stereotype. What's going on Blagre?"

The wizard simply smiled.

The princess appeared (visible) at the table and skipped her way around the tankards. "Well, *you* fools may not understand, but it seems – somewhat unusually – that *I* understand *everything*. And to be honest, I wasn't really paying attention for most of it – utter drivel if you ask me. I can also explain my presence in this whole farce."

"You do not know," said Art.

"I *do*," said the princess. "You see, *I* am here, so that this will *technically* count as a fairy tale (even if that is not the correct spelling of faerie). And the reason Master Blagre was concerned about *that* was because he feared being excluded – and that was because," she waited; a dramatic pause, "this is actually a *PARABLE,* and our unlikely escape is at the very heart of the matter. Am I right Mr Wizard?"

Blagre continued to smile.

"Ah ha!" said Art, "If you're so smart – and if I am supposed to go along with this nonsense – then what is the message? Surely a parable must have some sort of theme or lesson to be learned. Where is the moral?"

The princess sat cross-legged on the table, adjusted her skirt and then shrugged. "I must assume you are either deaf or stupid – and I favour the latter – because the message has been literally shouted throughout. Whoever this author of Blagre's is, he cannot be accused of subtlety."

"Gak, call me names if you will, but I still fail to understand any of this. Blagre, I feel a little exposition may be justified at this point."

The wizard settled back in his chair, stroked his beard and then, with a wistful look in his eye, touched the small bald patch at the crown of his head.

Eventually, he said, "Do you imagine this was all nothing more than second rate pulp fiction with the odd fart gag thrown in? There was much more to it than that but, until *you* accept *true* reality and your *own* fictional nature, you will never discover the meaning in anything. And... when you *do* finally accept it, so you will know the meaning of life, and you will come to understand there are fundamental principles that govern everything."

"Is that it?"

"I offer you the meaning of life, and you're not satisfied. By golly, you're a tough fellow to please."

"Pah... What meaning? What laws? It sounds like a riddle,

and you know how much I hate riddles. Nobody like riddles – especially not your readers, you barmy old fool."

"Well, the most important principle of all is *'show, don't tell'*; sadly, therefore I can't explain it all to you. The corollary of this principle is that one should never underestimate the intelligence of the reader. After all, *you* may not understand, but *they* most certainly will."

"What? Both of them?"

"Indeed."

Blagre turned to one side, "My dearest reader, am I right or am I right?"

S. Markem is an accidental writer of fiction. You cannot find him anywhere.

These Burning Bones
Laila Amado

1.

Once upon a time, in a town encircled by the shell of white-stone walls, nestled in the shadows cast by the golden onion domes of its dozen churches, in the tall terem of her father's house, lived a girl. You've all heard that story.

Beautiful and, of course, virtuous, as such girls are expected to be, she was known far and wide for her unsurpassed skill in lace making. Under her deft fingers, the silken threads twined and looped, fox and deer emerging, lifelike, from a landscape of fine white thread. So famous she became across the land for her art, that Koschei himself, the deathless ruler of the lands beyond the nine green forests, came to see with his own eyes if the rumors of magic in the hands of a mortal were true.

Disguised as a traveler—worn boots, gray beard, and a brown coat—he walked into town, joined the crowd queuing at the gates of the house where the girl lived, scoffed at the infatuation of gullible humans with the poor replica of magic that is human art. Yet, when he reached the vaulted upper chamber of the terem, with its spiraling columns painted red and green, and cast but one look at the delicate threadwork in the girl's hands, he was stunned. A mere mortal creating works of beauty so rare and precious, the likes of which he himself did not possess in his enchanted lands.

Awed and humbled by the wonder in front of him, Koschei bowed to the girl and offered to take her to that fabled land beyond the nine green forests where rivers of milk flow between the banks of sweet kissel and where she could weave her wondrous lace for all eternity.

The girl refused his offer.

Cornflower blue eyes cast downwards, she whispered that she would never abandon her parents, her beloved town, and her faith for the lands of godforsaken sorcery.

Anger flared in Koschei's deathless heart. Magic spilled from his fingers, turning the modest girl into a firebird, red of feather and gold of wings, so that she may never work her magic again.

The poor girl could not bear to be kept away from her art. She wept tears of fire, her body combusting into flames, and, wherever the ambers fell, crimson red flowers sprang from the ground, blooming for those that can admire beauty without seeking to possess it.

That story is famous, but none of it is true. I know better. That girl was me, and that girl was vain. Lace making had nothing to do with it, for I never cared for artistry.

And neither did Koschei.

2.

The first time I saw him he entered the terem as a merchant, scattering pearls and silk on the pillows propped beneath my feet. I suppose he did cut a splendid figure, in red boots of saffian leather and a fur-trimmed kaftan. My nanny certainly seemed to think so – I saw her cast an appraising look, cheeks flashing a faint pink.

One ride in a boat down the Volga river was all that he was asking for, just to be in the presence of my unrivaled beauty for a few hours of this warm summer day. I've heard it all before. Unwilling to listen further, I rolled my eyes, slapping the hand of the servant girl who had pinched my hair with a crooked tooth of a bone comb.

I didn't even bother to watch him leave, only heard the door bang, as my nanny frowned and shook her head.

3.

The second time, he came before me as a prince of a faraway land, peacock feathers gracing the tall turban. A cloak of azure blue silk flowed behind him like a river. He spoke of stars hanging low over the desert sands and of blooming pomegranate trees hidden in secret gardens, promising to build me a palace on the shores of a wide warm sea in return for one single kiss.

He looked so earnest, brows knitted in concentration, when he recited the odd, ancient love poems, and the vowels of his words carried the strangest echoes. I laughed.

This time I watched him leave, storm to the door in a cloud of silk the color of a vicious tempest. Nanny gave me her sternest look, but I just could not stop giggling.

4.

The third time, he came as himself. Shadows roiled around the gleaming crown of white bone on his brow. He spoke of his kingdom that lies in a far, faraway land, beyond the blue seas and the green forests, on the other side of the dawn, and I watched his face – the finely curved lips, the proud, hawkish nose, the darkness underneath his eyes cast by the long, black lashes. Now and again, in the light of the lanterns, a brittle edge of a socket or a yellowed hinge of a jaw showed through his features, like a ghost of the deathless skull hovering beneath the surface of his human face, bleeding through into the daylight world.

He offered me power and half of his immortal throne to go with it. I wasn't impressed. Words twisted on my tongue, sharp and poisonous, and as I opened my mouth to spit them out, nanny went pale.

"Why would I want your throne?" I hissed. "What's in it for me? I'm the most beautiful girl in this whole land. I can have anything I want, so why would I want your kingdom of cheap magic tricks and rotting bones?"

He swayed as if I slapped him, but this time he did not leave. Instead, he leaned close, bending over my hand, as if to plant a kiss, and said, "Three times I came and three times you rejected me. All I have to offer is not enough for you. For your vanity, I will turn you into a prize that everyone wants and no one wins, a harbinger of misfortune."

I tried to yank my hand away, but it was no use. Magic flowed through his fingers and into my flesh, cold like ice and hot like flame. It felt like fire burning in my bones. I opened my mouth to scream, yet nothing but a screeching caw of a bird burst from my throat. Hands flailing, I reached for Koschei's coat, but he stepped away, snapped his fingers and was gone, leaving behind wisps of black smoke.

Consumed by the burning pain, I crumpled to the floor, tearing at the fabric of my dress. Golden specks shone through my skin, merging into pools of molten lava, and then little tendrils of fire began to peel away, curling over my aching skin like tiny feathers. One final contortion and my human body was no more. Where a human girl cried and flailed, a firebird, its plumage red and golden, flapped its wings.

The servant girl, comb still clutched in hand, passed out, tumbling over a redwood bench, and the old nanny caught the bird with a tablecloth, swaddling it in heavy, embroidered fabric.

5.

Father moaned at the sight of me, but mother said, "Don't fret. Remember my sister living in the woods? Let's call on her, she would surely know what to do."

And so they did. A caravan of heavily laden wagons, loaded with wool, barley, wheat, and barrels of mead, rolled down the winding paths of the forest towards the doors of a hut teetering on a pair of chicken legs. Three days later my mother's sister walked into the terem, her bone leg clanking on the oak floors.

She stooped over the crate where I was pecking seeds, eyes the color of swamp water boring into the body of a bird. My parents hovered in the doorway.

"I cannot undo this spell," she said after a long pause. "But I can alleviate it." She turned to me and continued, "You will become free of this form, the day you care for someone other than yourself."

Enraged, I bit her hand and flew out of the open window.

6.

It's boring to live the life of a bird. No matter how bright your plumage, how melodious your songs, each new day is the same as the previous one and the one before it and all the other days, past and future. It didn't take me long to discover that flying high makes me dizzy and hopping from tree to tree provides a limited source of entertainment.

No wonder that one night, when a group of men set up camp in the forest on their way to the fair held in the capital city, I let one of my magnificent tail feathers fall to the ground between the trees.

Soon, I saw one of the men – a boy really – approach, staring open-mouthed at the treasure glowing between the gnarled knots of the roots. He was pretty, in a simple, hayseed way, with a swath of reddish freckles splayed across his cheeks and nose, and a soft baby mouth. Maybe the others warned him against venturing towards the strange light shining in the woods and he didn't listen. Maybe he snuck away from the group in secret, when the older men had sensibly gone to sleep. Maybe he didn't know any better. Whatever brought him here, he suited my goals perfectly.

He picked up the feather, cast a quick glance around to check if anyone was looking, hoping to keep the feather a secret, of course. So naïve. For a few seconds the bright plume of the feather burned in his hand, throwing sharp jagged shadows on his young face, and then its light was no more, hidden in the boy's coat.

I cannot know for sure what happened when he reached the capital, but there were rumors. I had to be patient and wait.

It didn't even take that long.

The boy got himself a job in the palace's stables, carrying straw and water, shoving out manure, brushing manes, mending saddles and, after each long and tiresome day, he climbed into the hayloft, where he had his bed, and pulled out the feather from its hiding place, unwrapping the bundle to gawk at the pretty light. He didn't know yet that if a secret is bright enough, you cannot hope to keep it to yourself. One night a laundry maid saw him and told the cook. The cook told the falconer. The falconer told the seneschal, and by morning the news reached the tsar himself.

Ushered into the throne room, the boy fell to his knees and took out the feather, its stem shaking in his sweaty hand. The bright, red and golden plume burned with a fire bright as daylight.

"Bring me the bird that left this feather," said the tsar. "I want my land to be a beacon of light for all the others."

"But I do not know where to find the firebird," the boy cried. "You have the feather now. Please don't send me on this quest for I will surely perish."

"In that case the executioner will have your head tomorrow," the tsar said and shrugged.

And so, seeing that he had no choice, the boy packed his knapsack and went in search of the firebird.

I made it easy for him, since I wanted to be taken to the palace and live out my firebird days in opulent luxury. He didn't have to travel far on that first quest – I made a nest in the branches of a sprawling oak he was bound to notice. After all, it also housed a talking cat and a couple of mermaids. All he had to do was cross the three rivers, one green, one blue, and one of fire, and then climb to the top of the highest hill wearing a pair of iron shoes. Sweet boy, he'd managed just fine.

He brought me to the palace of milk-white spires and arched doorways, to the tsar and his court, to the tastiest seeds, nuts, and berries. The tsar set me up in an elegant golden cage and the boy was sent back to the stables.

At first, the tsar came to see me every day. He fed me from his hand and watched my feathers glow, fascination softening his harsh features. Life at the palace was good and I was content, but the bliss didn't last long. Soon, the tsar's visits became few and far between and his eyes took on a haunted, hungry gleam. Then he stopped coming at all and was gone for weeks. Alone in the room, I discovered that the life of a bird was still quite boring even at the royal court and with the best selection of seeds.

One day the tsar came back to the parlor where my golden cage hung from the rafters, and when he did, he paced up and down the span of the room, muttering to himself, "I've heard, a sheikh in the south rides a griffin and a king in the west owns a deer with golden hooves, and I have nothing but a bird. A stupid creature with a pea-sized brain that can do nothing but flap its wings." I shrieked in indignation, but he paid me no heed. The next day he called for the boy again.

"Far away, in the malachite mountains lives a wondrous creature. A fox predicting the future with a swipe of its tail. Bring it to my palace and I'll let you keep your life," said the tsar.

The boy wept as he packed his knapsack, but he already knew that he had no choice. He was gone for a month and when he came back with the magic fox on a leash, the freckles on his face looked faded and dull.

This time, it took the tsar barely more than a month to get bored with the fox and its predictions. He called for the boy again.

"Far away, in a saltless sea lives a fish that can grant wishes. Bring it to me and your life will be spared," said the tsar.

The boy did not object. He left and was gone for a whole winter and, when he came back, there was no softness left in his mouth and his eyes turned the dirty gray color of melting snow.

The more wonders the boy brought to the palace, the greedier the tsar became, the hungrier his eyes looked at the world. Forgotten in my golden cage, I watched him spiral into madness and the boy fade away, his young face more haggard after every quest. Fire gnawed at my bones, blistering and cruel. In my fevered dreams, I heard Koschei's laughter echo in a land beyond the nine forests, on the other side of the dawn.

One sweltering summer day the tsar, drunk on greed and wine, left the cage unlocked. The latch slipped open, setting me free, and I flew away in search of a land less bleak and dreary. I don't know what happened to the boy.

7.

There was a kingdom, and in the kingdom there was a palace, and around the palace sprawled a garden, and in the garden stood a tree, and on the branches of that tree golden apples swayed and ripened. I came to like their taste, sweet and tangy. It was a lovely place. Until the king called for the apple thief to be captured, and his three sons – the angry one, the lazy one, and the handsome one – set out on a quest to find the firebird and win the crown.

Three young men began the journey but only two came back. The youngest prince was smart enough to catch me, I admit, but wasn't smart enough to understand his brothers' nature. Once he did all the work for them, they stabbed him in the back, chopped his body up into little pieces, and dumped the remains into the deep and desolate ravine. There was no raven nor the wolf to save him. Stories lie.

The two brothers traveled back to the palace and claimed the throne, feigning ignorance of their sibling's fate, and soon the kingdom went up in smoke, princes tearing apart the land in their quest for ultimate, undivided power. Day after day, locked in my gilded cage, I heard bone dice rolling from Koschei's long fingers, tumbling across the long table in a faraway land beyond the nine green forests.

One night, the fire – started by one brother or the other – burned the palace down. Invulnerable to the flaming tongues, I flew off into the pitch-black darkness, swearing to never be captured by a man again.

8.

There were other kingdoms, of course, tsardoms, empires, and duchies. There were men, young and old, clever and simple, handsome and not so much, who saw but a shadow of my flame and lost their peace, burned down their homes, sacrificed love, friendship, and life itself.

No matter how I tried to evade them, they always found me. In a plowed-up field and in a sacred grove, in the palace gardens and in a back alley. Fire burned in my bones, biting and bitter. In all the lands I roamed I heard Koschei's lips whisper words I couldn't quite understand, close but forever out of reach.

9.

Imagine a splash of light meadow green in the jagged rift between the malachite crowns of the trees. Imagine a horse in full gallop, flying like an arrow. Imagine a rider leaning forward in the saddle, fearless and agile.

From high up in the sky, I saw them racing across the field, a man and a beast perfectly fused together in one fluid motion. Transfixed, I could not help but stare, circling lower down to get a better look. By the time I noticed one of my feathers slip free and flutter downward into the shivering grass, it was too late. I cried out in despair, but the sound was lost, carried away by the wind.

He was a huntsman, favored by the tsar for his prowess in tracking prey. Of course, he saw the feather – red fire flaming in the grass – and raced to pick it up. His horse neighed, warning him not to touch the feather, as nothing good will come of it. But men like that don't listen to horses. The huntsman leaned down from the saddle and plucked the feather from the ground.

Unlike the others before him, he did not try to hide it. Instead, he took the flaming feather straight to his sovereign, hoping for a reward. The tsar, of course, wanted to have the whole wondrous bird and ordered the huntsman to fetch it for him. Strong and competent, the hunter was not intimidated by the task, or, perhaps, he lacked imagination to be intimidated.

He found me in the flowering branches of an abandoned orchard at the edge of the world. I know not how he'd managed to track me to these isolated lands, but then again, he was born and bred for tracking prey.

Fooled with the simplest trick – a handful of sunflower seeds scattered on the ground between the apple trees – I flew down and the huntsman's trap closed around me. His horse harrumphed in warning that nothing good ever comes from capturing a firebird, and I shrieked and cawed pleading to let me go, but men like that listen neither to birds, nor to horses.

He brought me back to the palace to be greeted by the satisfied nod of the tsar. "I see that you're a faithful servant, Huntsman, and will stop at nothing to serve me well," said the tsar. "Have you ever heard of Princess Vasilisa?"

And the huntsman answered, "Yes, my sire, I've heard stories of Princess Vasilisa, the beauty of the crystal towers in the middle of the ink-blue sea, daughter of the Moon, sister to the Eastern Wind. What of her?"

"Ever since I've learned of her divine beauty, I cannot sleep at night," said the tsar. "I wish to take her as my wife. Bring her to me and you'll be rewarded handsomely."

"Very well, sire," said the huntsman. "Every day at dawn, the princess you desire leaves her crystal tower in the middle of the sea and sails across the waves in her glass boat. It won't be difficult to bring her to you."

10.

And so, the huntsman rode to the shores of the ink-blue sea. Steps away from the breaking waves, he set up a tent of azure silk, served the table with honey crystals and sugared berries, all doused with sleeping syrup. He himself hid behind the tent.

When the first rays of light touched the surface of the water and on the horizon appeared a small boat gliding along the waves, the huntsman took out a simple pan flute and the notes of a melody, sweet and beguiling, floated towards the sea.

Drawn by the sounds of music, Princess Vasilisa stepped ashore. Curious, she approached the tent and peeked inside. The sight of sweets and red berries made her mouth water. She took a small bite of one treat, licked sugar off another, ate a handful of berries, and soon her limbs began to feel heavy and weak. When, drugged by the sleeping syrup, she sank onto the pillows strewn across the floor of the tent, the huntsman came out of his hiding place, wrapped the princess in a heavy blanket, and threw her across the saddle of his horse who harrumphed in protest. Princess Vasilisa begged the huntsman to let her go, but to men like that a woman is no better than a horse or a bird, and they listen to none of them.

11.

She was just a girl, small and crying, a child curled up on a cold, wide bed. She stayed where the huntsman flung her, waiting for her captors to seal her unkind fate – to be more property than a wife, a prize to be won, used, and then forgotten.

Inside my golden cage, I trembled with sudden anger. By now, I knew a thing or two about being a coveted trophy, an object of desire, and none of these things I'd wish on the child in front of me. Fire coursed through the veins of my bird body, roared in my ears, threatening to tear me apart. Still, I wouldn't back down and pacify myself.

Tears ran from my eyes in droplets of molten gold as the body I've lived in for a thousand years convulsed against the frame of the cage. One final spasm of blinding pain, and I stood up to my full, human height, the mangled remnants of the gilded bars broken on the floor. Fire danced around my body, crimson tongues enveloping me from head to toe. Princess Vasilisa stared up at me in awe, as the last of my golden feathers, the only one left, hovered down and settled at the foot of the bed.

"Take the feather and run," I told her. "It'll guide you through the night and keep you warm. When you reach your home in the crystal towers, throw the feather into the darkest pit of the ink-blue sea, so that it's never seen again." She nodded in agreement, and I believed her.

As for me, it was time for me to walk the path I should have taken long ago. To burn through the palace and its walls, the tsar and the huntsman. To burn through the towns and villages, prisons and cathedrals, the forests and the fields. When I reach the bone-white gates of Koschei's faraway kingdom on the other side of the dawn, they'll fall before me. Dressed in fury and flame, I will step through the smoldering ruins, kiss his cold lips, and watch the world – as we both know it – crumble in all-consuming fire.

Laila Amado writes in her second language and has recently exchanged her fourth country of residence for the fifth. Instead of the Mediterranean, she now stares at the North Sea. The sea still, occasionally, stares back. Her stories have been published or are forthcoming in Best Small Fictions 2022, Daily Science Fiction, Cheap Pop, Cotton Xenomorph, Aphotic Realm, and other publications.

VESPERTINE

Elanna Bellows

"The mind is not a vessel to be filled but a fire to be kindled."
- Plutarch

"Someday, after mastering the winds, the waves, the tides and gravity, we shall harness for God the energies of love, and then, for a second time in the history of the world, man will have discovered fire."
- Pierre Teilhard de Chardin

Only a fool would follow a will-o'-the-wisp when its hopeful glow pierces the dark heart of a thirsty forest. And only a fool would step into a dream out of another dream. And only a fool would fix steady eyes on the Sun and ask her to take as much as she gives. And only a fool would trade one memory for another, and in doing so lose the ability to forget.

What fool, you ask, would stand alone at the edge of dawn and give himself away for the answer to his heart's dearest question? For the question he longs for so deeply he does not know how to give it voice?

Certainly not you.

Yes, I remember the green, when summer was only a season—when it had a beginning, and an end, and the warm touch of the Sun on my back was something to look forward to while the whispering wind blew in winter.

But that was before—before summer swallowed more than its share of the year. Before the dream of castles in the air. Before the yellow Sun, close and seething in her course through the sky, sweated from the force of a truth nobody could bring themselves to see. Before a fawn born late in the damp heat of the solstice set out to seek the secrets—secrets that you refused to speak until the day when the winds became too wild and crushed your village with their screaming.

But that is getting to the end before the story has begun.

You asked for resolution to your quest, and so I will answer.

You asked about hope, about salvation. These ideas are not real. I cannot give you the hope you seek, for it is nothing more than a dream. Salvation is the same.

I have never been a savior.

So I cannot give you what you think you want—what you asked for. I do not grant wishes. I only provide answers. Instead, I will tell you about balance, and how I lost mine. And how you can find yours again.

* * *

In the forest, the ground was soft—a plush carpet of dead leaves and old pine needles giving way to summer ferns and irises. As the dawn light filtered through the canopy of young leaves, a yearling fawn stepped over roots and around stones as he made his way between the trees. His baby spots had long faded with the color in the foliage, and when his winter coat shed out, his summer hair had grown in orange like the Sun in autumn. On his brow, two stubby knobs swelled where antlers would soon burst forth.

He thought of nothing but the mud between his two hard toes and the lesson that his mother had told him, as her mother had told her, before she disappeared.

Do not trust fire. Your toes, though tough, are not made of flint. If the forest burns, it will take you with it. Only the Sun can hold fire without fear and know what she's made of.

And yet, every night when he slept in the dark underbrush of the forest, the fawn dreamt of fire—streaking through the sky from cloud to cloud, rising from the mists in the deep of midnight, peering down from the summit of noon, so bright and full of secrets that his eyes could not stand it.

And every morning he woke with yearning in his heart. He wanted to know those secrets, for the Sun had kissed him before he knew what it was to know, when the light dappled the ground like the white hairs of youth still dappled his coat.

And so, in his second summer, when the wisps found him and called him away, he did not hesitate, despite his mother's warning. He followed them, the tongues of ghost-fire, just as you now follow him—with a wish you can't help but speak to the wind. What else could you do if the wind spoke back?

But the wind speaks a language your tongue has forgotten, so you leave the crickets with questions you will never answer. And when the starlings gossip, you do not know whether they speak of the seeds in the meadows or the seeds in the feeders you hang in your yard. And when the snowflakes cry, you pay them no heed.

Yes, snow. Snow is a memory, not a figment or a dream, though perhaps you do not remember. There was a time when it was more real than hope, though no less cold, and you carved it into shelters to keep your skin from the wind. And you patted it into balls so you could play at war. And when it melted, it filled your lakes and reservoirs and kept your fields lush through the summer heat.

So it was in the flush of August, when green ferns still danced light and feathery on the wind, that the fawn, whose first set of antlers had sprouted in the spring, was a year old when the fire found him. Like a vespertine ghost, a wisp of a dream that sings a song too lovely to resist, the phantom flames led him away. He did not know then how they would change him. How could he? He was still too young to know what it was to be hunted.

Any hound worth half his salt would easily have tracked his path since he'd left his scent on the bark of the trees, rubbing the velvet from the fresh bone of his antlers, but he wasn't thinking about hounds then.

The will-o'-the-wisps, singing in his heart with their fiery tongues, led him to a cave in the middle of the mountain, and vanished. And their song went silent, for the cave swallowed all the sounds of the forest. When the fawn tapped his newly grown antlers against the stone walls, he did not hear the echo carry to the cave's heart, but a sparkling shape filled his vision, prismatic like the tiny shifting rainbows that dance when sunlight scatters through the spray of a waterfall. The rainbows resolved into the shape of the Sleeping Bear, her fur every color that had never been named shifting between every color that had, so that though she held a steady shape, the ombre of her fur was never the same from one moment to the next.

The fawn blinked, twice for the beauty of it, and bowed his head.

The Sleeping Bear raised her dazzling eyes and stared down at the fawn before her. *Which dream do you seek, child of the fleet foot?*

I wish to become an oracle. One who knows.

Knowledge is potent as fire is warm, and one who hoards this potential is not worthy of the holding of it. If you know, you must also speak.

Then I will learn to know, and know to speak.

Squinting through her depthless eyes, the Sleeping Bear shimmered in the shadows. *Very well. I will dream for you. Come out of the light so the dream does not drown in it.*

The fawn stepped into the cave and lay down on the cold stone floor, his body blanketed in shadow.

And the Sleeping Bear dreamed. Of a castle in the air and thin winking lights between blinks. Of a flaming river running parallel to death and forgetfulness, curling around the Earth, red and hot with the tears of voiceless ghosts who cannot cry out. Of one who did not know, but now does. Of the Sun searing summer out of spite for your silence.

When she woke, the Sleeping Bear shared her dream with the fawn. *There are trees made of glass that scrape the sky and burn in the twilight, and loud belching beasts that swallow humans and spit them out. The snails migrate in the wrong direction, finding heat where they sought the cool, and the sea swallows the beaches, strewn with the white skeletons of dead coral. The winds rage, and the trees fall with it. But the blueberries still bloom on the mountaintops.*

What does this mean? the fawn queried, but the Sleeping Bear shook her head.

It is not mine to know, only to see. The answer you seek lives in a castle in the air. You must go there. And she faded into the black night as quickly as she had come, as silent as the tongue that still slept in the fawn's young mouth, for he had not yet learned your thick language.

But he set out on his quest, as you set out on yours after the storms tore down your houses, and your people finally agreed to recognize that you were making a mistake. And so you sought me, for the answers you could not collectively imagine for yourselves, thinking that one creature has the power to stop something so exhaustive and inevitable.

Who did you think, child, would come to save the world? A single man, in possession of a great fortune, with the strength of a thousand arms? Or a fifty-pointed white stag with nimble tongue and the wisdom and honor of a god? These heroes you long for, they are the figments of your arrogance, and arrogance cannot save you from yourself. It never has, and it never will.

This is a lesson the fawn had not yet learned as he walked toward the sinking Sun, wishing her good dreams as she slept 'til daylight. With the Sleeping Bear's vision in his mind, he saw himself a hero much like you, but he could not imagine what he would become.

As he wandered, he found himself in a grove of hazel trees waving their flat leaves at the sky. Under their branches, dusk had fallen, and the sunlight winked in the shifting light that misted the floating dust golden. Between the shadows, the air shivered like heat rippling around a fire, though the day's warmth was fading with the light. And yet, in the split of a moment too small to count, the fawn thought he saw a flash of silver light, like a thin shard of iridescent mica twisting between seconds, one moment reflecting the crepuscular light on its flat face, only to spin into nothingness and disappear the next.

The fawn froze and focused on the slivers of hope. He felt his breath mingle with the summer wind, and his toes push into the ground, and his soul reach toward the light that was there and then not and then there again. The light that hung suspended in the air. The light that cut between the air. And in the light, he saw himself as I am now, as you will be in some *now* long distant from the one you are living. That was the beginning, as though memory recognizes the authority of such beginnings and endings. Knowledge exists beyond time.

There is only now, and now, and now.

And so the fawn stepped out of himself and into the fire. Joy, fear, surprise, melancholy, anger, confusion, inspiration, relief. The rush was overwhelming and everywhere. It was not a sound, for the fawn had no ears with which to hear it. And the twinkling mist that swirled around him was not something he saw, for he had no eyes. He was simply *aware*, and that was all there was to be. Beyond the swirling fog, the walls of a crystal cave enclosed him, and so the fawn felt himself contained still by boundaries, though those boundaries were no longer skin and bones and fur, but sparkling stone. And he was afraid, though he had no belly for fear to curl and no heart for it to chase.

But it was the kind of fear he had felt when he first saw rain dripping through the leaves of the forest—the kind of fear that split the sky like lightning when something was about to be revealed. So he followed his fear, willing himself toward the place where he knew the cave opened to the rest of whatever was on the other side of the river. The river of fire hurtling over the cliff's edge and tinting the castle red. The fawn imagined a shape for himself like a red ghost of who he had been before and stepped through the curtain of firewater into the castle, for he now saw that the castle was the space between the mountain and itself. Which is to say that the castle was not a castle—it was the idea of one.

I will not pretend that these ideas can be understood by your mammal brain. In the moment of learning them, the fawn became less of the animal he had been before and more like me. But he still had much to learn, and there are pieces of the universe too big for a human brain to conceptualize. Have you ever tried to visualize a seventeen-dimensional cube? Or understand time as anything other than a line? Or ask how the Sun feels that you squander her gifts, and burn the Earth's black blood instead? Or really, truly, tried to imagine the boundlessness of infinity? These ideas are too big to hold in the circuits of your soft brains and keep from floating back into multidimensional theory. Do not fight this. The universe has no obligation to bend to the concepts that your brain is capable of grasping.

Even the fawn struggled to hold them, though he reached out his mind in all directions, moving away from the simple uniformity of life and toward the all-reaching understanding that he sought. I do not recommend that you attempt to do this for yourself. It will bring no peace to you, or to your people. But the fawn was early yet in his knowledge and had not yet learned what it would cost him.

All around him—for remember he was no longer embodied—a Chimera appeared in bits and flashes and swirling ideas. As the fawn pulled his awareness back into the small space he had created in the imagined form of himself, the Chimera resolved into a beast only three times the size of the fawn, with smoke curling from the nostrils of their goat head. Their snake tail twisted, the tongue on his face flicking at the air as though trying to taste the fawn's spirit. The bearded face of the lion squinted, but it was the goat that moved first.

Before you can understand all of the things that are not named, the names of things must be understood. She opened her toothy mouth and bleated, and from her tongue leapt flames that wound around the fullness of the fawn's essence, in all of the spaces and dimensions he occupied.

The flames carried no heat, nor did the fawn have skin with which to feel it if they had. Instead, they filled the fawn's mind with words in all of the languages ever spoken. No more must he communicate through the silent-speak of the thing humans call nature; he could click to the dolphins and snarl to the tigers and know without interpreting through instinct what the birds meant when they cooed in the morning or chattered at dusk.

"Now you may speak, and speak you must. For we ask you to seek what it is you will say, and say what it is that you seek."

And so the fawn opened his mouth and called forth the words he had always longed to taste. "I want to know the secrets in seashell swirls, and the reason why the Sun sleeps at night, and why the Moon is shy some days and blushes on others. I want to know what the rain whispers to the Earth, and why the tides dance back and forth, back and forth. I want to know if the sky dreams, and if the lake hurts in winter, and if the fish ever wonder what it would be like to fly. I want to know why the ocelot eats mice, but the mice eat only seeds and berries. I want to know why the snow falls when the days grow short, and why the thunder bellows as it splits the sky, heavy and laden with heat. I want to know why the snails migrate backwards, and the beaches run red with the dead shells of lobster crabs cooked in warm currents. I want to know why the white bears cry and the black bears wake early and the brown bears curse the mountain pine beetles. I want to know why the sea hungers, and the winds throw fists at the tall glass trees that shine like red mirrors at sunset. I want to know what the humans sing in their plaster caves, and why they stopped listening to see if the stars sing. I want to know all of the great and terrible and beautiful things, and all of the small and wonderful and awful things."

He did not realize that there is no balance in knowing everything. There is only everything.

"There is no one answer to every question, and no one question for every answer," said the snake, curling around the lion to look past the goat head and the lion head in front of them. "There is only the truth, and the truth is all. You must know the question before the answers can find you. And the answers will find you when you the question is asked." His forked tongue darted from his lips, searching for answers or questions or both. "Things that are true must keep to themselves, just as you must keep to your truth. There is no honor in lies, and with infidelity lies no heart. The true answers come only for questions asked truly, and a promise that is broken will never see past the break in the truth."

And so the fawn betrothed himself to the light, and the dark, and the Sun, and the Moon, and the sky, and the Earth, to himself and to others, to the truth and the knowing of all things that it is, and was, and will be. And from his troth, an oath, a pledge that sprang from the true essence of himself, for he had never, as long as he had lived, been more than his quest for truth, from this troth sprang the fountain of knowledge.

The fountain—or was it a tree? In the castle in the air, all things are both formless and formed. In this translation, some truth is lost that cannot be caught by your unequivocal tongue. *True translation demands a return to the pre-verbal,* for your language exists in truths and lies, in real and unreal, in binaries. The castle in the air and all that is held there exist somewhere between all of these.

This is why you have come to me, crying, "I am become death, the destroyer of worlds," because you have stepped out of your dream and seen how you poisoned your air and warmed the seas. You think I will tell you, *all is well. Do this, and save yourselves. Save each other. Save the world.* It is not that simple. It is never that simple.

And so the fawn found that between all of the things that had been named, and all of the words that had ever been spoken, or thought, or wished, or dreamed—between all of these lay the questions that had not yet been asked, and never would, or would but haven't yet, or almost were, or could have been. And all of the answers that had never been sought danced on the tip of his nimble tongue, for he could now speak them, if only the question were asked of him.

He was joy. He was giddiness. He was light and hope and energy and song. He was the idea of dancing feet and prancing hooves. He was shade on a hot day and fire on a cold night.

But the thing that was the fawn, and had drifted beyond the shadow puppet ghost he had built for himself, stilled and calmed when the lion purred.

"Dangerous truths and dangerous lies, unknowing treachery is no worse or better than treachery known. The truth must be protected, and guard you must this truth. Never once let it fall in the hands of an unworthy soul, for unworthy hands must not sully its lustre. Many will hunt and many will seek, that which you sought they will follow and wish to keep. You must walk on the edge of the sword, and let it flay you if it wishes, for any sword that flays holds no hand you can answer. You must fight villainy by holding up the mirror of your pain, for only in your pain will the villain see his own truth, that you have seized true the principle of life, and he the principle of life has slain with his violence. This is *ahimsa*, and *ahimsa* you must be, with the graciousness of soul and a soul full of grace. This is the cost of knowledge. You will always be hunted, by those who wish to gain it, and those who wish to bury it."

I, who was not yet myself, knew, in that moment, what it was to be prey, not just of creatures with bellies to feed, but of minds with questions they could not answer. I felt in that moment the pain of every wound that would strike me, every arrow that would pierce my side and every axe that would remove my head from my neck. But I was no longer a fawn, and yet I was not yet me, for I was the castle that wove every breath to the light.

"You now know all that there is," said the goat from her place behind the lion head of the Chimera, "except how to return."

Indeed, I knew everything except for myself, for I was newly made, and far from my body. I was every dimension, and every color, and every word, and every time all at once. But if I did not return to my body, the knowledge would be lost along with myself. I held truths that must be shared, as I have shared and will share with you the truths that you need, if not the truths you sought when you hiked from your cities, and came to the woods, where you have forgotten how to be, and remembered to breathe. I will tell you because you reached out a hand full of sweet wild blueberries and said "please." But the body which you, seeker, did not harm, was still far away from myself. So I asked the Chimera how to return to its bounds when once I have been so vast and multitudinous. They spoke in sequence as a fiddler spins a reel from one note to the next.

"These things you have known, as knowledge has made them," the lion began, their mane shaking with the force of their speech.

"In the fire that makes your heart beat,

And the beat that gives your body life," said the goat.

"The beat that gives your limbs movement,

And the flutter that gives your lashes rhythm," said the snake.

"The twitch that gives your ears sound,

And the sound that makes your ears twitch," said the lion.

"The breath that trembles when cold wind creeps into your lungs,

And the lungs that pull the cold wind in to warm it by your hearth," said the goat.

"You are your body, and your body is you.

Here you are, and your body is here, for these things can never be left," said the snake.

And in harmony they chanted, "Kissik, be one, be one Kissik."

And so, as my being was summarized in one word, I felt myself compress once again to live between skin and bone, though bleached and ghostly like the wisps that had led me away. And among all the things I could now see, I felt my chest rising and falling with my breath—in, and out; give, and take—a circuitous transfer of energy. A closed loop. I breathed, and the Earth breathed with me, and we were one, and the stars were one, and in that moment I was everything and every time and everyone.

But in this great unity was a thorn in my tranquility—a catch in the breath when the Earth exhaled, a hand over her throat cutting her off. Do you see, child, how she holds her breath for you? Do you see how she stumbles when you ask her to dance, for you do not give as much as you take? You are the short in the circuit. And you must make it right.

But how, you ask as you teeter on the edge where the sky

meets the land meets the sea, can you repair the damage you have wrought?

For this, you set out for the white stag, but you asked the wrong question. No more can you repair the damage you have wrought to the Earth than Pandora could close her box on anything other than hope. You can only cease to wreak any more, and give the Earth the space to heal, to breathe, to remember herself whole.

You must remember how to think in circles instead of running down lines and digging dead ends. The light is the truth and the truth is the light, for the Sun gives you all that you need, and you have forgotten to thank her for it. Who would stare into the Sun with eyes full of fire and hope and ask her to take back the gifts she has given? A fool, only.

You must act as one, though you are many, and as one you must each care for the many instead of the one. For all that you take, you must give back, and when you make, you must consider what you will do when the thing you have made has lived out its purpose, and plan for its unmaking. And the unmaking must give back at least as much as was taken by the making. Who would build without thinking where the bricks would lie when the wall fell?

A fool, only.

And so in all things you will find the circle that is life and death, where all things are made and unmade and remade in new forms.

You will step out of your dream and look at what nobody wishes to see, and find answers to the questions nobody wishes to ask, or you will go on dreaming in ignorance and misery until your kind breathe their last breath, and the Earth crumbles under the weight of your exhale. You will remember what I told you here, in this grove of wildflowers where you offered your hand in return for an answer. You will remember, and carry truth in your heart, in your eyes, when you speak to each other—or you will trade one memory for another and carry only the knowledge that I answered a question different than what you asked, and did not give you what you thought you wanted.

And when the wisps call, you will answer them with hope, and listen to their song, or you will blink them away and carry on in your sweat and your thirst as summer grows ever more insatiable until it's the only thing left.

I know which you will choose, for I know all things and all lives and all deaths and all times, but you must not know which fate awaits you. You must choose for yourselves. Who would rather face down the knowledge of his future and weave it sideways than vanish from the race of mankind?

A fool, only.

I can give you no more than what I have learned, which is that bounty hangs in balance, and insatiable appetite in the arrogance that feeds asymmetry.

For, what fool, you ask, would turn away from the gifts he had been naturally given, and ruin himself in his heroic quest for more than is his due?

Certainly not you.

As a child, Elanna Bellows pretended to be a horse, wrote stories on the back of napkins to fend off boredom, and had the audacity as a third grader to try to teach her much younger brother multiplication. Now she teaches for real at a public school in Massachusetts, writes in notebooks instead of on napkins, and pretends to be an adult.

THE LAST ROSES OF SUMMER

Kate Longstone

Talia took another sip of water from her flask, the small break in trade giving her the chance to quench her thirst amidst the dust generated by market-goers in the busy square. She had received a steady stream of customers since setting up her stall that morning, many of them familiar, returning to purchase more of the goods that she offered. This was her final weekly trip to Ardburgh this summer, and her cart had been laden with the last roses from her cottage garden, and the remaining bottles of wine produced from the fruits grown on her land.

It was a bright morning, and Talia appreciated the warmth of the late summer sun on her bare arms while she served her customers, enjoying the chance to gossip and chat while she worked – it made a nice change from her solitary existence in the forest. She was half-listening to the tailor's wife, a neat woman with grey hair pinned tightly to her head, describe plans for an elaborate birthday party for her husband the following weekend – for which she simply must have six bottles of the peach and cinnamon wine, as it was his absolute favourite – when Talia spotted the Baron's daughter, entering the market square from the direction of the castle.

Talia hoped Astrid would visit her stall that morning; not

only would it be good for business to have the continued patronage of the Baron's daughter, but she desired the opportunity to talk with her again. The tailor's wife, noticing who had drawn Talia's attention, stopped her monologue to offer her opinion of the young woman.

"Such a pretty girl," she said. "It must infuriate her father that she isn't married yet. He keeps finding eligible young men for her, but she always seems to find something wrong with them." She shook her head as she added, "That would never have happened in my day."

Talia did not reply, but hurriedly wrapped the bottles in brown paper. Wishing her good luck with the party, Talia took the silver coins and placed them straight into her purse, and waited nervously as Astrid headed in her direction.

Talia wasn't sure exactly how old Astrid was, but assumed they were of a similar age, and would therefore be in her late twenties. She had to agree with the old woman though; Astrid was stunningly beautiful, which made the fact that she had never been married all the more surprising – and intriguing – for Talia.

Astrid was accompanied by two young women, who walked either side of her. All three wore loose summer dresses embroidered with flowers, and they were chatting and laughing together as they approached. Following a few feet behind them came three young men wearing the white cotton shirts with ruffled sleeves that were the latest fashion among the nobility.

Arriving at the stall Astrid pushed back her long black hair, revealing the thin straps of her green dress, and smiled at Talia. "Good morning, Talia, how has business been today?"

Surprised that the Baron's daughter remembered her name, Talia stuttered a little over her reply. "It's been going well, Miss Astrid. Most of the wine has gone, and I have only a few bunches of roses left."

Astrid studied the bouquets on display. "These are

exquisite," she said. "Even more beautiful than those I remember from last time I visited your stall."

"Thank you," Talia replied. "But compared to you, I fear they are rather plain." Even as she finished speaking, Talia could feel the blood rushing to her cheeks. What was she thinking, speaking to the Baron's daughter in such a manner?

Astrid smiled, but also blushed, while her companions gasped and laughed nervously.

"Thank you for the compliment, Talia. It is a rare and pleasant feeling to hear someone speak so directly. Most people only seem to see the Baron's daughter these days, and their comments and opinions are cloaked in formality."

Astrid picked up one of the dark red roses, and examined the flower as she lifted it slowly towards her nose.

Looking at Talia she whispered, "Such a beautiful thing to behold." Before returning her voice to its normal level to declare, "It smells delightful. You have exceeded even your high standards this year, Talia. I think these are perhaps the most wonderful roses you have ever produced."

Raising her voice slightly, she continued, "I'm sure it would make any woman very happy if they were presented with a bouquet of these roses. I myself would perhaps look favourably upon the courtship of someone if they brought some for me."

Astrid glanced behind her, where Talia could see the three young men looking slightly uneasy at being the centre of Astrid's attention. The man at the centre of the trio blushed and began fumbling nervously with his coin pouch, as Astrid turned back to her companions to add quietly, "If they can only keep out of the inns and gambling houses long enough."

Her companions laughed at her comment, but Talia noticed the noblemen moving closer to her stall to ensure they could hear the conversation clearly.

"Please, tell me, what is the secret to growing such glorious flowers?" asked Astrid.

Talia took a deep breath. The most beautiful and sought-after woman in the barony was spending more time than usual talking to her. She knew she shouldn't reveal anything of the process, which had been passed down from mother to daughter for generations, but she didn't want to disappoint Astrid.

"The last roses to flower each summer are the best of the season," she began. "But they are always kept back, and used to ensure the plants get what they need to flourish the following year."

"If they are more beautiful than these," said Astrid, indicating the roses in front of her, "then I would dearly love to see them." She placed the rose she had been holding back on the table. "But I have kept you long enough, and you have customers waiting, so it is time for us to depart," she said, smiling as she turned to leave. "I hope to see you again, Talia."

Talia did not have time to reflect on the exchange with Astrid, as there were indeed a number of people making their way towards her stall, eager to see what had kept the Baron's daughter engrossed for so long.

* * *

It had not taken long for the last of her roses and wine to be sold, even though she raised the prices to take advantage of Astrid's patronage. Spending most of the morning's profit on supplies for the coming autumn and winter, Talia had used the extra income to treat herself to a new dress from the dressmaker and a spicy trout dish from one of the nicer public houses situated around the edges of the market square. Now, as the heat of the mid-afternoon sun was beating down, Talia hurried back with her final purchases.

She was loading the last of the items onto her cart, when she spotted a young man with long dark hair approaching. Talia recognised him as the blushing man who had been following behind Astrid that morning, and went to greet him.

"I've come to buy the roses," he said, placing his hands on

the stall and leaning close enough that Talia could smell cheap wine on his breath.

"I'm sorry," she said, taking a couple of steps back. "All the roses have been sold."

"What do you mean?" he said, stumbling slightly as he tried to make his way around the stall to close the gap. "You heard what Astrid said, I have to give her some of your roses so she will look favourably upon me."

"Then you should have bought them in the morning, once the Baron's daughter left," she said.

"I... I couldn't. I didn't have the money then." He paused, and Talia sensed he was trying to find an excuse to justify his error. "I had to collect the money that was owed to me from a friend."

"That is a shame, but as I said before, all the roses have been sold," Talia replied.

"You'll be back tomorrow, or next week though, won't you?" The man reached into his coin pouch and offered Talia a handful of silver pieces. "I can give you the money now, and you can set them aside for me to collect."

Talia shook her head slowly. "I won't be coming back to market this year. I have no more goods to sell."

"What about the last roses? I heard you telling Astrid about them." He pulled the bag of coins from his belt and shook it vigorously. "I have the money. I will pay whatever you want for them, if you just bring them to me tomorrow."

"If you were listening," Talia said, hardening her voice, "you would have heard me say that those roses are never sold. They are used to provide the nutrients for the next year's crop. Now, if you'll excuse me, I need to be on my way. It is quite a long journey back to the forest, and I want to be home before nightfall."

Pounding his fists on the wooden stall, he shouted, "I am

Gregor, eldest son and heir of Lord Gaslin of White Hills. My father has paid the dowry to the Baron, and I demand that you bring me those roses so my courtship of Astrid is accepted."

"You may demand all you like, sir, but those roses are not for sale," Talia replied sternly, before turning her back on the red-faced Gregor, and making her way to the front of her cart.

Despite her hands shaking, Talia managed to harness the horse, before taking down the colourful cloth she had been using as an awning to shade her horse and cart.

Gregor had remained standing silently in front of the stall, alternately wringing his hands and fumbling with the coins in the pouch tied to his belt, before storming off in the direction of the nearest ale house.

Talia quickly dismantled the stall and placed it on top of the supplies, then, with her heart still racing, she shook the reins and began the journey home.

* * *

The sun, which had been dipping slowly towards the horizon, disappeared from Talia's view as the trees which lined the side of the road thickened. Taking advantage of a curve in the road to glance behind her, Talia spotted in the distance the mounted figure who had been keeping pace with her for the last few miles. Just past the bend was a small roadside shelter, the last resting place before she reached the old dirt track, which led through the forest towards her home. Talia pulled her cart to a stop beside the building and, leaving her horse to drink from the stone trough, she quickly walked the short distance back to where the road turned. Hiding amongst the roadside bushes, she waited for the horse and rider she could hear approaching.

Talia wasn't surprised when the rider stopped as he rounded the bend and saw the cart just ahead. She waited a few seconds, as the man struggled unsuccessfully to get his horse to walk backwards.

"Hello, Gregor," she said, moving from her hiding place to greet him. "I thought it might be you following me." She kept her eyes fixed on his, but he looked everywhere except at her.

"This is not what I would expect from a Lord's son. Why don't you join me in the shelter? Then, perhaps you can explain your behaviour."

Turning away from Gregor she began walking back down the road – the sound of the horse's breathing behind her indicating his acquiescence to her request.

When they reached the shelter, Talia climbed onto her cart to retrieve a leather bag, as Gregor dismounted and led his horse next to hers.

"You should probably tether that horse, Gregor." Talia smiled at him. "In case it decides to return to its owner."

Gregor did as Talia suggested, before turning to face her. "How did you know this isn't my horse?" he asked.

"It hasn't been groomed this morning, and the tack and saddle have seen better days," she said. "Not what the son of a wealthy lord would ride – especially one who was hoping to court the baron's daughter."

"I didn't have time to go home for one of my own horses," he said, gazing at his feet.

"No, I don't suppose you did," said Talia, turning to enter the shelter.

Sitting down on one end of the single worn wooden bench, Talia placed her bag on the floor beside her. The fading light coming through the open doorway was blocked by Gregor, as he paused in the entrance.

"Come in, Gregor," Talia said, indicating the bench with a swift movement of her hand.

After Gregor had sat down, Talia asked him, "Will you be returning to Ardburgh, or are you intent on following me?"

Gregor coughed but otherwise remained silent, so Talia

continued. "I will assume it is the latter, in which case we may as well travel together, and as you didn't have your own mount, I doubt you have any food or drink." She reached for her bag. "You are welcome to share mine, although I'm afraid it won't be quite what you're used to." Talia placed the end of a loaf of bread and a small wrapped cheese onto the bench, then rummaged around in her bag for a few seconds before adding a small bottle of wine, noticing how Gregor's gaze lingered on it while she cut the bread and cheese.

Gregor moved his hand toward the bottle, before retracting it quickly. He began gently rubbing his hands together as he spoke. "I was hoping to speak to you again. To try and persuade you to change your mind."

Talia poured some wine from the bottle into a small earthenware cup and handed it to Gregor. "By turning up at my cottage in the forest, late in the evening?" Talia asked.

"That's not what I intended," he said, quickly bringing the cup to his lips and taking a large mouthful of wine.

"Oh? Perhaps you were planning to wait until nightfall and just take the roses instead?" she asked.

"No, no. That's not what I was going to do. I'm sorry, I wasn't thinking ahead at all. I just panicked when I realised I wasn't going to be able to get the roses for Astrid. If I fail again, I think she's going to end the courtship, and my father will be so angry with me," said Gregor, taking another swig of wine as he finished answering.

"That doesn't excuse your behaviour."

"No, it doesn't. I don't suppose you have changed your mind?" he asked, drinking down the remainder of the liquid with an audible gulp.

"No," Talia said firmly. "As I said before, the last roses play an important part in preparing for the next year's crop. They are not for sale."

Talia poured the remainder of the wine into the cup and

offered it to Gregor.

"Are you not having any?" he asked.

"No, I think your need and appreciation are greater than mine at the moment," she said, carefully wrapping the remains of the bread and cheese before placing them into her bag with the empty bottle.

Gregor drained the remaining wine, and handed the cup back to Talia, who wiped it with a cloth before returning it to the bag.

"It's time to carry on," said Talia as she stood up. "I'd like to be home before dusk."

Gregor started to stand, but quickly sat back down again.

"Are you alright?" Talia asked.

"I just felt a bit queasy as I stood," Gregor answered.

"That wine was quite strong, and you did drink it rather fast. Perhaps you should rest here while I see to the cart and horses," she suggested.

Gregor yawned and stretched. "I think I might do that," he said, lifting his feet onto the bench where the food had just been.

Talia left the shelter, and after placing her bag on the cart, she went to check on the horse that Gregor had been riding. Taking the feeding bag from her own animal, she emptied the remaining grain at the feet of the other horse, before checking and tightening the knot that tethered it. No point in causing suffering to an innocent stranger's beast, she thought, as she harnessed her own horse to the cart ready for the journey home.

Before departing she went to check on Gregor, who had curled up on the bench with his head resting in the crook of his arm. Talia smiled at the sound of snoring coming from inside the shelter, before carefully closing the large oaken door behind her.

* * *

The gentle pealing of the small bell suspended above her bedside table disturbed Talia's thoughts. Rising from atop her bed already clothed, she only needed to pull on the pair of soft leather boots she had placed nearby in readiness. She did not light any of the candles as she made her way through the cottage – familiarity and the pale light of the moon seeping through the cracks in the curtains were enough to guide her to the kitchen door. Behind her, she could hear the soft padding of paws as her cat followed her out into the garden.

There was a slight breeze on Talia's cheeks as she made her way to the middle of the garden, where the rose beds were located inside a walled area. There were no clouds in the sky, lightened by the almost full moon which, Talia noticed, was lower than she had expected.

Positioning herself in the shadows of the nearest arched entrance, Talia watched as a slightly built figure in a white shirt emerged through the opposite opening. She listened to the footsteps crunching on the gravel path, as they made their way towards the solitary bush growing in the centre of the garden. This was the original rose, planted by her great-great grandmother, and the only one in the garden still to have its flowers this late in the summer.

Talia waited while the figure stepped off the circular path surrounding the rose and reached for the stalk holding the nearest flower. She stepped out of the shadows only when they quickly released their grasp with an exasperated curse.

"Be careful of the thorns, Gregor," she warned. "They are quite sharp."

"It's a little too late for that," Gregor replied, lifting his hand to his face to examine his finger. "How did you know I would be here?"

Talia, ignoring his question, moved closer to Gregor and asked, "Are you bleeding?"

"Yes," he answered, drawing attention to the growing drop of blood on his fingertip that glistened darkly in the moonlight.

"You should rub it on the stem of the rose that pricked you," she said. "It will help it heal."

A doubtful look crossed Gregor's face, but he did as she had suggested. "What now?"

"Well, as you shouldn't be here, I suggest you leave," Talia said, making a tiny beckoning movement with the index finger of her left hand, behind her back. There was a harsh hiss as her cat leapt from where it had been hiding towards Gregor's face. Stumbling backwards in surprise, he started to fall and instinctively stretched his hands out for balance, which only took him closer towards the rose bush. He tried to twist away, but as he did so his back pushed against the older central branches of the bush, and he cried out as the thorns ripped the flimsy shirt he was wearing, puncturing the soft skin of his back. There were further whimpers from Gregor as he tore himself free, before fleeing from the rose garden.

Talia followed Gregor at a measured pace, watching as he ran to the edge of her garden and hurriedly mounted the horse which he had picketed nearby. She waited for a time in the cool summer night until, certain that Gregor would not be returning, she made her way back to the cottage and her bed.

* * *

Talia placed the hoe on the gravel next to the spade, and walked over to the wall of the rose garden. Relieved to be out of the mid-afternoon sun, she sat down in the shadows and poured herself a glass of iced lemon water. The soil she was preparing for the new rose bed had been baked hard and dry over the long, hot summer and made digging difficult, but she needed to get the ground ready for that night; the last full moon of summer.

As she rested, her thoughts drifted to some of the many other tasks she needed to perform in the garden before autumn – collecting seeds, cutting back the chrysanthemums, and pruning the herbs. Her reverie was interrupted by the sound of muffled voices coming from beyond the garden wall. Rising, she made her way to the stone archway, walking on the flower beds to avoid alerting the intruders to her presence.

Peering around the edge, she could see three men standing amidst her apple trees. From the way their arms were gesticulating, they appeared to be involved in a heated discussion. Two of the men were standing together – they were well muscled and quite a bit taller than the other man, who stood facing them. This third man she recognised straight away by his slight build, dark hair and the white bloodstained shirt.

Unsure who the other men were, or why they were here, Talia decided to try and take control of the situation. Striding briskly towards the orchard, she called out, "Gregor! How lovely to see you again."

She stopped a few feet away and, as Gregor struggled to respond, she continued, "And I see you've brought friends to look at the roses."

Facing the two strangers, she said, "This way gentleman. Follow me." Turning, and without glancing behind her, she walked back to the rose garden.

Taking up a position near the original bush, Talia waited for the men to join her. They stopped at the point where the broad gravel path from the archway split to form a circle around the centre bed. Gregor, who had been following behind the others, pushed his way roughly between them, saying, "I've come for the roses. These men are here to ensure you cooperate, and to protect me from the beast that attacked me."

Talia laughed. "Beast? The only animal here is my cat Sooty." She pointed to the small ball of black fur curled up at the base of the rose bush. "Does she look like a beast to you?" she asked the two men.

"I can assure you, I was attacked," Gregor spluttered.

"You were startled by my cat, I think, and perhaps the moonlight was distorting things," Talia suggested. She smiled sweetly at Gregor as she added, "and you had had a bit too much to drink – before you arrived in the middle of the night to try and take the roses." Behind him, the two men exchanged a quick glance, which suggested to Talia that they were aware of Gregor's reputation where alcohol was concerned.

Not wanting to give Gregor the chance to intervene, Talia spoke again. "And of course you can have some roses. All you needed to do was visit during daylight hours and ask. I'm sure we could have come to an agreement. There really was no need for you to waste the time of these sturdy fellows."

"I can have some roses?" Gregor asked carefully.

"Yes," Talia answered. "However, tonight is the full moon, and the roses will be at their most beautiful in the morning, if you could wait until then."

"Well, I'd rather—" Gregor started to reply.

"But perhaps you gentleman could help me this afternoon while you wait," Talia interrupted. "I'll pay you well, and provide dinner and breakfast. How does that sound?"

"Hmm, don't seem too bad an offer, does it, Jake?" one of the men said.

"I'm always happy to make some extra coin," Jake said. "What would you like us to do?"

"Just a little digging," Talia said, pointing at the new rose bed behind them. "I've been trying to do it myself, but it's taking longer than I thought. It shouldn't be much trouble for two strong men like you though."

"Sounds fair to me," said Jake. "What say you, Karl?"

"Let's get started," said Karl, making his way to where Talia had left her tools earlier.

"Thank you," said Talia. "If you could dig down a couple of feet deep in the centre area, and pile the soil around the edges, it will be ready for me to use."

"Will do," said Jake, as Karl handed him the spade.

"What about me?" asked Gregor.

"Probably best if you just sit and watch," said Karl, laughing as he set to work.

"I'll go and prepare the food," said Talia, turning to leave. Behind her, Sooty stretched and, sensing the possibility of something to eat, rose to follow her mistress.

* * *

Talia stood beside the bush in the centre of the garden, her secateurs poised on the stem of one of the roses in full bloom. She paused to admire the tiny droplets of dew clinging to the dark red petals, glistening like drops of blood under the light of the full moon. Making the cut, she placed the rose alongside the others in the basket at her feet. Picking it up, she walked to the middle of the new rose bed. Kneeling in the freshly dug soil next to the remaining shallow hole, she took the five roses from the basket and carefully arranged them into the traditional pattern, before dragging the last soil heap over the top to complete the shallow mound.

As she stood, Talia heard a groan coming from the gravel path.

"Oh, you're awake, Gregor," she said. "I thought you would sleep for longer."

"What's going on?" he asked, struggling against the cords that bound his hands and feet. "What happened to the men I hired?"

Talia pointed to the raised earth behind her. "I put a strong dose of poison in their ale."

"I don't understand," he said softly. "Why did you kill them?"

"To feed the roses," Talia explained. "Blood and bones, as

fresh as possible, that's the secret to growing such beautiful flowers, and I should thank you for bringing me two fine sources of nutrients – next year's crop will be better than ever. And you made it so easy for me; you were so open to my suggestions, hardly needed the little something I put in your wine to make you more susceptible."

"You won't get away with this," he said, digging his feet into the gravel, trying to push himself away from her. "My father will be looking for me."

"No, he won't," Talia said confidently. "I'll be taking your body back to him myself. Tell him how I saw your horse wandering alongside the road, and found your body nearby. He'll make enquiries of course, but in the end he'll just assume those men you hired killed you for your money – which I will be keeping."

"He won't give up that easily," Gregor argued.

"Really? You're a drunkard, a gambler, and now a horse thief! I doubt he'll be that sorry to hear you're gone. Your younger brother seems a much better heir; at least he doesn't have any of your vices."

"But Astrid will miss me," he asserted.

"I doubt it," Talia smiled. "I don't think you're her type."

"Please, I won't say anything, I promise. I'll give you anything you want. Just let me go," pleaded Gregor.

"I don't think so," Talia replied, as she reached down and picked up one of the fist-sized rocks that bordered the flower bed. "This will be a lot easier if you can't struggle."

Talia dragged his inert body to the rose bush in the centre of the garden, and drew her knife, inflicting wounds comparable with those his men would have made. Leaving Gregor's blood to seep into the moonlit earth, she returned to her cottage to rest.

* * *

The following morning, after she had loaded Gregor's body onto the cart, Talia had washed and put on her new dress, ready for the trip to town.

Earlier she had picked the last of the deep red roses, and arranged them into a display that enhanced their beauty – there was someone in town that Talia knew would appreciate the gift.

Before leaving, she went to her workroom and opened a cupboard containing a large number of small bottles and vials. She lifted a bottle that had a tiny heart inked onto the label, and held it in her hand for a few seconds, then replaced it on the shelf. For once she was confident she wouldn't need any assistance from her concoctions.

A bottle of her finest wine and the last roses of summer would be enough.

Kate Longstone is a writer of fantasy and other fiction.

She has a passion for telling the stories of strong female protagonists overcoming adversity, drawing inspiration from her interests in myth, folklore, history and nature.

Kate lives in Essex in the United Kingdom with two adorable cats, and when not writing can be found enjoying the local countryside, or exploring fantasy realms in books and games.

LOVE, PRIDE, VIRTUE AND FATE
Bharat Krishnan

Content warning: this story includes some very brief descriptions of infanticide

On a hot summer day, with the sun beaming above the skies of Mathura, all the inhabitants of the city waited patiently even as they sweat through their saris and kurtas to witness the holiest and grandest of ceremonies: a royal wedding.

The smile on King Kamsa's face lifted his handlebar mustache. Curls of his black hair flowed in the wind. He was at his sister's wedding, and soon he would have a brother-in-law, Vasudeva, whom he could train in kingly arts. Kamsa had no heir and wondered if his future nephew could instead carry on his legacy. Ushering his sister down from her carriage, he heard a voice from the sky.

"Kamsa! The eighth child of Devaki will be your undoing! This boy will slay you and restore peace to these lands."

Kamsa believed in prophecies, and as soon as Devaki's feet touched the ground his sword was at her neck. "Perhaps I will kill my sister right here and now," he said to no one and everyone. "If there is no Devaki, there is no child."

"My king," Vasudeva said, bowing in fealty. "Please. It is not appropriate for a king to slay his sister, especially not on an auspicious day. What would the gods think of that? Let us marry, and we will give you our eighth child to do with as you please."

Succumbing to reason, Kamsa dropped his sword and let Devaki go. He wouldn't dare move against the gods during the auspicious season of summer – during a wedding when their eyes focused on the grandeur of this union as much as his citizens – but once his sister settled into a routine, he'd make his move. And so the wedding commenced, but neither member of the bridal party smiled during the ceremony.

Afterwards, the king insisted the couple live with him... forever.

* * *

A year passed without event. Though Devaki was a prisoner, the guards still allowed her to drape herself in richly colored saris that accentuated her lithe frame and capricious eyes. She and Vasudeva were not allowed to leave the king's guards, but they were not mistreated. Rather than live out their lives in a cell, they were even given the guest house on the palace grounds. After their initial frustrations, life seemed to have hit a new normal. That is, until the birth of their first child...

"What a darling boy," Kamsa said as he held the newborn in his arms just minutes after his birth. An exhausted Devaki smiled in their family room alongside her husband. Then Kamsa grabbed the boy's ankles and slammed him into a wall. Devaki dropped to her knees, a guttural scream echoing through the prison walls, and Vasudeva's eyes filled with tears at the sight of his son's insides smeared across the house's walls.

"There is no room for error," Kamsa roared. "My men will inform me whenever you have a child, and all of them will be dealt with the same way. My sovereignty will not be denied." He then left the childless parents to their sorrow, as Vasudeva clawed at the hairs on his head in an attempt to drown out his pain.

***

Five more times, Devaki bore children and five more times they met the same gruesome end at the hands of Kamsa. "My heart cannot bear another loss," she moaned when she discovered she was pregnant with a seventh child. "I would rather have my brother rip it directly from my womb than birth it and endure the death of another child." Praying that night, she asked for a boon from the gods. "My lords, I beseech you. Vasudeva had an earlier wife. Let this child go to her womb and live a bountiful life. Please, let at least one of my children live in peace."

Lo and behold, the next morning Devaki was no longer pregnant. They told Kamsa it was a miscarriage, and a week later Vasudeva received a letter from his first wife, Rohini, proclaiming her happiness that she was pregnant. The seventh child of Devaki, Balarama, was born from Rohini's womb and would go on to live a prosperous life.

Touched by the gods once, now, Vasudeva and Devaki allowed themselves to believe in miracles, and it was not long after that Devaki found herself pregnant yet again. On a rainy summer night not long after Balarama's birth, the eighth child of Devaki was born. The gods had protected Balarama, the parents thought, and so surely this newborn would also be protected.

Krishna did not cry when he emerged from his mother. Instead, the infant's smiling dark-skinned body bore four symbols upon his chest: a conch, a discus, a *gada*, and a lotus. And so the child's parents knew this was the boy of prophecy: the Hindu God of Love. Vasudeva would take the boy to the nearby village of Gokul, where he would be raised by Rohini alongside Balarama. Quickly, Devaki prayed to the gods again and they agreed to put the entire kingdom to sleep so that Krishna could be smuggled out.

Krishna was born in August, during the worst of monsoon

season, and so Vasudeva endured the elements, clutching Krishna to his body in order to keep the baby dry. Coming to a river, though, Vasudeva had to lift Krishna above his head in order to cross it. With each step he took, the river rose higher and higher until it was at his shoulders. The god of the seas wished to touch Krishna's body, for he knew that Krishna was a fellow god and the savior of Mathura. Finally, the water grew so high that Krishna kicked his feet playfully within it and the river receded once the sea god had been placated. As the waters went away, the king of serpents, Vasuki, emerged and Krishna smiled, for he knew his protection was the snake's reason for being. The serpent king had several heads, all hooded and as black as baby Krishna himself.

"Do not worry," Vasuki hissed upon seeing Vasudeva's terrified face. "The protection of your son is the responsibility of us all until the day comes when he will fulfill the prophecy." With that, the cobra extended his hoods over both father and son so that they would remain dry as the pair crossed the river.

When they finally reached Gokul, Vasudeva saw a frowning woman struggling to tend to a newborn girl. Drawing closer, he recognized her as the cousin of Rohini, Yashoda. The woman was trying to get her daughter to feed but stopped when she saw the man and his newborn.

"Vasudeva," she shouted from her house, smiling when she saw Krishna. "What brings you here with this beautiful child?"

At that moment, Vasudeva knew what must be done. "Will you switch children with me and raise this one as your own?" he asked. "Will you allow him to call you mother and play with his cousin, Balarama?"

Overwhelmed with emotion, Yashoda nodded before crying. She had always wanted a boy and welcomed them inside her modest home. All ate butter to celebrate this auspicious occasion, and Vasudeva explained where he had been the last few years.

"I cannot send my daughter to her death," Yashoda warned, already moving to take her girl back.

"Do not worry," Krishna's father said. "The gods will protect this one. They brought a sleep upon the entire kingdom this night so that we could escape, and they will not permit Kamsa to kill another child. The hour of judgment is finally at hand." He continued, "tell Rohini what has occurred, and be ready when the time comes for this child to fulfill his destiny. He is a special boy, and you must treasure him."

Taking Krishna in her arms, Yashoda began to feed him and Krishna took to her breast immediately. Then Vasudeva knew he had made the right decision and returned to his prison content.

When the sun rose the next day, Kamsa stormed into the chambers of his sister and tore the infant girl from her mother's arms. Grabbing her by the legs, he slammed her body into a wall only to find the newborn transforming into an eight-armed goddess before everyone's eyes. Each of her arms held a weapon in it, and Devaki smiled upon seeing Kamsa tremble in fear.

"He is born who shall kill thee, the mighty one amongst the gods," the goddess roared. "Your tyranny is not long for this world." And as quickly as she appeared, the daughter of Yashoda disappeared...

* * *

Kamsa searched in vain for weeks to find the eighth child of Devaki. And though the prophecy had already been set in motion, he insisted on keeping Krishna's parents imprisoned. After two months, Kamsa grew so desperate he ordered a woman named Putana to put trace amounts of poison in her breast milk and offer her services as a wet nurse to all newborns in the lands. Soon, an epidemic fell upon society with infants dying left and right. Eventually, Putana made her way to Gokul and found Krishna at last...

Yashoda needed help. She couldn't handle such an energetic infant. Young as he was, Krishna could already lift his head and crawl around. He wasted no time creating mischief, whether he was stealing butter from the table or falling into the river to splash around. When a wet nurse named Putana offered her services to help watch the boy, his adopted mother gratefully accepted.

One afternoon, Krishna grew hungry and Putana knew this was her chance, as Yashoda had gone to work for the day. Letting the boy drink from her breast, she waited in anticipation. Putana had witnessed the baby do remarkable things over the last few days, and so believed this must be the one Kamsa wanted dead. After several moments, though, Krishna was still breathing. Indeed, his grip had gotten tighter. And tighter. And tighter. Opening her mouth to scream at the might of Krishna's teeth, no words escaped her mouth. She had been robbed of her voice and could only watch in terror as Krishna sucked the life out of her. Putana collapsed, now nothing but bones, and when she failed to send her nightly report to Kamsa he knew that the eighth child of Devaki lived in Gokul.

* * *

A few more weeks passed, and aside from Yashoda wondering where her wet nurse had gone, nothing of significance occurred. Until one day, when the winds began to pick up an unnatural speed...

Kamsa now sought another way to defeat this child of prophecy. "Trinivarta," he said in prayer one day. "Heed my words, asura of the winds. My nephew will challenge you one day; he will become a problem for your kind before long. Lend me your strength so that we can end him while he is still a baby." Then the wind demon, Trinivarta, appeared and raced to Gokul.

Playing in the fields with Balarama, Krishna didn't notice

everyone else in Gokul fleeing in terror. A cyclone had appeared and was ravaging all the lands. Already, houses were being lifted up.

"Krishna! Balarama!" Yashoda and Rohini shrieked in fear as they tried to save their boys. Rohini plucked Balarama from the ground and continued to run, but when Yashoda tried to do the same Krishna refused to come, instead smiling at the oncoming cyclone as if it were a toy. Though Rohini tried to pull Yashoda, too, to safety, the woman refused. She would not just leave her son to die. Seeing her stand in the way of the cyclone, Krishna crawled with great speed to meet the wind demon before his mother came to harm.

Trinivarta seized Krishna from the ground and the asura rose higher and higher to meet the heavens. Once there, the asura would drop the child from the skies. The higher Trinivarta rose, though, the heavier the baby became. Soon, Krishna weighed as much as a mountain and the wind demon could go no farther. Trinivarta plummeted to the ground, dying on impact. Krishna, though, emerged unscathed and returned to his mother's arms. And Kamsa knew, now, that this was a boy that could already slay asuras with ease.

* * *

Kamsa realized brute force would never be enough to kill Krishna. Instead, he'd send a present to Gokul that resembled a large wooden Ferris wheel. Kamsa sent a small army to deliver it as a gift to all the children in the land, and as they played with it his warriors spotted Krishna and knew by his face that he was the child of destiny.

"Kids," one soldier said, "let's do something really fun now. My men will take this wheel to the top of a mountain and we can roll you down as a fun ride." The children roared their approval, and it took fourteen men to carry the wheel up a giant hill. At the top, the men spotted Krishna near his house at the bottom of the summit. "Oops," the soldiers said as they released the wheel down the hill, pretending to lose control of it. "Sorry."

The wheel rolled down and down, faster and faster, straight for Krishna. Yashoda saw it and screamed as she came outside to take Krishna in for lunch, but it was too late for her to stop it. Fearing the worst, she closed her eyes, but when she opened them the wheel had been smashed to bits. Krishna delivered a kick to it with both of his small legs, screaming in delight at this new game. For their part, the soldiers fled in terror as bits of the broken wheel soared through the sky and cut their skin.

When the broken wood was collected and the soldiers had all retreated, the mayor of Gokul spoke. "This land is cursed. First it was Putana, and then a demon, and now this."

Others agreed, and the villagers decided to leave for greener pastures. And so, the inhabitants of Gokul migrated to the neighboring village of Davana.

* * *

Years passed without Kamsa discovering his nephew's new home. Devaki and Vasudeva, though, had been informed of the child's safety by divine messenger. "Your child remains safe, though I cannot tell you where," the gods told them.

For years that was the arrangement, and all Krishna's parents could do was pray for the day when their child would slay Kamsa and free them. Finally, on Krishna's eighteenth birthday, the king of Mathura learned of Krishna's location and sent asuras to Davana...

Krishna was playing by the lake with his best friend and cousin, Balarama, when he saw a crane fly down upon them. It had a wingspan the size of an airplane and opened its gullet to reveal sharp teeth meant to crush his skull. Jumping aside, the boy barely dodged the crane's attack.

"It's coming around again," Balarama shouted. The crane crossed the lake and prepared to dive-bomb Krishna again, but this time he was ready. Rolling to the side to avoid the crane, Krishna gave it a kick, breaking one of its wings. The demon-bird lay on its back as Krishna jumped on its body and used his hands to stretch open its beak.

"Who has sent you? Why do you seek to do us harm?"

"King Kamsa," the crane croaked before throwing itself into the air with its last gust of strength and plunging itself into the waters of the lake. It chose to drown itself rather than face Kamsa's disappointment...

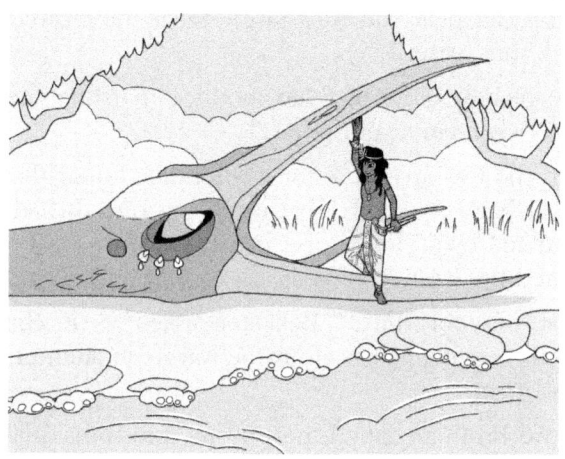

(Krishna fighting the crane demon, Meena Vempaty [2019])

* * *

A few weeks later, a wild bull charged at Krishna and Balarama as they worked on a farm, herding cows. The bull trampled over Balarama, causing him to roll down a hill bloody as cows escaped in fear.

"I will save you," Krishna said, chasing Balarama down to bring him to a halt at the foot of the hill. Then, seeing the bull charge again, Krishna dug his feet into the earth and seized the animal by the horns. Looking into its eyes, seeing the bull's hatred, Krishna knew this was no ordinary bull. Someone had sent an asura to slay him. "Tell me who sent you, and I will make your death quick," Krishna said.

"King Kamsa," the bull-demon replied. And with that, the boy threw the asura by the horns into the sun.

* * *

It had been two months since Krishna's eighteenth birthday, and he and Balarama had finally saved up enough money to go horseback riding. The boys had longed to do this ever since they were children, and now Rohini and Yashoda agreed to let them.

"I bet I can beat you in a race," Balarama crowed. "I am older and, thus, wiser."

"You are only older by a few months," Krishna said. "I bet you cannot even tame your horse."

When the two arrived at the stable, they found that all the horses had been released. That is, all but one. It had a black mane and red eyes. This horse had hooves made of obsidian and emitted fire from its nostrils.

"What magic is this?" Balarama asked as it charged at Krishna, dispensing flames along the way in an attempt to burn the young man.

The two brothers darted in opposite directions, making the horse choose whom to attack. Turning to face Balarama, it sped so fast that Balarama had to roll out of the way to avoid being trampled. Then Krishna jumped atop it and rode along as the horse tried to buck him. It neighed and huffed and thrashed itself against trees so that Krishna was eventually thrown off.

"This horse is surely an asura," Balarama said. Krishna nodded his assent before jumping on it again.

"Has King Kamsa sent you as well?" It did not answer Krishna, instead huffing fire to light the trees aflame. Bucking him again, the horse-demon shoved Krishna into the fire. With Krishna hidden in the flames, Balarama ran for help...

His son was eighteen, and though it was dangerous Vasudeva would not be denied. He had not seen Krishna since delivering him to Yashoda, and his sorrow could not be explained in words. Devaki was supposed to have come with him on this trip to Davana, but it was just too hard to smuggle both of them out of Mathura. Instead, Vasudeva would see his son and relay a message to him from Devaki. His mother was growing old and weak, and the hour was approaching when she would need to be liberated from Kamsa or accept the fact that she would die in captivity.

"Help! Help!"

Just then, Vasudeva saw a young man running towards him. "What is the problem?" he asked. Balarama filled him in, and Vasudeva realized he was speaking to his seventh child. And if that was true, Krishna could not be far behind.

Vasudeva was no god, nor did he possess any sort of superior strength or skill. Still, he was a father and so he raced to his son's aid without question. Arriving with Balarama, he saw Krishna beating the dead horse.

"There's no need for that," Balarama said. "You have done enough, and it is a very good thing."

"Why does the king focus on us instead of the wellness of his people?" Krishna asked.

"It is time to tell you all the truth," Vasudeva said. "Where is Yashoda?" Then the three men gathered in the house of Yashoda, with Rohini present as well, and Krishna the cowherder learned the truth. He was Krishna, the eighth son of Devaki.

* * *

Within days, everyone knew the truth about Krishna. The whole village of Davana was gossiping, and in that time Kamsa heard the news as well. Though Vasudeva had returned to the castle as quickly as possible, Kamsa knew it could only be he who had spoken to Krishna. "It is time to end this," Kamsa said. Realizing he would have to bring Krishna to him, he ordered Krishna and Balarama report to Mathura to participate in a wrestling tournament. The prophecy was delivered to

Kamsa on such a sweltering summer day so many years ago, and now with a scorching sun above Krishna and Balarama as they entered Mathura, it would come to pass one way or another.

A coliseum had been erected for all to witness the triumph of Kamsa over his nephew. In truth, though, the king feared fighting this warrior who had slain every asura sent after him. So, Kamsa tried one last time to have the boy killed. When Krishna and Balarama arrived at the entrance to the arena, they encountered an elephant. The beast swung its trunk at them, but Krishna dodged it while Balarama jumped on its back and began punching the beast. As blows rained down upon it, the elephant fell to the ground. Grabbing its trunk, Krishna pulled himself towards the animal and ended its life with a blow to the face.

Krishna and Balarama entered the stage soon after, each holding an ivory tusk from the elephant in their raised hands. As the crowd cheered, Kamsa ordered his two best wrestlers be sent to challenge the brothers. Within minutes, both were disposed.

"Uncle!" Krishna shouted. "Enough have suffered because of your feud with me. Face me now if you are not afraid."

Then Kamsa jumped from his stage and extended his muscles so that the crowd could see his might. "Impudent child!" he roared. "I should have ended your mother's life the day of her wedding." Enraged, Krishna raced toward his uncle to fulfill the prophecy at last.

Krishna and Kamsa traded blows for several minutes, until Krishna grabbed ahold of his uncle's toe and threw him over his shoulder. The king landed on his face in the dirt, and the crowd laughed. "See now, uncle," Krishna said. "Your people have no love for you. Amend your ways before it is too late."

"I would rather be feared than loved," Kamsa replied. He lifted himself up and charged at the son of Devaki, but the boy merely stretched out his palm and held Kamsa's head in it so that the king could not move.

"You are neither loved nor feared, for I have now exposed your weakness." Krishna dragged his uncle by the hair and ran around the arena, and the king's face grew filthy with dirt and blood as the people threw rocks at him from their seats. After fourteen laps, Krishna released his uncle's hair and watched as the king struggled to get up. "You who have reigned by cruelty, who have tormented my parents for so long, who has destroyed countless lives trying to end mine. Today, Kamsa, you are judged and found guilty by this jury of your peers."

The men and women of the stadium jeered and begged Krishna to end their torment at long last. "I am the eighth avatar of Vishnu, chosen by prophecy to end your reign, and today I fulfill my destiny!" Raising his left hand, bringing it down like a clap of thunder on Kamsa's back, Krishna broke both body and spirit.

The crowd was ebullient, but Krishna left their cheers behind to search Kamsa's castle with Balarama. Finding Devaki, mother and son embraced for the first time in over eighteen years.

"My son," she wept. "I knew you would return."

Then Yashoda, too, was invited to Mathura for celebrations, but though the woman came she could not enjoy the festivities.

"Why are you so glum?" Devaki asked.

"You have gained a son, and that is to be celebrated," Yashoda said. "But I have lost one."

Then Krishna, overhearing this conversation, came to greet them. He bowed to touch the feet of both women before speaking. "I am the most fortunate of beings because I have two mothers."

Then Yashoda smiled, and all partook in celebrations. And thus ended the story of Krishna's birth and the fulfillment of prophecy.

Bharat calls himself a professional storyteller and amateur cook. He's always looking to make a political statement with his writing because he knows politics seeps into every aspect of society and believes we can't understand each other without a firm, constant understanding of how politics affects us in all ways. He is currently working on a sequel to Privilege: A Trilogy, which won "Best Adult Fiction" for the Ohio chapter of the Indie Author Project. He's also been published in the award-winning anthology, Once Upon a Winter, and is a member of the Science Fiction & Fantasy Writers of America.

Juniper and the Upside Down Well

Ella Holmes

The Before.

The strangest thing about the well was not that it was upside down, but that it spoke.

I leaned against a moss-eaten rock, as I have since I found this place last summer, my back and brow dripping with sweat from the walk through the trees, carrying a pack with my carving tools inside. We could barely hear Whistler's Peak from here, a fact Lily-Fingers—named so because his talons were decidedly unlike the soft of a lily's petals—*cra_{ww}*ed at me the whole way into the woods. And louder again, when we passed the boundary trees with their trunks wrapped with iron wire. To keep him appeased, I threw him strips of dried fish, and he caught them as he swooped from branch to branch alongside me.

Lily-Fingers was a brave little crow, but he flew nowhere near the well.

The well hung stone-still amongst the oak tree canopy the way bees hover over flowers, voice echoing in her throat when she caught me staring. "Stop ogling."

I blew away the curled wood from the rose I had carved into the shoulder of a new lap harp, accustomed to her jokes. "How else am I to know you're *well?*"

Water gurgled, a maybe-laugh. "And some say you're not funny."

"My people say equally incorrect things about yours," I reminded her. "They call you good-folk nothing but tricksters." I've always hated the story of Princess Stiorra in particular—how the drought sucked the life from crops, turned our grass so dry it caught fire and choked the sky with smoke, all but powdered the cow's milk. Desperate, Princess Stiorra chose to give herself away, for a large favour comes at an enormous cost, especially with the good-folk. 'However,' I say, 'and I mean no disrespect by this, you don't seem so dangerous to me—what with being stuck in the air, made of rock and all."

A breeze blew through the woods, the slightest relief from the beating summer heat.

"I could fall on you, Juniper."

I arched a brow, lolled my head back as though she had eyes I could look into. "And rid yourself of my good company?"

The well's silence fell as heavy as cold water over me, though there was no explaining it when the water inside her never dripped nor dropped. It was a good thing there was water in there at all, for it we had been suffering through a throat-sandingly dry summer and the drought it brought with it for over a year.

"Will... will you return tomorrow?" she asked.

I smiled, all cold washed away by her question. "Of course."

As I carved, the sun dragged heavy golden fingers through the trees, clinging to what it could, and the sight was such that a sad song of longing came to me. I pulled out my starflowercarved flute and played it, with, I thought, no one else to hear.

* * *

Mother had lit the house to an orange glow with a soft, pine-cone fire, while father plated the stew, bread, and cheese for supper, humming a tune under his breath. Instruments were what my family was known for, but my and my father's true love lay in the tunes one might pluck or blow or beat from the harps and flutes and drums we crafted. It was a thing of magic, to beg from the trees a piece of wood with heart enough to hold the shapes we carved them into.

I was breathing in the savoury steam of my stew when a delicate knock rapped the door. The iron latch grated as Mother unlocked it and opened the door to the night and the black-cloaked man who blended with it. Rain jewelled his hood and shoulders, though there had been none yet this summer. "I am here to ask for your daughter's hand," he said before Mother had the chance to greet him.

He drew back his hood and looked at me, revealing blue eyes, curled copper hair, and skin warm and freckled as the embered fire. "You played the wood's tune this day, as it mourned the sun's farewell. I was told my love would do so. We're destined to be together." He produced a daisy from the air and held it out.

Mother pushed the door closed. "Get the iron!" she hissed.

I snatched an iron bar from the boot beside the hearth, fisted it as I added my weight to the door. "My answer is no," I called out, while mother, with her bark-brown hair and smile lines, looked at me as though I were mad. Perhaps I was—to displease the good-folk was to invite horror, but he was already here and waiting, and I'd be damned if I said nothing.

"I understand your fear," he said, "but I mean no harm."

What he said must have been truth, for all uncanny beings are bound by the words they speak. Still, I could not believe it. "I said no, so if you truly mean us no harm, you'll leave."

Crickets chirped outside, the only beings unbothered by his presence. If anything, they sang to it. Mother held an iron nail, while Father still hummed from the kitchen in complete unawareness. His hearing was not what it once was, nor was his heart, and neither Mother nor I were willing to let go of the door or frighten him.

The man took his foot away, and the door thumped shut. "It is the forest's decree that we should wed," his voice muffled through the wood. "I grew on its sap and soil and know this to be true."

I would not have my fate decided for me. "Anyone can wring a tune from an instrument. My father is more skilled on the flute than I am, and he sings right now—would you wed him for it?"

Mother hit my arm. If I had told her about the well, she'd likely have wrung my neck.

The good-folk's silence held all the tension of a weighted thread on the cusp of breaking. Then he broke it in the strangest way. "Well," he said, with the tone of thinking aloud. "No, I don't suppose I would. If you don't wish to wed, then I suppose that is that."

This was not at all what I'd been taught to expect from the good-folk, nor men, and he was both. "That is that?" I repeated, the iron bar warming in my palm.

"Yes," he said. There was a scuffing of footsteps on packed dirt, retreating, before his voice suddenly sounded again. "I'm sorry—you wouldn't have anything else for me to do, would you? I'm afraid I'm at quite a loss for what to do with myself."

Mother shook her head, but I opened the door by a hair. "What kind of good-folk are you that you wouldn't simply take what you want?"

"The good kind?" His smile was almost shy. "I'm an outcast among my folk, and this rejection will persuade nobody toward friendship with me. Besides, now that you have said no... I think marriage is not something I wanted either."

I stared at him. Despite his height and the strong set of his shoulders, he looked like no farm boy I'd ever known. His features were far too handsome and unblemished for a life of toiling fields, too kind and open for what he was. I was curious about him, and it gave me an idea. "We're about to eat. How would you feel about washing dishes?"

His brows quirked. "I've never washed dishes before, but I would try it."

"And you won't—" I waggled my fingers in between us, and shrugged at Mother when she frowned at the action. I didn't know how to phrase all the things he could do to us.

"I swear," he said. "I swear I will not trick, or harm, or try to beguile anyone here." He watched my mind pluck through his words, digging through confusion and surprise. Such was the nature of the good-folk, that anything spoken was truth, or binding, or both. What surprised me equally was that he was a man, taking my word as I gave it.

"Well, then." I opened the door.

* * *

The Now.

That is how I came to know Arden. Since he gave his word not to harm us, my parents' fear blunted to a dull uneasiness around him, which quickly softened. Arden took to the washing of dishes as softwood does to delicate shapes under a skilled blade-hand, and made himself useful in milking the cow and collecting eggs from our chickens, all the while speaking to me of his life in the woods. He had called himself an outcast, and it seemed true, for he does not play the mindless tricks his kin do. It set them at odds, like children crying when another refuses to play.

Lily-Fingers avoided him at first, *crawn*ing at me night and day when Arden was not around. Now, he accepts the fish strips and berries Arden offers him.

When Arden comes to the carving room, Lily-Fingers jerks his head to me as though to ask if I'm okay with it, and I nod, and we both listen to Arden's tales as I work.

"Destiny," Arden says as he watches me finish carving the last rose on the shoulder of a harp, "is a thing I never thought to challenge. When the forest speaks, we listen. What the old-folk desire, we give or take or create."

"And what good would it have been, marrying me?" I ask, looking for the needle-tip knife I put down before. "I have no desire for children, nor for the act it takes to make them, nor for being tied to one I don't love."

Arden stoops before me and picks up the tool, handing it to me with a grin. "I don't think it would have been so terrible. We get along nicely, do we not? What does that make us?"

I consider him, this honest trickster. "You may be my never-husband, so you can't forget my choice."

"Not the trusting type, are you, my never-wife?"

"I trust," I say, "when I can be sure a thing is what it is."

Arden nods. "Wise. And if a thing is not what it seems?"

"Then I'll hear its tale and decide what to do. Why? Are you not what you seem?"

"Not handsome and kind, you mean? Please, Juniper, I'm every bit as I appear." He grunts when I punch his chest, but his grin doesn't falter. "Scarcely a month not-married and you already batter me, without even knowing of what I speak."

I arch a brow. "What do you mean?"

"I will say it simply. Your well is not one of my kind. She is the Princess Stiorra."

Lily-Fingers swoops from his perch by the arched window and lands on the table in front of us. He *cawws* for food, which

Arden stands to give him.

"What are you saying?" I ask, rooted to my seat. "Everyone says she gave herself up to the Otherworld and is dancing forever in one of your courts, or some such fate." We laud the freshwater wells given in return for her, and thank the princess in our prayers, but it suddenly seems like an impossible tale—for even though women frequently enter into marriage bargains to the benefit of their family, it's not often done so happily.

Guilt gnaws my belly. Such is the tale spun so strongly, I never thought to question it.

Arden pulls a small wooden bowl from the air, overflowing with red berries. He pops one in his mouth before settling the bowl before Lily-Fingers. "Your people sacrificed her to end the summer drought," he says. "They forced her into the deep of the Old Wood, past the trees you wrap with iron, and she, instead of cowering and crying and cursing her fate, asked for water."

"Why turn her into a well?" I ask. "She's upside down, cannot even..." I wave my hands around, angry at my voicelessness. "She's alone."

"She has had you," Arden amends.

"She didn't tell me."

"She couldn't. My father was specific with his words—just like she tried to be."

I look at Arden, jaw so tight it hurts. Perhaps he is a trickster after all. "You saw it?"

"I heard it from the forest, though it would not tell me the complete tale. I have seen you talking to Stiorra, finding hearty wood and carving your instruments. You cared for her even when you thought she was one of my kind, and since she cannot tell you herself, I find I must tell you the conditions of her curse even if you can do nothing."

"Can I? Do anything?"

He shrugs, frowning. "The conditions my father laid on her are these: So long as she speaks not of this spell, nor this tale, she shall be returned to her body if she is filled with that which will not weigh her down." He purses his lips. "Whomsoever lays the curse has the answer in mind—though there are many possibilities, it is that one we must find. And there is but the last of summer to help her before she becomes the well she appears to be."

I shake my head, taking my harp back into my lap like it's a pillow that can bring me comfort. With my knife, I shave down the pillar with long strokes.

Summer will end in seven days. Stroke.

Where do we begin? Stroke.

"You would go against your father?" Pause. "How am I to trust you?"

"I swore I would not trick or harm anyone here, did I not?" He looks at me, blue eyes wide and earnest.

"I suppose you did," I admit. "Why did you wait so long to tell me?"

"You rejected what the forest destined for us, and it shook me, seeing all the paths I thought ahead of me wither. Can you blame me for needing time to recover my delicate sensibilities?"

I snort. "I think you should travel *this* path with me, if only so I might laugh."

Arden smiles. "What sort of never-husband would I be if I didn't?"

* * *

Arden knows the forest better than I and helps us avoid disturbing any of the good-folk with a penchant for biting, stealing, and riddling humans to disadvantage. Lily-Fingers calls out, and I announce our presence to Stiorra by stomping so she can hear us coming—not that she has any skirts to smooth or eyes to see us, but it gives her some choice in privacy.

"Someone is with you?" she asks when we stand under her.

"Yes," I say, and nod as I would in the presence of any royalty. "This is Arden. He is one of the good-folk, which is rather funny considering he looks like a young man, but then I suppose they all do." I shut my mouth, finding myself nervous and rambling for a reason I can't name. "He told me about your curse, princess. I'd like to try breaking it."

The water in Stiorra's throat rushes faster, as though the words she cannot say are running away. "You shall have my gratitude, Juniper," she murmurs. "And you, Arden, though I'm hesitant to accept help from..."

"I'm here to help," he says. "I don't play tricks as my father does."

Stiorra gives a flat hum.

"We'll do our best." I would lay a comforting hand to her stone, but she's too high to reach. "What can we fill you with that will not weigh you down? Have you any ideas, Arden?"

"My father never spoke the answer aloud." He scratches a hand through his copper-red hair, curled like wood shavings. "Air?" With the flick of his hand, a breeze whips up the leaves around us and flies into the well. Nothing happens. "Breath?"

I hang my head, half in exasperation at how difficult this is already turning out to be, and half so I can look at the well. "Not to ask a foolish question, but have you tried breathing?"

A water-logged snort. "I'm a well."

Sighing, I look at Arden. The very idea was ridiculous, if not something the good-folk would choose. I've heard tales of them using outlandish things as answers to their riddles and curses—bannocks, toe bones, three raps on a stone—and I think that's where we should start looking. "We should find a storyteller. They're good at taking threads of riddles and twisting them into answers."

Arden nods. "They have a penchant for imbuing wisdom and truth in stories. It's a talent my people fear."

"So, we begin in the village." I dust nonexistent wood curls from my skirt out of habit.

"Would you also look for my charm on your treks through the woods?" Stiorra asks. "It's a moon of silver-dipped iron, and precious to me."

Lily-Fingers *crawws* thrice and takes flight in a handsome swooping circle.

"Lily-Fingers will search for it," I relay to her. "We'll return soon."

* * *

A silver-haired storyteller sits on a bench by the hearth, several children gathered at his feet. The tavern sits in comfortable chatter, not loud enough to drown him out, only enough to keep a steady rhythm about the room, constant as the smell of smoke and roast meat. It makes me uneasy, this calm. With so little time, sitting and buying mulled wine as we wait for the storyteller to finish has me fidgeting.

As it happens, we don't need to approach him, for he comes to us. I offer him my untouched drink.

"Thank you," he says, and sips. "Telling stories often comes at the cost of a sore throat."

"It's the same with playing the harp," I say. "Sore fingers."

"I am Cole. What is it you wish from me?"

"How do you know we want something from you?" I glance at Arden, sitting tall and quiet.

"I am a storyteller. To everything, there is a pattern, and I see the weaving of life as and before it happens. And you," he looks at Arden, "you stand out to me like a stray thread."

Arden cocks his head and says nothing until I explain our purpose here, where he tells Cole exactly what his father said.

"So long as she speaks not of this spell, nor this tale, she shall be returned to her body if she is filled with that which will not weigh her down."

Cole nods. "I can weave a tale in which you may find an answer." He closes his eyes and drinks again, dirtying his purple sleeve when he wipes his mouth. His eyes dart beneath his eyelids.

"Where there was no wind, a woman danced,
her hair as brown as oak.
She volunteered her head to stone,
begged sailing winds from the good-folk.

For there was an army of leathered men
who wished to tread the sea,
but not a sail could billow when
the good-folk stilled the breeze.

Take from me what life I breathe,
she said, send these men to other shores,
And such a vision was she
that the good-folk could scarce ignore.

The king of old looked upon her,
and saw what she could be,
The very wind she begged for,
which her people now did plead.

He took her body, made it air,
and gave her rules to follow.

Fill her with something weightless and true,
to break her silence shortly after,
For how can joy be held without at least a little laughter?"

Laughter—have I made Stiorra laugh before? I thank the storyteller, though I dislike the tale he spun, and he smiles with a gleam in his eye only common in those who travel and tell the tales of it. "How can I pay you?"

"I shall simply keep this part of the story for my own," he says, standing. "If it does not work, seek my kin in the next town. They are a better weaver than even me."

I am inclined to agree, if only because I no longer believe anyone could sacrifice themselves so happily, even in verse.

* * *

Stiorra laughs. I laugh. Arden laughs. Lily-Fingers *crawws*.

And still, with only days remaining to save Stiorra, she remains stone.

I finish carving my harp, trying to dig comfort out of the wood.

* * *

The long-dry fountain, a galloping horse, sits in the centre of the village. It's from there that the second storyteller speaks. Their voice, though soft and melodic, rings out across the dirt yard for all to hear, even over the sound of cattle, carts, and sellers peddling iron charms. Though I'm sweaty from the long walk, I link arms with Arden as we approach the crowd. His steps are too smooth and soundless for the common-born human man he pretends to be, and he's so curious about the goings-on around us that his feet seem intent on carrying him away.

His body stiffens like a wood log when the iron peddler

jangles a fist of charms.

"Have you ever touched it?" I whisper.

Arden eyes the necklaces dangling from the man's pointer finger, each charm fashioned in the shape of nails, swords, and arrow tips. "When I was a babe. It's not pleasant." He turns the arm I'm holding so his palm faces up, a burn line running across the length of it. "Fear of iron is a learned thing."

"As is fear of you," the storyteller says, suddenly before us.

I plant myself between them and Arden without thinking. The storyteller's hair, dark as pitch and springing from her head in a cloud of curls, frames an unassuming smile. "Greetings," I say.

She waves a hand, telling us to follow her back to the fountain where folk have tossed coins to the waterless bottom in return for the tale. "I am Neryn. It is obvious you were waiting for me, and not to sing my praises. What is it you want?"

Arden seems speechless, so I relay our story, including what we learned from her kin, how his solution didn't work, and how we only have three days left.

"Forgive me," Arden says, "but you're quite beautiful."

I elbow his side with the arm linking me to him. "You cannot just say things like that. Even if it's true," I add, a blush creeping up my neck.

"When one speaks the truth, there is nothing to forgive," Neryn says around a smile. Her reddish-brown cheeks glow brighter as she says to me, "I will weave this tale for you, but only while you play a song. I've not made enough coin this season, and you have the fingers of a songstress."

A song is a thing I can give, but I'm wary of the time we have left. "A quick song," I say. A half-question.

When Neryn nods, I pull the flute out from the pocket of my skirt and unlink my arm from Arden's before sitting on the pale ledge of the fountain. I test a high note. It echoes beautifully inside the bowl of stone.

So, I play. The tune comes to me of its own accord, the fountain whispering in my ear, the lilting chorus of a time with water and without, of glorious golden sun in summer and delicate dancing snow in winter. My fingers rise and fall with the grace of the breeze it tells me about, with the ease of heat clinging to stone.

Neryn stands beside me and begins her tale.

"A field of wanting wheat did cry,
for leaf and stalk and soil were dry.
Strong farmers, high-born, men of all,
Mourned the life-giving touch of rainfall.

They thought what thing might grant them water,
 might be to gift the great king's daughter.
 For a daughter is a natural victim,
 to what or whom she's given."

"There is no heroism without the drawing of swords,
 a silver cut of valour
 But if she keeps her silence,
 she may yet take on its pallor.

So the story spun is one of thanks,
 for what she stood to do,
 For the choice she had was hers, of course,
 and nothing but the truth.

The princess hangs against the sky,
  cursed to carry the water for which men cried,
  It's in their bones and in her stone,
  where the weightless-heavy secrets lie."

The last notes canter from my flute, tumbling around the fountain's bowl until they slow and fade into a silence broken almost immediately. Hands in pockets and purses, the clink of coins into stone, the clapping of hands—it brays in my ears as people shake my hand and compliment my playing. They say my flute is beautiful, a thing of envy. They ask where they might purchase such instruments, and I sputter that my family carves them, quite overwhelmed by the compliments. Some push coins in my hand, others tug at my sleeves for another song.

Arden plants himself between me and the swell of people, and nods to Neryn with something more than farewell and thanks in his eyes. I think a part of him stays with her, a part of her with him, and a part of me in the fountain.

* * *

When I make it to Stiorra the day after next—alone, for sharing secrets is hard to do even with one person—I glow red-cheeked with giddiness and heat from running. The excitement of freedom, the elation of having done something and loved it to chest-bursting happiness, the hope her curse might end today. "I played the flute for them, and they acted as though I'd spun gold from it. They even asked to buy anything I made. Me!"

"Of course," Stiorra says. "You play so beautifully, I'd think it a wonder if they didn't."

I cannot stop smiling as I build a small fire for light rather than warmth. "Thank you. I've not even told my parents. I had to tell you first." When the fire clings to the kindling and the air smells richly of burning wood, I tell her the tale Neryn spun, and how the answer she gave was *secrets*—for what else is weightless and heavy at the same time?

"Are you sure?" Stiorra asks. "I shall hold your secrets forever, Juniper, but it's still much to ask of you."

My hand goes to my pocketed flute, a source of comfort. "Nobody knows me as well as I'd like," I admit. "I think... We've spent enough time together that I'd like it to be you."

The water in her rushes faster, rather like a tumbling heartbeat. "Then I'll share mine first." A pause. "I don't wish to wed a man."

I wait for the magic, for something to happen. Nothing does —and it stings, for I see myself in her admission, feel it like a warm blanket. "Nor do I," I whisper, then shout it so it echoes in her throat. "And I don't like Cobbler Farlan's shoes. I said I did, but they're too pointed in the toe. I don't dream of having children, even if it's expected of me." Shouting into the night and Stiorra above me, my chest relents the tension I've always had coiled there. "I resent that people listen to my music more than they do my words."

"I like the sound of your voice, Juniper," Stiorra says. "I look forward to your company and think of it when you're gone."

I smile, quite forgetting the purpose of our secret-sharing. "Sometimes when I'm carving in the shop, I imagine myself sitting against this rock, talking to you like this. In my head, I tell you everything. How I eat the carrots on my plate only to please my father, how I wish to play music until the ground takes me into herself, how I have never seen the ocean but often dream of sailing far away so I might see new things and plant them in my songs."

Losing ourselves to the shouting, our voices echo several times over, the same way hopes dare to grow roots in my heart. We spend the afternoon like this, stopping only when dusk bruises the forest and night soothes it to darkness, and Arden comes with Lily-Fingers perched on his shoulder. Their arrival stings, for it reminds me of what I hoped would happen tonight, and what has not, and what we have only tomorrow to do.

Tears come far too easily to me—my mother has always said this. But Arden settles at my side and hugs me without judgement. He folds his cloak and tells me to lay my head upon it, and together we rest under the canopy, the stars that appear through the needles of it, and Stiorra who is still a well.

Lily-Fingers *crawws*, and I make an almost-nest out of the crook of my arm for him to stand in.

"I never thought I could trust one of the good-folk," Stiorra says after a while. "But you seem a good friend to Juniper."

Arden grins at me. "Anything for my never-wife."

"While I do some things sometimes for my never-husband," I reply, earning a laugh from both of them. Lily-Fingers narrows his eyes, disturbed from his sleep.

"I'll share a secret," Arden says. "I've always seen myself fitting more with your people than with my own. It's that, perhaps, that outcasts me."

I look at him. "Is this a safe place for you to admit such a thing?"

"No good-folk will come here until the curse is broken, or... set," he whispers to me.

"How do you know this?"

"I bargained for it," he says. "Privacy." There's a shine in his eye I can't name the meaning of, and I thank him. "Another secret I hold is that I get drunk off milk and honey—"

"Everyone knows this," Stiorra and I say.

"—and turn into quite the talented dancer," he finishes the funny admission that turns sad with every echo.

"Then you must show us," Stiorra says.

"No." I frown. "We should think of answers."

"Juniper—"

"No," I say again, sitting up and disturbing Lily-Fingers so much that he perches himself in a nearby tree. "We can't waste any more time."

"Happiness, laughter, none are a waste," she says. "In fact, I desire it. Dance for me. Let me hear your laughter, the thump of your feet on the earth, the heaviness of your breath as you move. This way, I may fill with joy and hope that one day I might dance with you."

Arden stands first and offers his hand to me. "Will you hum for us, princess?" he requests, and Stiorra agrees.

"In the morning, we do all we can," I say to them both, unable to deny her request.

I take Arden's hand and let him lead us into a dance, led by the wind-blown tune of Whistler's Peak and Stiorra's rushing-water hum. Around the fire, we sway with the grace of leaping deer, and the closeness of otters holding hands as they drift downriver, and the happiness of bumblebees finding golden pollen in springtime. Our booted feet meet the earth again and again, a rhythmic beat in the heart of the forest. We hold hands and spin and spin and spin, kicking up summer-dry leaves until joy swells and laughter bursts from us, and we fall asleep in the dawn-lit echo of it.

* * *

I wake to a cold drop on my forehead, and slight pressure on my stomach.

Not rain, for it's solid, and Lily-Fingers *crawws* at me excitedly, jumping on my belly. I pull Stiorra's silver moon charm off my face, and I hold it up before I remember she cannot see. "Lily-Fingers found your charm, Stiorra." I pat his head. "Good job."

"Thank you," she replies. "It's yours now, in return for all you've done for me."

I don't know what to say, for she speaks as though she has given up. Arden is gone too, only his cloak left behind. I strain my ears, but hear only wind and Lily-Fingers's flight as he takes to the trees. The sun is high.

Too high.

Arden appears at the treeline, a small bag hanging across his shoulders.

"Why didn't either of you wake me?" I ask, springing to my feet. "It's nearly midday!"

He pulls apples, a small loaf of seeded bread, and a waterskin from the bag, laying them on the cloak. "You needed rest, and to eat, and I've been doing all I can to find answers."

"I could have helped," I say, looking between him and the well. "Don't go quiet now. You're frightening me. We still have time, don't we?"

"Until the sun begins to fall," she says, too slow for my liking.

My heart feels like the apple in Arden's hand, cut into the wedges he urges me to take. I only eat because my belly betrays my hunger, and I've little else to do but sit and think. His hands make quick work of the bread too. "I tried to ask my folk if they knew my father's answer to the riddle, but they would not help. On the way back, I had thought it could be anger, for as women, that's a thing you're taught to refrain from, is it not?"

"I have been angry," Stiorra says.

"Of course she has. She's a well, and made thus without choice," I snap. It claps through her stones, and I close my eyes at myself, not least of all because it does nothing to return her to herself. "I'm sorry, Arden. My anger is not toward you."

"I know," he says, and squeezes my hand.

I wrack my mind like a child ripping whatever flowers they can from a garden. "Love," I say, "the answer must be love." What else could it be? "It weighs nothing, but your heart may be full of it. Mine is. That must mean something."

A sigh echoes through her stones. "I do love you, Juniper," she murmurs. "But if that were the answer, it would have changed me back already. Just as I was hopeless before you came, less so when you declared you would like to help me. Now, the hopelessness does not hurt so much, for I was happier here than I was elsewhere."

My heart cracks at her confession. It beats inside my chest like a great bird, desperate for flight. "Happiness. Sadness. Something!" I fling guesses to the trees. "I don't know, Stiorra. I don't..." The sun peaks, taking my voice with it.

"It's alright," she says. Her voice grates like rock on rock, flat and cold and lifeless. "It was not near enough time, but I'm glad we had any at all." Her stones dull, like a green stem turning grey with death. "Did you bring what I asked, Arden?"

"I did," Arden says, pulling my lap harp from the bag.

"Would you play it for me?" Stiorra asks, her voice heavy with emotion, or water, or the sudden stiffness of her shape. "Please."

My eyes water. I take the harp from Arden, and he offers an encouraging smile. "Of course," I say. How could I deny her?

I begin by plucking the strings along its length with the gentleness of a bee coaxing pollen from little flowers, thinking that if Stiorra is to go, she should go with all the gifts I have to give. So I sing the story of us, of Arden coming upon my door and begging marriage, of us saying no to destiny. The tree canopy sways with a strong breeze, kicking up the sound of rattling leaves and the smell of dry wood. In it, I hear more.

The story of that summer, of the blinding sun and sweat-wringing heat. I relay what the forest tells me through its every rustling leaf and creak of wood. The true tale, the one Stiorra lived, but could not tell. The song fills Stiorra's stone throat until I'm singing back to myself several times over.

"Taken by men into the forest was she,
A princess who asked from the old-folk, the key
For the people she begged, water to cure
Thirst and throats, all summer-sore.

She said, 'Bring water back, end this summer-spell.'
Not knowing the cost was becoming a well."

A well-stone falls to the ground before us, but I don't stop singing, for though she is gone, it's too important. Arden joins in with a melodic hum, his hand on the chest of the great oak beside us.

"She did not curse those who forced her to stand,
In a place she might suffer for the healing of land.

She sarcased, 'If it means men might drink of water again,
what is one woman's life in the tapestry of things,
but a deciding thread, yet the weakest of strings?'"

I repeat her words as a chorus. And there, a low whisper of wind through the trees. The well-stones break apart and drum a beat into the soil as they fall.

"And the old-folk did laugh,
and the old-one did say,

> '*Not one of those men*
> *would be half as brave.*'

But still, he magicked her heart to stone,
  her soul to water, and hung her alone.

He said, 'So long as she speaks not of this spell, nor this tale,
  she shall be returned to her body,
  if she is filled with that which will not weigh her down.'

And it was the old-one alone who knew the answer to this charm.
  May the truth of her story now undo the harm.

'If it means men might drink of water again,
  what is one woman's life, in the tapestry of things,
  but a deciding thread, yet the weakest of strings?'

The stones rain down until there is nothing left. I drop my harp. The trees around us settle, the breeze having died with the last note of our song. Silence claims the forest, and sadness claims me. Arden holds my hand as I stare at Stiorra's remains.

If truth was the answer, we told it too late.

I don't know what to say. If Stiorra is not around to hear me —I think I might not speak again, for she's the one I would tell all to. Ardan's arms come around me when my first tear falls, his own eyes glassy and wide.

Craww. Lily-Fingers swoops down from his summer-dry oak perch, landing by the remains. *Craww.*

The fallen stones clatter together, piece by piece. Edges

over edges, thumping, thudding, and cracking as they press into each other. The grey blanches to a vivid white, softens to fabric.

And there—the gold of wheat in sunlight, curled and long and brilliant. Little stones become pale fingers, become an elbow, become shoulders.

Stiorra crawls to life, finding her feet before they're truly hers and stumbling right into my arms. I cling to her, rubbing the cold from her body, throat tight as the tuned string of a lute. "Stiorra," I cry. "Truth. It was truth."

Her laughter is like a song, so beautiful and joyous I cry for the hearing of it. "Yes," she says. "Juniper, Juniper, Juniper."

"I know. I had the answer all along." My neck and cheeks blaze with embarrassment.

"No," she says. "I just wanted to say your name with my own mouth—you've no idea how much I've longed to do so." She smiles brilliantly. "Might I also kiss you?"

I nod, and her lips press to my mouth, soft and sweet. At first I think my skin is tingling, but a dollop of cold water splashes over my forehead, one more, and another, and we look up to see a sudden grey sky full of rain. It buckets down, soaking us in an instant.

The first true downpour in years, marking the end of Summer, the end of the drought. The soil turns dark as it drinks of the rain, cupping it in rippling pools.

"How is this happening?" I shout at Arden, who grins at us, red hair plastered to his face.

"My bargain," he shouts back, and laughs. "I bargained with my father for rain, believing you could solve his riddle. I may not trick as he does, but I play games just as well."

Together, we laugh and dance until Whistler's Peak calls us home.

Ella T. Holmes always dreamed of being a Mad Hatter, Trojan horse, or a cunning princess who is definitely not a witch but reality intervened. Fortunately, she's got a knack for escaping it.

Born and raised around Australia, Ella spends her time avoiding bush turkeys, and drinking enough coffee to bring down the moon. Her work has been published in or is forthcoming in Coffin Bell Journal, Antithesis, and Macfarlane Lantern Publishing Seasonal Anthologies, among others.

LOVE IN THE TIME OF VOLCANOES

Jake Curran-Pipe

"You got any honey rum?" Gara whispered to the old man.

He looked astounded that a princess from another island would even bother speaking to him. She had slipped away from the festivities by the black-sand shore to a small copse of pine trees to marvel at the fresh, woody smell and towering verdant limbs. Nothing on her island of Ghomara evoked such floral beauty: all the plants she had ever known were vicious and hard. Embracing the thick trunk she closed her eyes and inhaled the bright aroma.

"It's strong," the man said whilst the princess hugged the tree in an arboreal trance. She was enamoured by the ridged grooves of the bark.

"No matter. Anything's better than that ghastly milk they're serving," she replied.

"Here you go, Princess," he said, handing her a conch filled with the homemade concoction. Gara peeled herself from the tree, her eyebrows twisted in curiosity.

"How did you know?"

"No commoner could afford such patterns on their tunic."

She looked down at the swirling patterns that had been

embossed by her father's leather worker. She took the ornate shell and thanked the man before knocking back the sweet, deep rum.

"Much better. Why aren't you at the festival?"

"My body cannot seem to handle the heat anymore. I like to stay here in the trees now," he said. "I've already made my prayers to the Sun Mother."

"Good old Chaxiraxi," smiled Gara as the old man lay at the stump of the tree.

"And why aren't you at the festivities, Princess?"

Gara sighed and stared out to the distant beach where folk from all seven islands were laughing and dancing and gossiping. She saw the prince from Benahoare that her mother was trying to get her engaged to; he was juggling some custard apples to amuse the children from the far eastern desert isle of Tyterogaka. The sun was gradually sliding down toward the sea, and soon enough there would be glosses of orange and purple painting the brilliant blue sky. Gara sighed once more and looked down at the rum-filled conch.

"Thanks for the drink, mister. What was your name?"

His eyes were closed, a gentle snore emitting from his nostrils. Gara smiled and placed the conch gently next to him before fixing the ivy on his straw hat.

Meanwhile, in the blanket of vibrant bougainvillaea, Prince Jonay hid from his persistent mother. The ornamental vines were a proud labour of love for his mother, the Queen of Southern Achinet, who adored nothing more than getting her hands dirty and making art from the flowers of this rich island. "Soil might be messy, but what beauty can come from it!" she would always say whenever Jonay flinched at the idea of getting his fingernails dirty to care for some bright yellow foxgloves.

The scorching sun was beginning to set, sending a ripple of fluid shadows across the coastal village. Jonay's chest tightened with anxiety at the thought of going back to the beach. His whole life was about to be upended, destroyed by his parents. And they wouldn't even know why.

He sighed and busied his hands with the bougainvillaea to stop them from shaking. Thoughts of running off into the hills never to be seen again dashed across his fraught mind. If only his mother wasn't so protective of him, he could easily spend the rest of his life up in the rainforest. Instead, his destiny was to be in charge of everyone that lived by the blistering shore. Too hot, too frigid. A life in the forest would set him free of the constraints put upon him by *tradition.*

Something scampered past him in the corner of his eye. He flinched, his arms raised ready to fight off a drunkard wanting the attention of a prince.

"Who's there?" he said, his voice cracking.

Nothing. Just the sound of waves, canaries, and distant laughter.

Then, another rustle.

Intrigued, Jonay followed the sound. Funnily enough, the anxiety he had been feeling was getting pushed further to the back of his mind to make room for curiosity and excitement. *Someone doesn't want to be seen. What are they up to?*

Following the rustle of leaves and snapping of twigs, he furthered into the woodland. The hot sun was filtered by the thick needles of the ancient pine trees. The air was cleaner, less fuggy in here. It was a welcome respite to the asphyxiating feeling of parental disappointment and August sun.

There was a large snap followed by a high-pitched shriek, and then a thump.

"Ouch," moaned a voice not far from him.

Jonay pulled apart some low-hanging, mossy branches to find the Princess of Ghomara lying on the woody floor. The river nearby blocked out any sound from the Celebration of Beñesmén.

"Are you OK?" asked Jonay, offering a hand to the girl.

Gara looked up at him, partly embarrassed, partly annoyed. The look in her eyes evoked the same of a child who had just been caught cheating in a game of marbles.

"I'm fine, thank you," she said curtly, ignoring Jonay's help.

"Why were you running away? Hate the party that much?"

"You wouldn't understand," she replied, brushing off the twigs from her tunic.

Gara turned her back on Jonay and continued her voyage into the forest.

"Do you even know where you're going?" Jonay called after her.

"I don't care," she bit back.

He could hear pain in her voice.

"I'll ask again, are you OK? Because it's not every day you see a Princess running into the forest when she's supposed to be getting engaged."

Gara stopped in her tracks.

"What business is it of yours? I could say the same thing to you..."

She turned around and their eyes locked. Both sets a rich shade of brown, marked by sadness. There was a spark of energy that flitted between them the moment they both realised they shared something.

"Who's yours?" he said.

"A prince from Benahoare. Yours?"

"The daughter of a chief from Tyterogaka. Bloody rabbit catchers..."

"I've heard it's nothing but volcanoes there. And camels. And sand. Wouldn't you like that, to get away from all this?" she said, gesturing sarcastically at the lush greenery of his home island.

Jonay chuckled.

"I want nothing less than to leave this island. It's perfect," he replied.

"It is," Gara said, sitting down on a hollow, mossy log by the river. "So much life. My island has nothing. No animals, no flowers. Just shrubland filled with palm trees and cacti. My cousin loves it; she finds beauty in everything. But to me, it feels empty, and vicious. Like we're not supposed to be there. I wish I lived here."

"Well, didn't your people come from my people? I guess it's in your blood to want to be in the forests. I heard Benahoare is packed to the rim with trees, no? You'd get exactly what you want there."

"Not exactly what I want..."

Jonay moved over to the log and sat beside her.

"Well, what do you want then?"

"How can you ask me that when you don't know either?" she replied, Jonay's eyes

looking confused. "You're hiding out here, just like I am."

Gara and Jonay looked at each other in the eyes once again before turning their gaze to the gentle stream before them.

"Seems like neither of us want to get married," he whispered.

"And, yet, we have to. Not for love, but for politics," she replied, putting her head into her hands.

Jonay's eyes fixed on the flowing water. His mind was usually frenetic with feelings, emotions, thoughts, worries... but right now, sat on this log with a princess he had never met before, he had never felt so at peace. He knew what to do.

"I don't even know what love is supposed to feel like," he said.

Gara looked up from her sulk.

"In fact, not even attraction," he continued. The Princess's face and the loud river made him feel safe in expressing his feelings.

"What do you mean?"

"I just think I'm meant to be alone. And not in some tragic, woe-is-me way. I just... don't think love is for me. Is that how you feel?"

"Um, well... no. Not exactly. In fact, I believe quite the opposite. I love people far too hard."

"Then could you not find it in yourself to love your prince?"

"Not my type. Which would be fine if I was a commoner but princesses must marry princes. I tell myself it's because people would be scared of two women ruling –" Gara's voice cracked and she put her head back into her hands.

Looking out to the rushing river, Jonay's soul felt as vibrant as the cascading water. He had never told anyone about how constricted he felt by the concept of love. Romance and sex was never on the cards for him. All he wanted was solitude. He often thought the Guayota cursed him at birth — for whatever reason — to be born amongst the busiest, most social kingdom in the seven isles that valued sex over everything.

That malignant god who dwelled in caves with his black-furred hellhounds. What did he do in a past life to deserve such a hex? Jonay never felt like he was a born 'right' and his whole life up until now he believed he was unworthy.

"Let's get engaged," he said.

Gara's head shot up.

"Pardon?"

Jonay turned to her, smiling like a mad March hare. In that river he saw hope. Life charging through a forest, making everything in its path part way for it.

"You heard. Let's do it! Why not? We're both of noble birth, both being harassed by our parents to marry, both being pressured into marriage –"

"We can live a life that pleases our parents. Yet, behind closed doors do whatever we like?" Gara laughed, the idea at first preposterous but the more she thought about it, the more excitement grew in her stomach.

"If you want to put it that way..."

"Well, if it's a chance at happiness," she said, "I do."

***

In the royal hut, the Queen's handmaid was spreading the smoky, spicy cheese onto some crusty bread. Jonay's eyes were hooked on the amber paste with its flecks of bright red chilli. Nothing like this had ever been made on his island, but the deep, nutty smells of the mature goat's cheese unlocked an almost opiate infatuation. He wanted to demand more from the handmaid but always felt guilty about using his royal status for personal gain.

Gara and Jonay's parents were delighted, eventually, at their children's surprise engagement, and Queen Kaza had quickly got to work to planning the wedding. However, the chief of Tyterogaka wasn't particularly pleased that it meant his daughter now had to marry the prince from North Achinet with body odour that could fell a camel. But they didn't care. It hadn't even been a month and Gara and Jonay were edging ever so closer to freedom they never thought they would have.

"This is the best thing that has ever passed my lips. Did you make this yourself?" Jonay asked the handmaid.

"My mother makes it up in the hills with her goats."

"Well," Jonay looked at his future mother-in-law, "I demand the goats of Ghomara be knighted for their service to cuisine!"

Queen Kaza chuckled as her daughter groaned.

"It's good but it's not *that* good," said Gara.

Jonay jokingly batted her away before helping himself to more almogrote. There was a knock at the hut wall and another handmaid announced that a florist from Achinet had come over with a sample of flowers for the wedding ceremony. The Queen ushered the cheese-maid out of the hut as she left: a hint that she wanted her daughter and son-in-law to be alone.

"Finally," sighed Gara, as she flopped down on the bedding. "There's only so many pre-marriage rituals a girl can take!"

"*That* was a ritual? Cheese was a ritual?" Jonay said, his mouth agape.

"Something about fertility. They were making sure you get me pregnant in one go," she replied.

Jonay choked on the cheese he had just scoffed from the rest of the plate.

"Careful, the villagers will run amok if a Prince dies before his wedding day. They probably have a superstition for that," Gara laughed.

"This is superstitious cheese?"

"Everything to do with marriage is superstition, really, isn't it? I can't believe I have to do that stupid water ceremony in the morning." Gara shot up and walked over to the royal hut's window.

There was a commotion of excited townsfolk preparing everything for the big day tomorrow. Commoners and royal staff from both Ghomara and Achinet coming together to create one big, gaudy celebration.

"Are you looking forward to it?" said Jonay. "The party."

"Looking forward to it being *over*, so we can get on with our lives," she said, her eyes fixed on two men digging a barbecue pit on the black sand beach.

"Come on, this is a once in a lifetime event! It may be our

day but this is also *their* special day. Our parents', our people's. We all have the need to feel special and our wedding will bring them so much joy!"

"Yeah, I suppose," she said. "We're moving to your island, by the way. I can't keep living here."

"You're too hard on this island, Gara," sighed Jonay. "I've never seen cacti or date palms or all those spiky bushes before I came here. They're *so* beautiful. Just because they aren't colourful and soft and fragrant like the plants on my island doesn't make them ugly."

"Your island is so *full* of life. So many places to explore."

"So is this place, if you give it a chance. My dad and I had a great time up in the valleys yesterday. I bet you've never even been."

Gara sighed.

"I just wish we had a jungle. When it gets really hot here, fires can start and everything gets turned to ash. Takes years to recover. A jungle would be perfect."

Moving over to the window, Jonay put his hands on Gara's shoulders and began to massage them. Her muscles were ridden with tight knots, no doubt caused by the constant chip on her shoulder.

"Come on, just a few more little traditions, the grandiose wedding, and then we can live the most glorious life in the forest."

"Promise?"

"Cross my heart. But we *are* going to be spending our winters here. Well, even if you don't come, I will anyway. Those goats and their cheese have me wrapped around their little hooves."

***

It was a stiflingly hot morning in Ghomara, the coastal caves in which Gara's people lived filled with all the mothers and babies of the village whilst the men cooled themselves off in the ocean. Gara, however, was not taking part in such respite. Her father had booked her in with an appointment north of the island to speak with the Soothsayer of Agulo.

It was tradition, on the day of the wedding, for an engaged woman to look upon her reflection at the Soothsayer's well. Should the water remain clear then the marriage shall go ahead; should it turn cloudy then misfortune will befall the family.

"This is so pointless, father. What are you going to do if the water turns cloudy? Surely any god's wrath isn't as fiery as mother's if all that wedding planning has gone to waste," said Gara, in the rickety carriage taking herself and her father up to Agulo.

"Enough of that cheek, young lady," he replied. "Besides, I've already paid the Soothsayer."

Truth was, Gara was anxious about leaving Jonay alone in her village. She feared the worst among the townsfolk interrogating him before he married the heir to the throne. He was a nice lad but buckled easily under pressure; any hint that their marriage was a sham would cause unbridled chaos.

"You know, when I become Queen, I'm getting rid of this tradition. Mostly because my bum really hurts," she laughed, shifting in her seat.

"Oh, when you become Queen, my dear, I shudder to think what will become of our future," he laughed in return.

She examined the smile of her father. He had a glint in his eye she had never seen before. All her life she had felt like a burden, someone who didn't fit the mould of how a princess should act or how a princess should feel. All her life she had felt like a liar. And today was no different. Guilt panged in Gara's chest; her parents had always been so giving and understanding, why couldn't she tell them the secret that had rooted itself inside of her?

Arriving at Agulo, Gara leapt from the carriage, massaging her bottom.

"How very royal," chuckled her father.

"Dad!" Gara hissed back, annoyed he drew attention to her trying to rub life back into her behind.

Whilst standing behind the carriage, the midday sun beat down on Gara. She spotted the grotto where a small spring, as old as the island itself, formed at the mouth of the cave. Hunched over the running water was a wrinkled woman, probably also as old as the island itself, wrapped in a colourful shawl dyed with the bright carnelian beetles that resided on the mountainside cacti.

An image of Chaxiraxi stood before them. The statue was around seven-feet tall; her white robes, dark skin and golden halo all glistened with the summer heat. Gara thought it almost looked like the goddess herself had appeared in a mirage. The Sun Mother had a serene disposition Gara had never appreciated before. In that small moment she understood why some people turned to religion.

Gara made her way down to the grotto where the Soothsayer stood grinning by the stream. As Gara reached her destination, the Soothsayer began to chant in a deep, low grumble. Her aged hands, calloused by the heat and hardness of the island, took Gara's softer ones and held them tightly. The Soothsayer closed her eyes and King Geran gestured to Gara that she do the same. Gara's mind was a flurry of nerves and excitement: once she and Jonay tied the knot, they could live the lives they had always wanted in pure, arboreal secrecy. She prayed to Chaxiraxi that this ritual didn't hinder her wedding.

The Soothsayer stopped her chants and squeezed Gara's hands.

"It is time," she smiled.

Gara knelt down at the water's edge and looked upon her

reflection. The lazy current distorted her face but the water remained clear. The Soothsayer clapped her hands together and cheered. King Geran sighed with relief.

"Is that it?" Gara said with shock. "All of that for half a second of me looking at myself?"

The king chuckled to himself before thanking the Soothsayer. She nodded and returned to the shade of her grotto. Gara looked around at the scorched earth of Ghomara, the statue of Chaxiraxi beaming at her, and she felt for the first time in years that everything was going to be okay. She was going to get her forest.

Before Gara and Geran could get back to the carriage, a deafening racket pummelled through the air. Gara, Geran, the Soothsayer and the carriage driver looked on in open-mouthed disbelief as blackened clouds rose from the island of Achinet on the horizon. Clouds darker than anything Gara had ever seen before. The rumbling air shook the onlookers' ears as if thunder was forming above their heads. Gara squinted toward the blackening sky and saw tinges of burning red and orange emit from the mountain. She was once told that ancestors said a fiery demon dwelled within it but she thought that was nonsense.

Clearly not.

***

"It's him! He's cursed!" shouted someone nearby.

The townsfolk of Ghomara had gone into a frenzy and Jonay could not believe he was seeing his home island erupt before his very eyes. Screams from children rang in his ears as he tried to push himself through the crowd toward the royal hut.

"A demon comes forth from his island! Look how the sea glows! They're not meant to marry!"

"The ancestors said this day would come!"

Jonay's heart and breath constricted through his chest as he elbowed his way through the throngs of panicked people. He ducked his head so the hysterical persecutors couldn't see him. *What are they on about? What curse? What day?*

Meanwhile, Gara and King Geran raced down the valley as fast as the carriage driver could go. Queen Kaza tried to calm the madding crowd. But nobody would listen. Non-believers were quickly converted into raging heretics determined to exile Jonay from the island before the gates of hell spread to Ghomara. She had found him hiding in the royal hut and distracted the crowd so that he could run away into the valley until King Geran arrived back from the grotto.

"Enough with this nonsense! There is no such prophecy! You're all acting ridiculous!" Kaza yelled over the mob's noise and the rumbles of the distant volcano. She, too, was frightened by such a monstrous sight. But right now, her daughter's future was more important than her own anxieties. She wasn't having the future of the kingdom jeopardised by ancient tales of the Hell Prince.

Gara and her father pulled up by the royal hut.

"Where is he? I know you're hiding him!" demanded one of the fishermen. Queen Kaza struck the man as he approached the family with a spear. He fell the ground, screaming, as the handmaids grabbed him by each kicking and punching limb.

"Take him to the jail cell!" boomed the Queen.

"What's going on?" shouted Gara.

"They've all gone mad, it's like they've been cursed," said Queen Kaza, taking her daughter's hands, trying to control her anger.

"It's that stupid Hell Prince legend, isn't it? How can they believe such rubbish?"

After seeing the fisherman struck down, other townsfolk were now grabbing weapons. King Geran began climbing to the top of the royal hut.

"Where is he?" said Gara.

"I sent him into the valley to hide," whispered Queen Kaza.

"SILENCE!" roared the King.

The Ghomarans stopped in their tracks. Gara knew this was her chance; all of their attention was drawn to the King. She had to go into the valley and find him before it was too late. She had to save him; nothing was going to stop them from getting their new life in the forest.

As the King and Queen tried to calm the crowd, Princess Gara ran toward the valley, not noticing the tiny embers that were beginning to descend from the dark sky.

***

Sprawling across the charcoaled trees, the raging, bulging fire licked the edges of the cave where Gara and Jonay hid. Gara had found him hiding in the caves but a rogue group of angered Ghomarans had broken free from the monarchs' imprisonment. The fleeing betrothed then scaled the valley to a cave Gara used to hide in as a child.

Gara scrambled over rock and rubble, desperate for a glint of summer sky to guide her to an escape route, whilst Jonay knelt by the cave's mouth praying to the gods he didn't believe in. Embers from the fire mountain had set Ghomara alight, enraging the townsfolk more, and calling for Jonay's execution.

"We need to find them now!" shouted a voice from the distance, fighting over the crackle of burning date palms.

Jonay, his eyes closed, could feel the growing heat prickle on his skin. It was getting closer. Smoke hadn't reached them yet, but soon there would be no air to breathe. Soon enough, the desert hills would become too scorched to risk scouting for the prince and princess. Looking down at his torn clothes, Jonay marvelled at the robust leather tunic that had been battered by sea, forest and fire yet remained strong and untorn.

A date palm creaked and groaned into submission as it fell across the cave's mouth, sending a swirl of embers, sand and soot into the small cave. Jonay shot upright and scarpered back before the searing sand burnt his flesh. He ran to the back of the cave where Gara was frantically throwing small rocks away from a nook in the ceiling.

"Any luck?" he asked, his words catching in his throat as they mixed with dust and old vomit.

Gara grunted in return as she pulled away a rock that had been lodged in a cranny.

"I'm almost..." she groaned, her fingernails digging into black volcanic stone.

"Do you need –"

With an ear-splitting scream, the rock broke free from its cradle and tumbled down with the princess. Jonay tried to catch her but her unexpected heaviness brought him down too. As the dust settled and the sharp rays of sunshine burst through the cavity, Gara and Jonay giggled in their crumpled state.

"Ouch..." Jonay groaned.

Gara's smile was struck from her face when she clocked the approaching fire making its way into the cave.

"We need to get out of here," she said, pushing herself free of Jonay, their leather tunics sticky in the baking heat.

The fire hadn't reached this side of the rock formation and Gara scrambled out from the barely-there hole she had managed to form. Jonay cringed as the jagged igneous cut like little daggers into his skin.

Appearing on the side of the rocks they clambered to the top of the mound. Ahead of them they saw the full extent of the violent fire. The delicate, dry shrubland engulfed with the blackening rage; date palms quelled and succumbed to the flames; skeletons of spiky bushes buckled under the heat; cacti curled and cracked like overcooked meat. Faint yells from the villagers muffled by the blazing chaos. Gara prayed her parents weren't among the flames.

Atop the cliff face, the summer's sun beat down on them with oppressive fervour. The stark, blue sky overhead offered no sign of respite from the cracked earth. Gara glanced behind her to the deep blue Atlantic Ocean that beckoned a welcome, watery haven from the island's soaring temperature.

"Fuck it, let's just jump," she sighed.

"It would kill us!" he replied.

"Like life would be worth living after this? They won't stop until you're dead, anyway. And my parents could be dead for all we know."

Jonay looked to the east where he saw the silhouette of his island's volcano. He could still hear the screams of terror from Gara's villagers when the towering beauty rumbled deep from its core and the hysteria of an ancient prophecy ran rampant like wildfire.

"There! By the caves!" shouted someone.

"Where did that come from?" said Jonay.

"I think over there," Gara replied, pointing south toward the mouth of the cave. The prince and princess glanced anxiously at each other. In mutual agreement, they turned west and hurried along the cliff side, all too wary of the sheer drop to the jagged rocks and pulsing waves below.

Gara and Jonay ventured further into the island where sharp plants bit at their ankles and loose gravel threatened to send them over a valley edge. In the midday sun, their eyes were beginning to ache with the glare of its rays upon exposed arid rock. The rustle of the fire grew louder the further they moved away from the crashing waves and whistling wind.

Ahead of them was a looming rock formation that formed like a colossal stalagmite. The barren, beige landscape around them lay dormant, oblivious to the approaching fire that would soon turn everything black.

"There's some more caves up there we could hide out in," said Jonay, pointing to the volcanic plug he had heard the islanders refer to as Agando.

There were similar formations on his own island, Achinet. His mother had told him that they were created long before humans existed, when the earth was a fiery sea of magma and brimstone. Certain smaller tribes on Jonay's island of Achinet resided near these plugs and often conducted rituals there. He wondered if the people of Ghomara had the same rituals.

"If they find us there, there's no escape," said Gara, glancing back at the fire.

"Here!" a voice screamed.

"Shit," the prince and princess said in unison.

Gara looked back at the angry villagers that stood on the crest of the valley. Dozens of Ghomarans stood with spears and daggers, their faces aflame with hatred. How quickly they turned on their princess. Gara froze in place, her chest tightening, her throat closing as if she was being asphyxiated by the fumes from the forest fire. Despite the sweeping loneliness of the arid landscape, she felt enclosed, entombed. Trapped in her own fate. Jonay had started to run toward Agando but stood still when he saw more Ghomarans appear at the valley's edge closest to the rock. Surrounded by fiery vengeance, Gara and Jonay moved closer together and held hands.

Jonay squeezed Gara's hands to fight back the tears forming in his eyes. The sharpened spears glistened in the sunlight that baked down on them like the churning lava pools of Achinet. Gara figured it would take the mob at least five minutes to reach them. Five minutes to try and escape a fiery death.

A shrill whistle rattled down the valley; with various others responding, their piercing cantation echoing across the shrubland. The villagers began their descent, weapons raised. Jonay nudged Gara's ribs. She turned to him, her eyes as wet as his, her dark brown skin radiant with the midsummer sun. They examined their surroundings, swarmed by flames and townsfolk who wanted them dead. There was nothing they could do. As the rage of villagers and fire swarmed toward them, Gara and Jonay embraced each other and lay down to rest on the hot, lifeless earth.

***

As years turned into decades and decades into centuries, Gara and Jonay's story altered with time. Some say the crowd went crazy due to a curse put on them by the King of Tyterogaka; some say the heat of the island had finally made them all snap. Insignificant discrepancies were debated amongst islanders, but there was only one thing everyone agreed on: what had happened once the fire consumed the supposed lovers and the rabid townsfolk.

A survivor of the mob told of how when he watched Gara and Jonay lie down to accept their fate, a vision of a woman glistened in the island's heat. She was towering yet calming, strong yet graceful. A halo of bright white light encircling the rich, dark hair on her head. Her face was glowing with love and protection. The islander knew she had come to save the souls of these unfortunate lovers.

Something shifted on the island of Ghomara in the coming centuries. From the blackened sand and soot of the raging fire, new life began to sprout. At first it was delicate white flowers. Then, all of a sudden, there were orange, pink and blue ones. Spindly trees with meandering limbs; rivers sprouting from the rocks in every valley; bright yellow birds flocking to the verdant canopies. After hundreds of years, the island was engulfed in rich, humid forest filled with succulent moss and lichen. The once barren and inhospitable island now offered shade and cooling mists from the beating sun, and the ground was soft and welcoming for explorers to rest on.

Gara and Jonay lived their lives as strangled as the roots of the laurisilva. In life, they didn't get the chance to grow, but in death their forest did.

<u>Jake Curran-Pipe</u> Jake Curran-Pipe is a horror and fantasy writer from Manchester. He enjoys writing scary, exciting, and intriguing fiction about underrepresented people and communities. Jake currently lives in Glasgow where he is the assistant producer of a theatre that used to be a Neo-Gothic church!

Love in the Time of Volcanoes is an interpretation of the legend of Gara and Jonay from La Gomera that is used to explain the existence of the Garajonay National Park. Being born in the Canary Islands, Jake wanted to showcase the archipelago's history and folklore in this anthology as he has never seen it represented anywhere outside of the islands.

BLUEBEARD'S BEACH HOUSE

Jenna Smithwick

Josephine lit the last tapered candle and gently let go of the wrought iron bar, careful not to let the candelabra swing back too quickly. She stepped down from the table and watched the garnet baubles knock together with the motion. The article had been right; in the soft light the formal dining room looked the way she imagined it must have years ago, before the salt air caused the wallpaper to warp and peel. Henry would be impressed. She adjusted the fixtures on the table until they were evenly spaced; the flames flickered and the shadows from the sconces stretched across the walls like claws reaching for the windows.

Perfect, she thought. *Tonight will be perfect.*

It had to be. They needed the money, and Josephine knew she could help her husband charm their dinner hosts into a successful partnership. She'd been preparing for weeks now. She pored over the open pages on the counter and ran a fingernail beneath the task she'd completed. *Set the mood. The soft glow of candlelight will make any woman look prettier.*

The magazines were her little secret. She'd found them in a drawer in one of the empty rooms and kept them stuffed under her bed. They were full of good advice on how to wow your husband and keep the flame alive in a marriage. Judging by the date, they had belonged to Danielle. Mary had died shortly after the war, years before the latest issue had come out, but Danielle, she'd only drowned five years ago. Josephine couldn't help but wonder if Henry's second wife had also felt the pressure of maintaining a home that would never be truly hers.

Make sure your husband feels relaxed after a long day. Make him his favorite drink and let him tell you about his troubles. Don't forget to smile! She paced her way to the foyer, the bloated hardwood creaking beneath her heels. They could only afford to keep the place looking nice on the surface in an antique fashion. They patched up the places where guests might stop in, but the foundation was rotting away.

It was fine; they'd close the deal tonight, and there'd be plenty of money for repairs. They could put linoleum floors in, maybe they'd even get one of those fridges with the built-in ice machine. Panic fluttered in her chest. Ice. She'd forgotten the ice, and now there was no time to freeze a tray. She felt the evening crumple around her. How could things go to plan if she couldn't even manage to make Henry feel at ease before they went out?

She grabbed the crystal tumbler from the entryway table and poured two fingers of whiskey in. Her eyes caught on the two portraits hanging at the top of the stairs. Mary's picture hung in the large gold frame, a constant reminder that the house belonged to her. Danielle sat to her left, too beautiful for anyone to question whether or not she belonged in any place. Josephine looked down at her pink shift dress and thought she was too bright, too loud for the muted palette of the place. Henry's late wives looked down on her like she was an unwanted guest.

"At least I'm not a pile of bones in an outdated dress," she said, taking a swig of the drink. Acid stung at the back of her throat. It was bad enough she'd had the thought, worse that she'd said it aloud. Josephine never thought of herself as a mean person, but she felt the unbearable weight of their beauty every time she passed the paintings. Heat bloomed across her cheeks as she studied them. Their hair fell around their shoulders in dark waves, and she felt the urge to touch her thin blonde hair, her scalp still sore from all the backcombing and teasing.

Her eyes were glued to the portraits. Henry had loved them more than he could ever love her. He called out to them in his sleep, so often that the women had become frequent visitors in her own dreams. They perched alongside the bed and whispered against her hair, words slipping through the sieve of her mind, so she woke up exhausted and confused each morning.

"What is your secret?" she whispered. The paintings stared back, but Mary's lips curled up in a smile, her chin tilting at an angle, so she was looking right at her.

The glass slipped from her hand and shattered at her feet.

She jumped back, her heart pounding in her chest. She reached for the dust cloth and dabbed at the liquid, trying to usher the glass bits into the palm of her hand.

"Oh no. No, no, no."

An engine whirred in the drive, the gears shifting to park. In a last-ditch effort, she clawed at the shards, fisting them behind her back as Henry's Oxfords scraped against the welcome mat.

"Ow," she breathed and loosened her grip. Crystal dripped red from her fingers. There was a gash across her palm.

The door swung open, and Henry filled the doorframe.

"Josephine, what are you doing?" he asked. Her heart slowed its pounding. Maybe he would see that she was hurt, she thought. Maybe he would look at the wound and drive her to the hospital for stitches.

His eyebrows knit together when he saw what she was holding.

"Was that one of Mary's tumblers?" he asked, and she felt the storm brewing between them. She hadn't been aware of how hot the house was until this moment. Her dress clung to her back, and the smoke from the candles seemed to sit in the air, unwilling to dissipate. It was hard to breathe.

"I thought I told you that those wedding gifts were off-limits," he said, his voice still low.

He stepped in close enough that she could see his clean-shaven skin. She'd only seen him stubbled once, after their own wedding when they'd sunbathed on towels. He'd spent the days telling her stories of pirates, how their souls roamed the beaches looking for the treasures they'd buried and lost years ago. "You look a bit like a pirate yourself. I think I'll call you Bluebeard," she'd told him, stroking the odd blue-black whiskers along his chin.

That had been a year ago, and those moments had withered along with the blossoms in her June bride's bouquet. Now she had come to expect an air of tension, a constant feeling that she was on the edge of something bad happening.

"I'm sorry," she said. Her heels clicked as she scrambled back. "I didn't mean to. I don't feel well." Henry made no move to close the space she made when she fled to the bathroom.

The illness was an excuse, yes, but it wasn't entirely made up. Josephine had been sick as a dog since the Independence Day crowds had cleared out. It was an awful combination for her: the relentless heat of summer and the lack of sleep. She'd read the chemicals from cleaning supplies weren't good to breathe in. That explained the lightheadedness and what she'd imagined in the foyer. Portraits didn't move.

The doorknob turned, catching on the lock. She forced a deep breath through her nose.

"Josephine, my lamb, come out now or we'll miss the party," he said. The words were drenched in sweetness, but she could feel the heat rolling beneath them, the thunder threatening to break. She could open the door, but she didn't know which version of Henry to expect tonight. As much as she wanted to go out, she couldn't face the risk. It had been a close call with the broken glass.

"I'm sorry, babe," she said. "I feel really bad. I think I'll have to miss this one," she sniffed and squeezed her eyes shut. She could sense his fist poised ready to knock against the door, louder than necessary.

He sighed instead.

"Ok, then. I'm heading to the Tait's house. I might be back late. Wish me luck."

That was it. Josephine resented the relief she heard in his voice but mustered as much brightness as she could to say, "Good luck!"

His footsteps moved away from the door, and she let out a breath.

"Josephine," he called. Her shoulders hunched up by her ears again. "Don't even think about rummaging through the attic."

She kept her forearms braced against the sink until she heard him leave. Of course, he'd mentioned the attic. He always did. It was the one room in the house that was for his eyes only.

The lights flickered on the vanity. The harsh lighting made her look strange; the cat-eyes she'd drawn across her eyelids seemed too bold, her skin and lips too pale. She ran her bleeding palm beneath the tap water, picking the shards out and splashing her face until the makeup ran down her face in dark streaks. Nothing could cool her down.

Mary and Danielle probably never had a night like this, she thought, wrapping the wound. They were too perfect to feel this bad. Josephine was sure everyone had adored them. The pipes groaned within the walls, and another sick sensation ripped through her. She was alone, but she didn't feel like it when the house sounded alive, when the wood boards seemed to draw in soggy breaths. She shook the thought away, trying to enjoy the peace that came with having the house to herself. Rest. She needed to rest and hope the night went well without her.

Make sure you don't stay up later than your husband. You'll fill his mind with doubts.

Josephine lay awake in bed, staring at the ceiling. She'd slipped into a nightgown, but the room was too hot. She'd lived there a whole year, had marked the pages of her calendar throughout each of the seasons, but she couldn't remember a time when she existed outside of the heat. She thrashed the covers away, but the humidity pinned her to the spot. She'd have to lie there and be still if she ever wanted to get comfortable.

A breath tickled the shell of her ear. She glanced at the clock; it was half past two, the same time she always woke up in the night. She rolled over, expecting to see her husband, but a woman filled the space between their pillows. She sat upright, her heart hammering against her ribs. He'd come home late before, smelling of perfume, and sure, she'd scrubbed smudges of lipstick from his collar, but this was different.

"Who are you?"

The woman laughed, and Josephine struggled to compose herself while her eyes adjusted to the dark. The pale curve of the woman's cheek, the cut of her mouth, and the sway of her hair all seemed familiar. She blinked. She must have fallen asleep. It was impossible that Mary was sitting next to her in bed.

"Little lamb," she cooed, her voice as cloyingly sweet as the times Henry worked to soothe her after a rough patch. "You want to know our secrets?"

Her voice rang through Josephine's mind. This was a dream; she'd gone to bed wondering about his wives. She was safe to answer truthfully here. Henry couldn't know the thoughts that ran through her mind.

"Yes."

"You need to look in the attic. The secrets lie there. You know it's true."

"But he'll—" she froze. Mary was gone; she was speaking to an empty space. She looked around the room. She was sure she'd been dreaming, but it had felt so real. Her skin was still pebbled from the breathy voice in her ear.

Don't pry. A good wife respects her husband's privacy. A housekeeping article had given the advice, but she was sick and tired of following the rules. She had followed them all perfectly, and nothing good ever happened for her.

The key was on Henry's nightstand, a horrible place to keep it if he was really concerned about her snooping. She swiped it up with the flashlight, but she didn't need to turn it on. She knew where it rested in the dark; she'd stared at it so many times on the nights she'd spent alone, wondering what secrets were locked away. Tonight she would find out. Henry wouldn't need to know. The idea of her having her own secret hidden from him gave her a strange thrill.

She walked lightly, sucking in a breath so her feet wouldn't land too hard on the warped wood. She clenched her jaw tight when she pressed the key in the hole. She didn't dare to breathe. It was the last chance to turn back, to be a good wife, but she knew she couldn't. Sleep would never come if she didn't peek.

The lock clicked with the turn of the key, and she pushed too hard on the door, sending it creaking on its hinges. She gasped and looked behind her, waiting for Henry to rush up the stairs. She could feel her pulse in every extremity, but the loud noise she heard was only her own heart pounding in her ears. Mary and Danielle smiled from their portraits, urging Josephine on.

A rancid odor floated on a wave of hot air when she stepped in. Josephine pressed the back of her hand to her mouth; the whole room smelled like their street on garbage day. She tried to remember which way the pipes ran in the house. Maybe the plumbing was bad, or something had curled up and died in there. She shut the door behind her before clicking on her flashlight.

Something skittered behind her. A rat, she thought. Maybe they had rodents nesting and dying in these walls. She sighed. It had happened before. She shone the light where the noise had sounded, spotlighting a recession in the wall. Dresses hung from a rod, a fabulous assortment of fabrics and furs from the looks of it. She stepped closer: she wanted to look.

Something scratched along the floor. Frowning, she dropped the flashlight lower to where two pale things stuck out beneath the mess of skirts. She dropped to her hands and knees, crawling toward the objects. They looked like...feet. There was a tang of fear in her mouth. She was lightheaded again, crawling towards the feet that flopped in an unnatural angle.

"Hello?" she asked, trying not to let the sob jump into her throat.

SCRITCHHH. She paused at the sound, her hand shaking on the flashlight as the feet slipped further into the closet, out of her sight. Going back to her room and pretending she saw nothing seemed the safest option, but it was out of the question. Curiosity would kill her if she tried to shove it down. She moved forward on her knees, pushing the outfits aside. She held the flashlight up, looking high and low. There was nothing, only the wood-paneled wall at the back. She pushed on it. Nothing gave. There were no secrets in here; she was imagining things again.

The light hit something sparkly in front of her. She slid her hand forward until it bumped up against the frock on the floor. She picked it up, running the flashlight over the beadwork etched into the cream silk. It was more elegant than anything she'd ever worn, she thought with envy gnawing at her insides. There was an interesting red pattern at the collar. The flashlight flickered off, but when it came back on, she could see that the red poured down from the high neckline. She scratched at it and studied the flakes beneath her nails.

Blood.

She dropped the dress and got to her feet.

Her stomach flopped over; queasiness reared its head again. She needed fresh air. It was too stuffy, and the smell was unbearable. She staggered over to the window, pushing at the lift. She was desperate to leave but felt trapped in that room, like hot air in the lungs dying to be exhaled. The window wouldn't budge. It was far too old and heavy.

She leaned her forehead against the glass and closed her eyes. Something terrible had happened here. She knew it. It was the heavy feeling in the room, the warning in Henry's voice, the way he snapped if he even caught her looking at the attic door. It was all she could think of as she listened to the sound of the tide rushing in. She lifted her eyes to look out at the ocean.

There was one woman walking along the shore, her white night gown trailing in the sand. Josephine wiped the coat of dust away so she could see more clearly. The woman stopped in her tracks, arms dangling by her side. She stepped slowly, turning toward the house. Moonlight glinted off her pale skin as she craned her neck, her chin pointing up at the window.

Josephine stepped back in a panic. Surely the woman hadn't seen her, not with it being so dark in the room. But it felt like she was being watched. She backed up until her knee knocked against something hard, and she had to catch herself from stumbling over it, her hand braced against the top of the structure.

She pushed off it and shone the flashlight over the obstacle. It was a perfect replica of the house. The colonial style with bone white shingles, perfect in its symmetry with black shutters that closed and blotted out the lights. The pitched roof in the back where the attic faced the Atlantic. She walked her fingers through the home, opening doors and peeking inside.

A figure sat in their bedroom. She shone the light on the doll, the blue-black hair and briefcase on his lap. *Henry.* She left the thing where it sat and paused when her fingertips brushed the attic door.

"Go on," a voice whispered from the makeshift closet. Her heart stilled for a moment, then began to bounce wildly in her chest. She pushed the small door open. Two dolls were inside, resting flat on their backs, a thin strand of black ribbon wrapped over their mouths. She scooped them up and untied them, touching the delicate paint on their faces. Mary and Danielle. She'd searched the whole house; there wasn't one of her.

"Aren't they pretty?" the voice asked, and Mary appeared beside her, translucent in the night.

"You aren't really here," Josephine whispered.

"Maybe not, but you're not in there." Mary waved a hand and stepped toward the dollhouse. "His greatest treasure." She knelt before her, tracing her hand down Josephine's cheek. She squeezed her eyes shut and only felt the lightest ghost of a touch. "Can't you see? You'll never be enough. Leave while you still can."

When she opened her eyes, Mary was gone again. The dolls felt warm in her hand. She peered down; the dresses were smeared with red. Blood had seeped through her bandage. She wiped at the tiny frocks, but the stains spread out on the white fabric. Henry would know she'd been in the attic.

She stuffed the dolls back inside and lifted the house, ignoring the bite of pain in her hand. She needed stitches, but that was the least of her worries. Holding her breath, she ran down the stairs as fast as the weight in her arms allowed. The dining room seemed the safest place to hide it until she could clean it up. Henry would probably go straight to bed. She hoped he would. She could put it back and pretend she'd never seen a thing.

The flames flickered in their sconces when she dropped the dollhouse on the table. Wax dribbled down to the drip pans and hung over the sides. Josephine wet a cloth and swiped at the dolls. The red stains spread and turned pink around the edges. Tension ran up her neck and pressed at her skull. She'd used hot water like the magazines had said. Or maybe she'd remembered wrong, was it supposed to be cold?

It was no use. She thought of her sister who had always been able to get their brothers' shirts looking clean. Anne would know what to do.

Josephine eyed the phone hanging on the wall. What would she tell her sister? They hadn't spoken in months—not since they'd fought. It had been easier, not talking to her. She didn't need to worry that Anne might see through her smile or hear the cracks in her voice while she pretended to be the happiest bride.

The tone rang clear when she picked up the phone. She pressed her finger into the dial; it sounded incredibly loud each time it turned and snapped back before cranking another number. She hoped Henry wouldn't come home now. She needed a few minutes to ask for advice. Or a ride. She didn't know what she needed or if anyone was willing to help.

"You're just jealous," she'd snapped at her sister when she'd commented on the age gap in her marriage. She couldn't blame her if Anne wanted to stay away for good.

The ringing sounded in the earpiece, and Anne's voice crackled through the line.

"Hello?"

"Anne," Josephine whispered. The words spilled out. "I think something terrible has happened. There's blood. I need help."

"Josie?" Anne asked, the line popping with static, "What's... on...Josie?"

Her words were drowned out by another sound. Breathing. Wet rasping breathing that gurgled with liquid.

Josephine's breath hitched in her throat. Had someone on the party line picked up? She placed the phone back on the receiver, desperate to make the noise stop. She couldn't hear it anymore, but she could feel the wet fog of an exhalation against the back of her neck.

"I'll leave," she said.

Tears stung behind her eyes, but she turned around. There was no one, only the empty dining room and the touches of Mary's presence all around her. This wasn't Josephine's home. She didn't belong.

Through the window, framed by the light of the candelabras, she could see the woman still walking the beach. Maybe she would help her find a phone. She could leave tonight, find a job, or beg her siblings to let her stay with them. She had no money of her own, but she could figure it out.

The moment she stepped outside she felt the rush of the wind moving in from the sea. If anyone saw her out here, they'd think she'd lost her mind for traipsing around in her babydoll nightgown. *Be modest, some things are for your husband's eyes only.* But she didn't care anymore; the night air was cool against her thighs, and she was so tired of the suffocating heat.

"Wait!" Josephine called out. The woman never turned around, she kept her steady pace, marching forward. "Please!"

Josephine ran and fell in the wet sand, water rushing up over her knees and hands and soaking her hemline. It wasn't so long ago she'd stood in this place and felt the ocean was as vast as the world waiting for her. Now she could only think of lost treasure and dead things drifting about the bottom of the sea.

Water dripped down her back. She turned back, and there she was—the woman she'd followed out into the night. Her hair was wet and plastered to her face, and her nightgown was soaked through. Her dark lashes stuck together making her look doll-like. Josephine blinked at the freckles across her chest and the bridge of her nose. *Danielle.*

She made such a lovely image, ships would wreck themselves against the rocks at the sight of her, Josephine thought.

Danielle opened her mouth, the outline of her pale limbs blurring as water gushed from her lips.

"Want...hurt..."

"Do you want to hurt me?" Josephine asked.

She shook her head. "Wanted... help..." Greenish water bubbled from her nose, and her words were lost, thrown back into the crashing waves. "Help... her...her house," she coughed and lifted her hands to her throat, and Josephine spotted the necklace of bruises there.

Danielle stared up at the single window at the very top of the house, where Mary stared back at them.

"If she wants the house, she can have it," she said, but she didn't mean it. She didn't want to stay, but she had nowhere to go. Henry would be back soon, and he'd find out she'd been in the attic. She'd have to live there until she was a ghost herself. She'd spend eternity in that house where the air stayed stagnant all summer long. There was no escape.

"Help...*her,*" Danielle rasped, stretching an arm out. Seaweed dripped to the ground. Josephine didn't understand but looked to where she pointed. There was a cherry red car parked up by the curb. A Pontiac Bonneville with the top down. *Anne's car.* She ran for the house, her feet moving slow against the sand.

"Anne," she called, pushing the door open. She gripped the banister, looking up the staircase. The attic door was open. Without a thought, she raced her way up and stepped in. "Anne?"

Her sister was pressed against the corner, a cast-iron pan in her hand. She'd tied her scarf over her nose and mouth, and her hair stuck to her forehead in a sheen of sweat.

"Josie. What is going on?" she hissed. "I looked downstairs. There's blood everywhere. It smells like death in here." She moved forward, throwing an arm around her. "What did he do?" She pulled back to study her face, touching the streaks of makeup on Josephine's cheeks. "You know what? Tell me on the ride home. We're getting out of here."

Josephine laughed in relief. It would all be ok. They could get through this together. She didn't need any of her belongings if her sister had her back. She'd leave the magazines and their bad advice for the next wife.

The joyful reunion was cut short by the slamming of the door. There was a breath of silence, then the shuffle of Henry's boots across the floor. Josephine could hear his staggering step, the clunky timing of his pace. His boot creaked against the first step. She hoped he would be too drunk to notice the door. She squeezed her sister's hand and shut her eyes tight.

"Josephine?" he called, his steps thundering up the stairs. No such luck.

"Hide in the dresses," she said, pushing Anne in the fluff of organza and lace. "You shouldn't be here."

Henry stood in the doorway, his eyes going past her to the spot where the dollhouse had been.

"Where is it?" he asked, running his fingers through his hair. It stood up in tufts where he pulled at it. She backed up, her knees wobbling. He was impossible to calm when he was like this.

"It's...I was just cleaning it," she squeaked.

He stopped then, as if he had only just noticed her.

"Come here, Josephine," he beckoned. "You were such a good little lamb, and now you've gone and spoiled it."

She took another step back and bumped up against the wall, her head hitting the corner of the window frame. Hot tears spilled down her cheeks. He looked at her, but then blinked, his eyes moving past her.

"Danielle?" he breathed, his eyes wide.

Josephine shook against the wall. She didn't want to think of her ghost wandering next to the watery grave. Another face appeared behind Henry; Mary smirked and ran a finger down his spine. He shuddered and faced his first wife. Josephine could see him trembling.

"Mary. No." He looked back to Josephine. His hands clawed at his hair as he pleaded with her, "You know you're my favorite, little lamb. We can forget any of this ever happened if you just make them go away. I'll make you all go away."

Can't you see? You'll never be enough. Leave while you still can. Josephine replayed the words in her mind. It had been a warning, not a taunt. She braced herself for the worst. She'd heard all of Henry's lines and sweet promises before; she would never leave this place.

Clang. Everything went still. Anne stood where Mary had just been, the pan poised above her head. Henry fell to the ground, his hair flopped near her feet.

"Come on, let's go," Anne said, gripping her hand and pulling her toward the stairs. Josephine saw the key in the lock and turned it. She didn't want him racing down the street after her. She needed a clean getaway. They skipped steps as they raced down, hand in hand.

The door to the dining room creaked open and shut.

"I forgot something," Josephine said, thinking of Mary and

Danielle and how they were bound to this place.

"Hurry up!" Anne screamed, but Josephine had already pushed the door open. Mary and Danielle's pale figures stood next to the table, their outlines faint. They looked on as they did in their portraits, but she was still nervous as she lifted the dollhouse.

"I'm sorry for all of it," she said, backing up. The house was unwieldy, forcing her off-balance. Her elbow connected with the iron arm of a candelabra, knocking it to the ground as she adjusted herself. Flames kissed the pages of the magazine and danced along the hardwood floor. The ghosts faded from her sight. Everything really did look prettier in the glow of candlelight, she thought, taking one last look at the place.

She held the dollhouse in her lap as they rode off. The top was down and Josephine closed her eyes, letting the wind whip through her hair.

"What is that?" Anne asked. Josephine opened her eyes and watched her sister adjust the rearview mirror. From where she sat it looked like the ocean would swallow up the orange ball of flames. Her sister clutched at her scarf, a look of horror on her face.

"Josie, what did you do?"

***

"I'm sorry it took a few years, but I'm glad the insurance company finally came through," Eddy said. He wiped the sweat from his brow and leaned against the balcony of the wraparound porch where Josephine was tapping the ashes from her cigarette off the side. It was a nice new build on the old plot—a sizeable chunk of oceanfront property that most people couldn't get their hands on these days. It made her the talk of the town and the envy of her neighbors.

The place seemed quiet now that the construction crew had cleared out. Eddy stayed behind as he did each day, but Josephine could feel the shift in his easygoing nature as he struggled to keep a conversation going with her. He fidgeted with his work gloves and turned his face away from hers. She looked at him. His eyes were soft, a pale green beneath the brim of his hat.

He'd asked her what happened that night. Everyone asked. She couldn't blame them for it; she knew how morbid curiosity worked. She had repeated the story enough times that it didn't feel like a lie when she stripped it to the bare bones, made it a skeleton of a tale that danced and sang about a perfect marriage. She had to, or people might suspect. They might avoid her eyes like Anne had for months after, or worse.

"At least he can be with his late wives now," he said, then clicked his teeth together. "Sorry, that was inappropriate. I'm not great at talking to women, but I was wondering if you'd like to hire a sitter. Maybe we could go out to the Peppermint Beach Club..."

She eyed him. His skin was tanned from the sun and strands of grey hair poked out around his temples. He seemed nice enough, but she was always cautious around people.

"EEEEAHHHH!"

The scream cut off her train of thought before she had time to consider. She pushed the door to the house open and saw the little girl playing with the dollhouse on the cream carpet.

Eddy crouched down next to her.

"Mommy," the little girl cried, strands of blue-black hair sticking to her cheeks. "Daddy is saying mean things again."

Josephine pulled the doll from her daughter's palm. Henry's scowl stared back at her.

"Well, that's not very nice of him," she *tsked*. "Here, he won't bother you again." She placed the doll back in the miniature attic, shutting the door.

"Jeepers, is this what the beach house looked like? I'm surprised you didn't want us to replicate that," Eddy said, crouching to take a better look.

"I like this better," she said, looking around. "You can feel the breeze in here." She walked to the window and lifted it, sunshine and salt air filling the open space. She glanced back at the dollhouse, where Mary and Danielle's figures sat. They must have found the peace they were looking for, because she hadn't heard from them since the night it all went down in flames. Sometimes she wondered if Henry was still out there, searching for his treasure, his soul tethered to the place where he'd left it. It didn't matter now.

It all belonged to her.

Jenna Smithwick is a writer living in Virginia Beach with her husband, two sons, two wild cats, and one sweet pup.

She has an M.A. in International Studies, but she's more interested in the stories that tie communities together than foreign policy these days. Jenna writes Gothic romance and horror for adults and is always interested in new spins on old tales.

When she's not writing you can find her teaching yoga or reading a romance novel on the beach.

The Knucker of Lyminster

Katherine Shaw

"I don't care what is *expected*, I will not do it!"

The king pinched the bridge of his nose. "This is not one of your little games, Orellane. This is the future of our kingdom!" He let out a heavy sigh and knelt by the bed, taking Orellane's hand in his own. The princess looked down at her father through a veil of tears. "Sweet daughter, I don't ask this of you to give you pain, but it is what has to be done. You must marry someone of suitable standing, and any one of those fine men would ensure your future is secure."

"But Father, you don't understand!" She took a breath, trying her hardest to sound calm. If she sobbed and screamed, he would think her irrational. "I don't love any of those men, I *couldn't* love them."

King Eadwine let a gentle smile pass over his lips and his bright blue eyes shone with what could have been sympathy. Orellane allowed herself to hope. "You are not the first princess to say that, but you will grow to love the one you choose. These are good men – I hand-picked them myself."

Orellane's heart sank to her stomach. *He doesn't understand.* Fresh tears burned the back of her eyes, threatening to burst free. She couldn't break down now; she would lose all credibility with the man who controlled every aspect of her sheltered life.

"I—" she began, choking back the sob which threatened to escape her throat. "I cannot and will not do it, Father."

The king's demeanour changed. His eyebrows knitted together in a firm frown and his face flushed pink. Orellane braced herself. He spoke with slow, hard words which turned her stomach to ice. "You *will* do it – that much is out of your control. I am trying to be generous and offer you a choice of suitors. If you continue to disobey, you will marry the man of *my* choosing without so much as seeing his face ahead of your wedding day."

Orellane couldn't take it any longer. With her rising sobs threatening to burst free, she rose from the bed, pushed past her kneeling father and ran out of the room before he could attempt to intercept her. It didn't matter that tears blurred her vision; she had escaped this mansion enough times to know her route by heart.

Her unprotected feet scraped painfully against the hard dirt path, but Orellane didn't stop. She continued to sprint away from that overbearing, suffocating house, through the village and beyond. The powerful summer sun beat down on her brow, but she didn't slow until she approached the sanctuary of the forest. The locals would probably be gossiping for weeks about the princess darting through the streets barefoot, her long, silken dress trailing in the dust behind her while the soft soles of her feet blistered on the hot, dry ground, but she didn't care. As she ran, the breeze pulling at her loose, tangled hair and her tears flowing without restraint, she felt freer than she had her entire life.

As soon as Orellane felt the soft moss of the forest floor underfoot, she allowed herself to stop and dropped to her knees, panting for breath. The canopy overhead provided blessed respit from the heat, and for a moment Orellane knelt motionless, allowing the gentle coolness to temporarily wash her worries away. She wiped the tears from her cheeks with the back of her hands and looked up to find herself beside a sparkling blue pool, its shimmering surface laced with dappled sunlight. She stood and peered into its waters, and her breath caught in her throat. It was crystal clear, with no bottom in sight. The water simply darkened to a beautiful indigo blue, its depth seemingly endless.

A knuckerhole?

Orellane had heard rumours of a knuckerhole around Lyminster, but they were just rumours – something to keep the village children entertained as they drifted off to sleep, nothing more. She pondered for a moment about how wondrous a world might be which had such creatures in it, but her thoughts soon collapsed into an image of her father, and the parade of suitors she would be expected to choose from in the coming weeks before they left their summer home and returned to the palace. They were probably decent enough men, but Orellane had no interest in any of them, and she was certain she never would. She would be forced to marry, and spend her entire life living a lie.

It is so unfair.

She dropped onto a nearby log and buried her head in her hands, quiet tears seeping through her fingers. She would have given anything to have someone, anyone, who understood her.

As if in answer, the pool began to bubble and churn, and Orellane lifted her face to see its surface roiling with small sapphire waves. Her heart pounded in her chest and she sat frozen in place, too terrified to move. She had been warned to stay out of the forest, told to stay in the safety of the confines of the mansion, but she hadn't listened, and now she was going to pay for her disobedience.

Orellane's entire body trembled as the waves slowly parted to reveal a figure rising from the surface of the pool. It stepped out slowly onto the mossy bank and stood, glistening in a shaft of soft sunlight filtering through the forest canopy above. For a moment, Orellane couldn't breathe. She just stared, wide-eyed and slack-jawed, at the creature standing before her.

She's beautiful.

The Knucker wasn't like anything or anyone Orellane had ever seen, and a world away from the mythical draconic beast the village children feared would gobble them up if they misbehaved. She was human height and, despite her reptilian facial features, remarkably feminine. Her entire body was covered from head to tail in stunning blue-white scales. Her striking golden eyes settled on Orellane, and she felt a shiver run down her spine. But it wasn't fear the princess felt. It was...something else. Something new, and exciting.

The Knucker took a step towards Orellane and, without thinking, Orellane rose to meet her. They stood face to face, the air around them alive with an energy Orellane had never experienced before. It was like magic, but not the magic from stories, used by old wizards and witches. Something...*primal.*

She wanted to speak, but no words came. She was enraptured. The Knucker raised a clawed hand and brushed her fingers against Orellane's cheek, causing an explosion of butterflies to erupt in her stomach. She felt a fresh heat spreading across her face in answer to the Knucker's surprisingly soft touch, and couldn't suppress a broad smile creeping across her lips. The Knucker moved closer, her face just inches away now, and Orellane's chest tightened with anticipation. Her eyes had just fluttered closed when the loud ringing of the village bell reverberated through the trees.

Damn it!

She opened her eyes. The Knucker looked at her curiously, tilting her head in a most endearing fashion. Orellane wished she could stay and spend more time with this entrancing creature, but her father had been very clear about the consequences of staying out past the toll of the evening bell. It wouldn't do either of them any good to have the Royal Guard tearing through the forest, decimating the area in the hope of capturing the princess and dragging her home. No, she had to go back. But, at the same time, she didn't want to end her time with the Knucker.

Orellane reached out and took the Knucker's hands in her own. "I have to go home, back to the mansion." She gestured her head towards the village, hoping the Knucker would understand. She nodded, her golden eyes sullen. "But I'll be back, I promise! I'll return tomorrow, earlier in the afternoon, to this spot. Is...is that okay with you?"

The Knucker smiled. It was a small smile, not giving too much away, but it was warm and sweet, and Orellane's butterflies returned. She lingered a moment longer, then reluctantly turned and ran all the way home.

***

Orellane was true to her promise, and returned to visit the Knucker the next day, and each following day. She never spoke, but Orellane didn't mind. They had a connection that meant no words were needed, and it was a pleasure to simply be in each other's company. Orellane would sing while the Knucker braided her long, raven-coloured hair, or they would stroll through the trees together, hand in hand, listening to the chorus of visiting swallows, taking a break from hotter climes in the south, and breathing in the sweet scent of honeysuckle and foxglove as they bloomed in the summer sunshine. It was perfect.

On the seventh day, Orellane surprised the Knucker with a picnic, and they sat together on a woollen blanket eating bread, salted fish and freshly picked berries. Away from the confines and pressures of the royal mansion, out in the open with the Knucker by her side, Orellane felt a peace she had never experienced before, and wished it would never end.

As the sunlight dwindled and the toll of the evening bell loomed, Orellane reluctantly began to pack up her things. Her father hadn't yet questioned her frequent visits to the forest – she suspected he was simply relieved her mood had improved

– but she couldn't risk arriving home late and rousing suspicion. The Knucker knelt beside her to help fold up the blanket, her soft, scaled hand brushing against Orellane's. The princess looked up at her new companion, her smile dropping as she noticed a look of shock shining in the Knucker's eyes.

"What's the—"

"Oh, Gods! Oh, Gods!" A shrill voice punctured the air, and Orellane spun around to see a hysterical village woman pointing at their serene picnic spot, eyes wide with horror. "A monster! A monster! It's trying to take the princess!"

"No, it's okay, there's no need to—"

"DEAR GODS IT'S A KNUCKER!"

Before Orellane could say any more, other villagers burst through the trees, forming a circle around Orellane and the Knucker. Large men carried pitchforks, shovels and scythes, holding them up as if preparing for battle.

"She's not dangerous!" Orellane shouted, holding her arms wide to try and protect her friend. "She means me no harm!"

"The demon has bewitched her!" the woman shrieked. She lurched at Orellane and grabbed her with rough hands. "I will save you, child!"

Orellane struggled in the woman's grasp, but she was remarkably strong and soon had the princess pinned against her. The Knucker's eyes widened and her entire body tensed, ready to spring forward and wrestle Orellane free.

"It is for your own safety, princess," the woman said gently, not loosening her grip on Orellane's arms. She raised her voice at the men, who stood as if paralysed, staring at the confused and startled Knucker. "What're you waiting for? Kill the beast, before it resurfaces and charms her again!"

The men advanced on the Knucker, her eyes wide with fear. She looked past her would-be attackers towards the sanctuary of her pool.

"Go!" Orellane cried out, tears pricking the back of her eyes. "I'll return to you tomorrow, I promise. Just go, while you can!"

The Knucker locked eyes with Orellane, who wanted more than anything to reach out to her, to hold her close and tell her everything would be okay, but the woman held her tight against her stiff, woollen coat, trapped. Finally, the Knucker nodded and, like lightning, she slipped between two of the men and dove head first into her pool, sending a wave of water crashing over the confused onlookers. She was safe.

***

"So it is true! A Knucker, in *our* kingdom, attacking *our* royal family! I will not stand for it!"

King Eadwine paced up and down the hall, his booming voice echoing around the vast room. Before him stood his Royal Guard, flanked by the group of villagers who had brought Orellane kicking and screaming back to the mansion. She had argued the whole way, but it didn't do her any good, and her father had called for his men as soon as he heard what had happened. Orellane had been sent to bed immediately but, in all the commotion, no one had noticed her creep back downstairs and peer through the doorway to eavesdrop on their meeting.

"It had her charmed, Your Highness." It was that damned woman again. "She's been venturing into those woods every day this week. We felt it only proper to investigate. By all that is holy, we got there just in time."

"You did very well, Aldreda, and your assistance to the crown will not be forgotten. But is Orellane safe? How far does this black magic reach?" Her father's concern was genuine; perhaps he had some care for his daughter's wellbeing after all. Orellane had to repress a bitter laugh at the thought.

Aldreda frowned. "Who can say, Your Highness? It has lured her to it each day. Its power must be great."

"Then it must be destroyed."

"NO!" Orellane burst from her hiding spot and rushed into the room. "She means no harm! She wouldn't hurt me, Father, I know it. You can't kill her!"

"Orellane, you forget yourself." King Eadwine's cheeks reddened. Whether with anger or embarrassment, she couldn't tell. "You are the princess, and heir to the South Kingdom, you must see that your life is of higher value than that of this monster."

Monster.

The words cut through Orellane like a knife. They saw the Knucker and immediately assumed she was a menace, when they were the ones brandishing weapons and threatening murder. It was so very wrong. She couldn't let them kill her.

"Please, Father, leave her be. I'll, I'll…" Orellane knew there was only one thing that would calm her father's ire and save her new friend. "I'll do as you wish. I'll take a suitor and return with you to the palace, ready to be married."

The king stood silent, his blue eyes shining in the torchlight. Orellane held her breath as her heart pounded in her ears, the Knucker's life hanging in the balance. Finally, her father's face broke into a wide grin.

"Orellane, you bring joy to this old man's heart." He strode to his daughter and embraced her, his strong arms pressing her against his chest. Orellane breathed in his lightly spiced scent, wishing it brought the same comfort it had as a child. It was a relief when he withdrew.

"It shall be done! Men, send word to my chosen suitors, they shall each visit tomorrow and Orellane shall choose her husband. But," His face hardened and Orellane's stomach clenched. "Should the Knucker be seen with my daughter again, you will kill it immediately, without hesitation."

***

Orellane adjusted her hair in the mirror and scowled at the overdressed doll staring back at her. The formal gown her father had insisted she wear was not only uncomfortable, but adorned with so many ruffles and jewels it was like moving around in a suit of lead. She felt like a court jester. *More like a puppet, moving to their strings,* she thought bitterly.

She grimaced as she tugged on a curl and a hair pin bit into her scalp. Why did that damn servant have to tie her hair so tight? Orellane sighed. She shouldn't blame Eda; this was all her father's fault. If the man wasn't so hot-headed, she could have continued seeing the Knucker and this farce could have been avoided.

The Knucker.

Orellane's heart dropped at the thought of her friend, waiting for her to return, as she had promised. Perhaps she wouldn't care. Perhaps she would move on and find a new companion. That thought only made Orellane feel worse. She hadn't known the Knucker for long, but their time together had felt special. With her, Orellane's world came alive, and all her confusion and frustration melted away, leaving her free. She remembered the look the Knucker had given her when she had been grabbed by the villager woman, how she had readied herself to save her. The Knucker *did* care, she was sure of it, and Orellane only hoped she would forgive being abandoned

It will be worth it, to save her.

Orellane took a deep breath to force back the tears threatening to break free and strode out of her bedroom, heading downstairs towards the parlour.

King Eadwine had wasted no time ensuring his preferred suitor would arrive first to woo the bride-to-be, and Orellane had been instructed to be on her best behaviour. Lord Roland was no different to the rest of the peacocks her father had paraded in front of her in recent weeks. Each was an eligible Lord of the kingdom, rich in power or wealth or both, and as dull as dishwater. He was handsome, she supposed, but he stirred nothing within her.

For the first time in her life, Orellane was happy her father had insisted on chaperoning every visit she had. He and Roland sat chatting about the politics of the kingdom while she tried not to fidget in a particularly uncomfortable ornate armchair. Sunshine streamed in through tall glass windows, heating the room like a greenhouse. Orellane felt suffocated, and absurdly unimportant. Roland had been as charming and courteous as ever when he greeted the princess, but since they had been seated his attention had been firmly fixed on impressing the king while she sweltered in her many layers and ruffles.

Orellane couldn't blame him; they both knew this would be a political marriage. She had expected to be relieved that she didn't have to worry about holding a conversation with this tedious man, but instead she felt isolated, and desperately lonely. She was a ghost, haunting a life she would never have more than a supporting role in. She would marry Roland and spend her days drifting through the palace grounds while he ruled over the South Kingdom. It would be easy, but it would be empty.

She tried to focus on the present, to cement herself in this life she had already committed to, but her mind wandered back to her time in the forest – the time she had spent with the Knucker. It had been exciting, yes, but there was something more, something she couldn't quite put her finger on. The way she felt when she was with the Knucker, the way her body reacted to her touch and the way heat filled her cheeks under her gaze…Well, it was how she expected she should feel when Lord Roland kissed her hand or complimented her appearance. But she didn't. Only when she was with the Knucker did Orellane feel…herself.

That's it.

A sudden clarity washed over her, and she knew what she

had to do. She rose from her seat and strode forwards, caution thrown to the wind. At first the two men didn't notice her approach, too engrossed in their conversation, but as she reached her father they turned and frowned at the princess, the confusion evident on both their faces. She leaned over the king and kissed him softly on the cheek.

"I love you, Father. I hope you will remember that, and forgive me."

"Orellane, I do not—"

She was out of the room before he could finish his sentence. When she reached the front door of the mansion, she broke into a sprint, kicking off her shoes as she ran.

Orellane ignored the cries of the villagers as she tore past their houses, leaving a trail behind her as she pulled out her hair pins and shed her heavy jewellery. She had no need for any of it now.

As she reached the edge of the forest and slipped between the trees, she ripped at the bodice of her dress, tearing off great strips of bejewelled fabric and tossing them over her shoulder. She heard the shouts of the Royal Guard behind her, summoned by the king to retrieve his wayward princess.

"You're too late!" she laughed, slowing to a halt as her destination came into view.

Her pounding heart drowned out any sound of pursuit as she stepped out of her remaining garments and felt the gentle caress of the cool breeze passing over her bare skin. A broad smile spread across her lips and a new joy blossomed in her chest as she ran forwards and dove head first into the pool's crystal clear waters.

As a crash of cold serenity washed over her, Orellane's grasping hands met with those of the Knucker. Their bodies entwined, two becoming one. A new heat flooded Orellane's senses, and she knew. This was right.

This was home.

Katherine Shaw is a multi-genre writer and self-confessed nerd from Yorkshire in the United Kingdom, spending most of her time dreaming up new characters or playing D&D. She has a passion for telling stories of injustice and battles against oppression, often with a focus on female protagonists. She has published her debut novel Gloria, a contemporary domestic thriller, and has work appearing in multiple anthology collections.

You can find out more at her website www.katherineshawwrites.com

Summer Dreams

R. A. Gerritse

In the beginning, there was light, sharp as needles, cold as silver—it was everything, everywhere, endless as if it had ever been. In the beginning, that was me, back when I was alone. Then, once upon an end of days amidst a thousand passing lives, forged in tongues of burning sky, reality crashed into me —or I into it—but I was one no more.

A dying wish, a mother's love, an infant's dream, a will to be—that slice of time, that single, fearful moment caught in a grain of sand, my first memory, my very first dream. Warming my light, gifting me sense and sight, silver turned to gold.

The dream felt overwhelming, impossible, incomprehensible. Like the newborn that I was, my world grew from sounds and colors, smells and instincts, moving, changing, shouting, screaming, in an endless loop of a mere lifetime's worth of memories—a fearful, hostile place, laced with a tiny edge of hope.

Through the eyes of a giant, kindred and primal, set on nothing but survival, I learned what it is to live below an endless summer sun. Grazing, feeding, procreating—a simple life, a chain of moments on repeat, where tomorrow meant nothing but the promise growing inside her womb. A promise that was not to be, for at the end of every viewing from the heavens came the fire that was me.

The day the last of the dinosaurs died, I came to life.

Lodged inside a dying mother desperate to save her unborn, in a moment stretched eternal, two lives in perfect harmony as only mother and child could ever be, reached for their last remaining brightness—the star shard, the sky fire, the harbinger of death, the one to end an age—and inside me their hopes, their souls, their consciousnesses merged into something even reality could never have believed.

We became I, and I could see, be it not with eyes, but with dreams. At first, only mine, but as time moved on and my core dislodged from the decaying body that birthed me, there came others. I walked the dreams of all the lives I touched, which were many—a natural thing for a mind the size of a grain of sand, drifting ageless, unaffected by the never-ending winds of change, from one vessel to the next.

Animals of every kind, plants, and trees with ancient wisdom, each of them granted me a glimpse of what it meant to live like them, how the world appeared, witnessed from their perspective, how it felt to walk their path through the ever-cycling seasons.

I loved each marvel that was Spring, the promise of every new beginning. I loved each Autumn's melancholy, as nature winded down its cycle. I reveled in the warmth of closeness as life pulled together in the deepest, coldest heart of every Winter.

But my favorite season, my most treasured dreams have ever been those of Summer.

May it have been the season's warmth, reminding me of days forgotten? A time when I was naught but dust and flame? Maybe so, but call me a romantic for believing it to be the memory of a loving mother's heart and her little one, alive in me, still reaching for the light. Grateful for their sacrifice, as parts of me, I found them the best summer dreams, days of warmth they never had the chance to share, and through them, felt alive.

Time moved on, and my summer dream collection grew. The world around me healed, changed, and came into sharper view. Life evolved and changed into endless new forms and shapes, and it was good. All of it, but somehow, it felt wanting.

Watching life in all its glory, it is wonderful but lonely. As the first of humanity began to leave their caves, as their social structures changed and their societies developed, as I watched the birth of speech, I hungered for communication, longed for the spark of connection that set humanity apart from all other species. I longed to be more than an unseen eye, a silent witness spying on their lives—a desire so strong, that unconsciously, over time, my soul learned to speak.

Don't get me wrong, there were no words involved—not then, not yet. No, there were sensations, impressions. There was wonderment and awe. There were waves of amazement and shivers of contentment, and for the longest time, I did not realize that these were mine, my reactions, projected, transmitted onto others—and I was felt.

It was a summer—of course, it was a summer—on a cooler, rainy day beneath a sky cloudy and gray while reveling in memories of warmth, walking the shadows of days beneath the blue, when something shifted. I felt it, the exact moment my summer reverie connected, long before my vessel turned her eyes to the darkened sky. For the first time, I knew that I was a spectator no more—my longing had sprung from my thoughts to those of another, irrevocably changing her path.

"Ah Kin?" she asked in an unknown tongue, and with fateful, cosmic coincidence, thunder answered.

I'll never claim to have created the sun religions, I was too infinitely small. I still am, I don't deserve that credit. And yet, the moment my connection to the world opened both ways, there was an impact, perhaps bigger than my crash from the stars, but just as unintended.

My vessel began to speak to me, addressing the sky, trying to please me whenever the weather seemed angry—leaving me offerings on hilltops to convince me to shine and bless their lives. It was overwhelming. Had I instilled in her this obsession with the sun with my fanciful dreaming? Had I steered this life into the worship of a force of nature deaf to her pleas—a force even muter than me? It felt like a disaster.

Sunny days are bliss, but rain serves its purpose. Summers are great but need their contrast to Winter, the proper perspective to appreciate its highs and lows, to reap all bounties, to heed all warnings. All types of weather and all seasons are but slices of this wonderful chaos called life. Placing the lens of worship over one enforced a balance bound to fall—it left me devastated and wordless.

For many lifetimes after, I was afraid to interfere, to steer the world even further from its intended path. For many lifetimes after, I cowered in the backs of minds, in the darkest corners of consciousness, afraid to be sensed or seen, keeping distant from the living's dreams, far out of touch with reality. For many lifetimes after, I felt miserable, my world cold, bleak, and lonely.

It was not until, after spending years in a desert, under mounds of burning sand in the buried ruins of a long-forgotten city, that an excavation team unwittingly freed me—both in body as in spirit—for on a wind of change I drifted into a new mind that was the very definition of happiness.

There were no words in this mind. There was no hate, no fear, no worship—only a vast appreciation of everything it saw, felt, tasted, and heard. It felt hard to believe, but there seemed to be no other emotion in this vessel than joy. This small, hairy creature saw life like no other I'd ever known, and he pulled me from my darkness.

For the first time in so many decades that I lost count, I allowed myself to share the sensations of the living, and as I did, it reawoke the memories of all the moments I once witnessed and so loved. Carefully, hesitantly, I once more dared to open myself and was greeted with naught but boundless joy.

This simple animal with a silly, given name, this carefree bundle of energy, man's self-proclaimed companion, showed me a side of existence I had yet to see, and its simplicity healed me.

When I dreamt of beaches, he ran blissfully in the sand. When I dreamt of rain, it took me swimming in the creek. When I dreamt of my roots in the stars, we howled at the moon. Sharing the wonders of past and present, I had made my very first friend. This unexpected, too-short slice of time was the best summer of my life.

Of course, like all dreams, this one did not last, for they all end—as all things must—but I still carry it and treasure its warmth. Especially when I share these memories, for I've learned that through the emotions in these brightest, frozen moments, we are all connected. I've learned that sharing the light we all carry is our most precious gift.

We may turn to the sun, but it's the warmth we seek, not the heavens—a warmth we live and breathe. After all, what is existence, but a summer dream?

As a rock journalist for Metal On Loud Magazine, Randy watches the world in search of both rhythms and answers. As an author, host of the Twitter poetry prompt tag #vsspoem, and a lyricist for four different bands, poetry is part of his every day – it even found its way into his novels.

His first self-publication: a collection of micro poetry forged into a single, two act epic poem called The Rhythm of Life, is now available on Amazon.

Randy's first published short stories Rain Must Fall and Days Gone By are now available in the anthologies Of Silver Bells and Chilling Tales and Of Mistletoe And Snow by Jazz House Publications.

The Witches of Dogtown

A. J. Van Belle

Eye of toad and horn of newt.

They get the eyes and the horns wrong in the stories they tell. Some things have horns even though you wouldn't expect them to. Such as dreams and notions. Mossy corner joists in old log cabins. Buttered toasts, shedding crumbs.

And newts.

Which we have here in Dogtown. The dogs eat them. Those and the mice dart into woodpiles, making games for dogs. My cuddly, fur-covered babies are monsters to the small things of the wood. All a matter of perspective.

I dust pollen and mushroom spores off my hands, finished with another concoction, ready to start another day.

There's a young woman in a blue T-shirt in my yard, toeing the old maple stump with a worn running shoe.

Strangers don't happen into my yard often. When they do, there's always a reason.

I poke my head out the front door, and the woman looks up at the creak of the hinges, mouth a startled O. They don't see my house unless they're meant to find it. Or unless I make myself known.

She has hair past her shoulders, no makeup, a leaf stuck in her hair. A creature of the woods. As am I. The factory-made clothing she wears doesn't fool me. The costume gets her through times in that "we're better than we used to be" world out there but she's a part of the Earth, sprung up from the soil.

"Come in!" I say, in my best warm-granny tone. I don't curse travelers, no matter what the legends say.

A salt-studded wind blows up from Gloucester. It sways the trees and sends hair across the woman's line of sight. She shakes her head and clears her view. I know what she sees: me, a medium-old woman. With a halo-mane of gray and brown. Wearing a simple loose dress with sleeves pushed up past the elbows, made of brown fabric with white flowers. Could be early factory made or could come from one of the latest designers. Doesn't matter.

"I'm Tamara Whitt." It's what I call myself these days. "Won't you come inside?"

She doesn't identify herself. Her gaze traces the cottage's edges.

I grip the doorframe but there's little friction in the contact. I see through my hands. It happens more often than it used to. Once I found my roots and learned to draw strength from the earth, I lived nearly two hundred years without a flicker. But that's changed now. For the last few decades, at times the wind blows through me. Even the heartiest witch can't live forever.

I'm not worried for myself. My concern is for the travelers who pass by this place.

Old forces are at work here, rumblings from the Earth that lead to accidents and conflicts. Here the energetic lines of the Earth converge and give off invisible sparks. Those who pass through feel an inexplicable pressure like the opposing poles of a magnet repelling each other. For generations upon generations, I've been here to ease the tension.

I won't be here much longer.

All the more reason to talk to this stranger. She must be able to see me for a reason. I wave to her. "I suppose you weren't expecting to find anyone living here."

She looks up at the treetops as if answers might live there. "I didn't, no. It's public land."

"Right you are. What better place to live for one who hasn't any money?"

Her eyes narrow. Her cheek twitches. She's half-amused, half-suspicious. "Are you saying you're a squatter?"

"I have the right of longevity to this land. The city's resigned itself to letting me be. Throwing a witch out of Dogtown would be like banishing heat from a flame. Can't be done."

She props a foot on the stump and opens her palm to a beam of sunlight falling into the glade. Catching light rays is the province of one who knows the arts. "So you're a witch. You practice Wicca?"

"I don't give a name to the water that flows through the stream. And I don't practice – I *am* the water."

"Water. You mean that as a metaphor for magic."

I wave a hand. "Metaphor. Words. What are they?"

She glances up, face sharp, eyes shrewd. Measuring me without a yardstick. She's got no clue what I am or how I came to be in her story today. That much is clear.

"Tell me a tale," I say. "Tell me how you came to be in Dogtown this summer's day, Liese. That's your name, isn't it?"

She draws in a sharp breath. "How did you know my name?"

I only smile. "Tell me what brought you here."

She closes her fingers. Opens them again. Catching the light. Drinking it in through the center of her left palm. "We were just out for a short hike."

"We? How many of you are there?"

She laughs. "Two. Ren – that's my boyfriend – he's back near the parking lot. He said – it sounds crazy."

"Everything's crazy."

"He started down the trail with me, but he said the land was pushing him out. He's sensitive that way. An intuitive. He's been teaching me."

"Teaching you, has he?"

She nods. "He said the witches' spirits are here. Not like ghosts. Nothing that – sentient. But their echo. It's here. Living among the trees. And it – their collective essence – doesn't want him here. It's not personal, he thought. Just men. They don't want men here."

I must tread carefully for my next few sentences. "Men are all right. If they follow the rules of Dogtown."

"What are the rules of Dogtown?" There's a hint of challenge in her voice. A ripple of amusement.

"Respect the land. Don't fear the dogs. No human tells another what to do. Follow those rules and you're golden." As golden as the light in the treetops.

She opens her palm again. With my mind's eye, I see sunshine stream in through her pores and flow through her veins. All the way to her heart, where it glows and whispers. She's meant to be here, all right. She's a witch herself.

She sighs. "He tells me what to do all the time. Maybe that was the rule he couldn't follow."

"What does he tell you to do?" I can't keep the sharp concern from my voice.

She looks up, hearing my thoughts. "Nothing like that. He's more advanced in witchcraft than I am, that's all. He teaches me. It's what drew me to him in the first place."

With a sweep of my arm, I invite her into the cottage-that-isn't. At least it isn't there to the ordinary eye.

She follows me and gapes at the purple toadstools growing from the rafters, the moss creeping over the tabletop, the vines encircling the turned-wood chair legs.

I sit at the table. "Join me!"

My two mortal dogs get up from resting in a shaft of sunlight and wiggle their way over to greet her. She pulses with currents of energy that run beneath her skin. A powerful witch even if she doesn't know it yet.

She sits and puts down an absent hand to pat a furry canine head. "How is this...possible?"

I look down through the backs of my wavering hands at the tiny phyllids of moss growing over the table. "Possible? You've already seen stranger things, I'll warrant."

She narrows her eyes at my hands but I can't tell if they're as ethereal to her gaze as mine. Tricky thing, truth. Doesn't show itself to everyone all the time.

"Not really."

"Then tell me," I say. "Tell me what this boyfriend of yours means when he says you're not advanced."

"Well. Okay," she says. "Here's an example. I was sitting on the floor of our apartment one night holding hands with Ren with a candle between us. We were doing a simple practice: raising energy and blessing our space. We said the words of the spell – a little rhyme he taught me, and I can't remember it now. See how hopeless I am? And I felt so hot, and the candle flame burned up so bright it lit up the whole room like daylight.

"I felt like I was floating. I was sitting on the floor with my legs crossed, but I could see us from above. Ren grunted and scooted back from me, and I saw right away what the problem was: there was a stinkbug crawling across his wrist. You know those really big brown ones? He's afraid of them. Well, he grabbed it with his other hand and I knew he was about to crush it even though it wouldn't do him any harm. I'd seen him squash them before for no reason. I felt all that heat in the room rush into me, and the next thing you know the stinkbug was halfway across the room on the carpet. We both saw it.

"I got up and coaxed it onto a piece of paper and put it outside. As soon as I did that, all the energy I'd been feeling – it rushed through me. I don't know how else to describe it. I was like a funnel and the energy poured through me and went down, out through my feet and past the floor, all the way down to the foundation of the building and then into the ground.

"Ren didn't say anything about the bug. Neither of us asked how it ended up so far away from him. He just said I ruined the ceremony because I wasn't ready yet."

"Not ready? Too ready, I'll wager." I open my palms, give her a questioning look, and she lets me take her hands. My fingers might be ghostly, but hers are warm and strong. "Let's see," I croon like a mother to an infant. "Let's see what brought you here."

With my eyes closed, I can see the box she's in. It's like glass around her. She may laugh on the outside and tell me all is well, but she can move hardly an inch to the left or right.

I squeeze her hands and close my eyes. The sunlight streams through the window and warms our intertwined fingers. I send my senses in every direction, feeling the summer breeze outside these walls. The hawthorn berries ripe on the bush by the door, the broad oak leaves of the forest canopy soaking up light, the young fisher cat dozing in its hollow off the trail. At the same time, my sight goes inward to the heart of the young woman in front of me.

At first, all I see is blood. Confused, I have to open my eyes and see her again to know she's whole. Her eyes are closed, long brown lashes against bronze cheeks. Outwardly peaceful. But inside, there's turmoil. A memory of pain, too much to bear. A feeling of loss and failure like fog that eats her alive, threatening to make her vanish. An inner world vastly different from my sunny summer cottage.

I let my mind cross paths with hers again. The blood doesn't come from a wound; it comes from within.

"There was a baby," I say.

Her lashes flutter and I look into her eyes, which are startled and sad at once. "How did you know?"

"I see it." I see the too-early, bright red flow and the baby no bigger than a fist. I feel all the pain of labor but leading only to death. I hear the echo of a man's voice but not the words. "What did he tell you?"

She looks confused. "What did who tell me?"

"Ren. What did he say? What did he tell you about the baby? I can hear there was something but I can't make out the words."

She grips my fingers. "He said if I'd known how to ground myself, the baby would have lived." She sheds no tears. Her voice is as stiff as a tree trunk. The emotion has been squeezed out of her like water from a cloth. "He said my magic isn't strong enough yet. He said *I* wasn't strong enough to keep the baby alive."

It's not your fault. The words won't go to her heart. Not yet. "Like most people, Ren is neither all good nor all bad," I say instead. "In this case, he's dead wrong."

Hope flits cloud-like over her face. "You think so?"

I know so. "It's my turn to tell you a story." I know she's here so I can tell her; I knew the moment I saw the sunlight enter her heart.

I release her hands, get up, and pace to the window. With my hands clasped behind me, my cloud of hair trailing down my back, and my dress so simple it could belong to any age, I doubt she notices anything out of place. When she does – when she sees I'm living proof the world has more dimensions than she previously knew – she'll see the door in the glass house that holds her prisoner.

"A long time ago," I begin, "these trails led to houses where dwelt women fed up with the rules placed on them by society. Or women who'd lost the protection of a man – which people believed necessary in those days. Or women who'd simply felt drawn to the hum of the woods here. Women who kept dogs as friends and guards. The dogs let them know when someone was coming. They drove out anyone who looked suspicious – and dogs always know who looks suspicious. Strong judges of character, dogs are. The hearsay was that these women cursed those who wouldn't help them. That the people of Gloucester gave them food to avoid the old hackneyed curses: soured milk, illness, stolen babies. The truth was the women traded herbal remedies with healing powers more powerful than herbs alone can provide. They traded wisdom not found outside their woods. And they traded spells of protection for ships at sea and crops at home.

"But before that came an in-between time. First this was an ordinary town, filled with busy families. Then they all left and it was a ghost town. Except for one person. There was a first witch who lived here. Alone and half-starving."

As I continue my tale, I relive it in my memory.

I lived alone in a house with the roof rotted through. When it rained, I sheltered in the root cellar, which was nothing more than a hole in the ground, cold even in summer. I ate what I could catch and gather: rabbits and squirrels caught in traps, berries and roots in the summer. Potatoes grown from half-decayed cuttings that somehow sprouted and made new fleshy tubers for me to eat in the spring. It was scant at first. But the people passing below on the roads had carts full of goods. I didn't dare approach them at first. I was alone, and alone is a hard habit to break.

A half-bred creature came around in the nights, a thing as skeletal as I was, with rough, gray fur hanging from its bony frame. I heard it on warm summer nights when I slept in the open cottage with the ragged hole through which starlight fell like the dust of broken glass. At first I thought I dreamed the snuffling. There were no bears here, and the coyotes would yip and sing and let me know their presence. I must be imagining the presence of another living thing coming close enough for me to hear its breathing.

I stayed awake the night of the midsummer's full moon. The light made me restless and made something strange and foreign flow through my veins. Something like hope. Though it couldn't be hope. Couldn't be because there wasn't hope, not for me, not anymore. Nothing more for me but surviving another day, until one day I wouldn't anymore.

I sat for a long time without moving on the broken front step. The half-dog, half-coyote came into my yard. I held my breath. A strange, liminal creature, neither domestic nor wild. Neither beautiful nor ugly. Neither free nor captive. An outcast, like me. A creature of night because the day wouldn't have it. The animal nosed through the burned skeletons of my recent scant dinners. Femur of hare, charred scapula of squirrel. A little marrow must have remained, because my visitor snapped up my discards and crunched the bones.

It looked up mid-crunch, made eye contact with me, and froze. I smiled for the first time I could remember; this was the first eye contact I could remember in ages. The animal looked silly with a small bone sticking out the side of its mouth like a cigar, afraid to stay and afraid to go.

I crept inside to my dank kitchen. When I returned with a sliver of squirrel meat I'd dried in the sun, I half-expected my canine visitor to be gone. But he was still there and ducked his head without taking his eyes off me. I squatted and offered him the meat.

We've been friends ever since. I call him Midsummer Moon.

He's not here yet. Doesn't come out in the daytime.

The light has faded and the world is deep blue outside the

windows.

Liese reaches down and pets one of the dogs, a fluffy mutt like a cotton ball come to life. "Aren't all your dogs here now?"

I smile. "No. These are the flesh-and-blood mortal dogs. Midsummer Moon only visits at night."

She gives me a sidelong look, more intrigued now than skeptical, I think.

I glance into the darkness. "Midsummer Moon may join us soon," I say, and then I tell her the rest. What it was like once woman after woman joined me here, drawn to bushes heavy with berries in the summer, trees lush with sheltering leaves, and magic thick in the air.

We were the ones who refused to be part of it all. The cycle of unforgiving subjugation and colonization. To escape oppression our ancestors sailed far and wide and in coming home to these woods they claimed what was never theirs.

The subjugation of women's bodies. The colonization of lands with tales already long and true.

They cut down trees to build the port town of Gloucester, but we up in Dogtown made homes between the trunks. The maple in my front yard fell in its own time. With the land, not stealing from it.

But. Massachusetts winters are long. Especially in those days. Especially when you have dogs to feed. Dogs who keep the townsfolk away. Dogs who ruin the spells by running wrong ways 'round the fire but they're so cute you don't mind. Cold. Hungry. Days on end with only old dried berries and rabbit meat frozen since November.

But the summers. Oh, the summers. Long too. Golden and ripe. Coming home to yourself day after day, angling sun through tree branches long after the evening cook fire's put out. My dogs and I sing tunes to the chirping crickets and joyfully creaking frogs. We've done this for ages and do it today. I have a piccolo made of tin, given to me by my father before he passed away. Midsummer Moon likes to sing along. And when a traveler's wagon wheel breaks, I hold it together with my magic from afar until the traveler reaches safety. When a hiker is lost in these woods after dark, I send fireflies to light their way home.

My story done, I squeeze Liese's hands and let them go. Outside the window, fireflies spark, telling tales in light patterns to wake the witch inside Liese.

I hold out my hand to her. "Come. The trees are calling."

She takes my hand. Stands. Blinks at the window and the darkness outside. "What? It was morning."

Her fingers pass through mine and she's left holding only air. Her startled gaze darts around, frantic. First she looks at me and into the shadows in the corners of the room.

"It's whatever time it needs to be," I tell her. "Come! The hour is now. The trees won't wait. They're telling me someone needs me."

Outside, the humid summer wind blows strong. A harsh creaking sound comes from somewhere far down the path in the direction of the Dogtown Commons parking lot.

The whites of Liese's eyes are pale by starlight. "What's that sound?"

I peer down the path and see beyond what my physical eyes can possibly know. "An old tree about to be blown over. A large one, by the sound of it." The wind blows through my breastbone and batters my spine. I don't have long now. "Follow me."

I lead the way through the woods until a junction between two paths comes into view. A thin young man stands there, hands in his pockets, shoulders hunched. He has short, spiky, dark hair and he's all angles. "Liese?" he calls out quietly. "Where'd you go?"

A stronger gust of wind blows up. The creaking sound fills the air as an enormous oak next to Ren tilts sideways and threatens to fall.

"Liese?" Ren calls again, oblivious to the tree looming over him. Its trunk is so big around a person's arms couldn't encircle it. The wind gusts hard again and the tree tilts over Ren's head.

Dogtown doesn't like people who aren't meant to be here. He didn't heed the warning he felt in his bones, and now the woods are a true menace to him.

In the warm night wind, my cloak billows to one side. Barely clinging to my shoulders, it sweeps across Liese's chest. Although she's solid, my magic blows through her as surely as the breeze cuts through my insubstantial torso.

"Ren!" she calls out. A sharp, wild cry. If not for the magic, he would hear her. But he looks up into the treetops as if he might have heard an owl.

I try again to warp the earth and tilt the tree away. But reaching my mind into the soil gives no strength. As if instead of roots and rocks I can find only shifting sand.

"I'm fading," I tell her. "You'll have to stop it from falling."

"I don't know how!" She sounds like a lost child.

"You know how to do it," I whisper in her ear. "If you're ready to claim your power and all that comes with it." When I wrap an arm around her shoulders, the last of my power flows into her. I fade to no more than the scent of wild geranium on the air. My cloak falls to the dirt, empty.

Liese glows.

She raises her arms. I can't see my own arms in front of me, but I feel her power. Sweeping lines of energy run from her fingers and toes deep into the ground beneath us. The blue-gray clouds swirl above the treetops against the black of night. Stars that wink beyond them echo the blinking of the fireflies that gather along the trail of her power and rise to circle her head like a crown.

The earth shakes. Ren loses his balance and catches it again, half-crouching and looking around wildly. The soil ripples, throwing him to the ground and tossing the tree's roots high so they break from the ground and arc like crooked fingers into the air.

The tree falls the other way. Away from Ren.

He pants on the ground, eyes wide.

Liese folds her hands in front of her and walks to his side. Spirals of fireflies follow her, green and gold sparks of magic. When I blink, I can still see the glass box around her, but the glass is as thin as a soap bubble now. The fireflies circle her, and the box shatters.

A dark smoke rises from her and disperses in the night air, leaving her shape bright and clear against the darkness: her trauma and the pain of a toxic relationship no longer hold her captive. In the place of the darkness, threads of light wrap themselves around her:

Forgiveness for losing the baby.

Freedom from a sour relationship.

The realization of who she really is.

Glowing, she stands over Ren, calm and sure of herself.

I no longer feel the ground beneath me. I see the two people from above. I do not have a body any longer.

"Did you see that?" Ren gasps.

Liese smiles. Again she's childlike, but this time with pleasure instead of uncertainty. "I'll find my own way home."

Ren scrambles to his feet. "Aw, come on, Liese. I'm sorry. I was harsh earlier. About – you know, about everything."

"I don't think we should see each other anymore," she tells him in a thoughtful tone, "but I'm not angry. It's just that – I belong somewhere else now."

She turns and leaves him, and like a warm breeze, I follow her. She doesn't look for me. She seems to understand what's happened. That I've changed but I'll never be gone. That the cloak is hers now. That the cottage is hers too. Finders keepers, or my gift to her. Whichever way she chooses to see it.

From my vantage point as wind among the tree branches, Liese looks like a force of nature herself. She takes up my cloak from the path, dusts it off, and slings it across her shoulders. She strides up the path with Midsummer Moon prancing at her side and jumping up to lick her hand. The last echo of Ren's footsteps fades along his path toward civilization. Neither I nor Liese look back.

***

She strides along the dusty ways that were once the streets of Dogtown. The cloak ripples in the wind. In its wake, whorls of magic swirl from her shoulders and blend with the night.

She walks to my - her - cottage. Midsummer Moon trots at her side, wagging his tail. She ruffles his fur and tugs his ear as if they've known each other all their lives. She goes into what was my home until now. Watching her through the window, I whisper a blessing to the summer sky.

Inside the cottage, she strikes a spark from the flint as if she's been doing it all her life. The kindling at the hearth springs to bright life. She crumbles a handful of dried lemon verbena into a lopsided stoneware mug, as sure of the herb as if she dried it herself. Soon, the water in the kettle reaches a cheerful boil. She makes herself a cup of tea.

She's finally home. As am I.

We will be here always: the witches of Dogtown.

A. J. Van Belle is an author living in Massachusetts with their husband, teenage daughter, and two very personable dogs.

They write for teens and adults in multiple genres, including sci-fi, fantasy, horror, and contemporary lit fic. Across all genres, their work incorporates themes of trauma, healing, and a hint at something beyond the senses.

When not writing, A. J. works as a professor and researcher in biology. They often bring their scientific expertise to their fiction and have a blast using real knowledge of fungal ecology and evolutionary history to help build speculative worlds.

Check out their work at www.ajvanbelle.com.

CONTRACT WITH A MERMAID
M. J. Weatherall

There's a maid has sat on the green mereside
These ten lang years and mair;
An' every first night o' the new moon
She kames her yellow hair.
— Allan Cunningham

Once upon a time on the outskirts of Delbeattie, Scotland, there lived a *Maighdean-mara* called Morveren. The most enchanting mermaid to ever venture inland.

Morveren had been coming to her seat in the burn on the night of the full moon for decades. She'd lost her cap and could not return to the sea without it. The crimson, feathered hood protected merpeople from battering waves and allowed them to roam the vast oceans freely. She spent her lonely existence searching for her missing cap. Bargaining with the townsfolk for her lost hope.

Many desperate people struck bargains with the mermaid over the course of her stay. But this focuses on her last contract.

***

Fenella's maw forbade her from seeing Morveren. She told her the mermaid was wicked and lured men to their deaths. That she played tricks and would prophesize death to those who spoke to her. Fenella could see some of this being true. Folk who worried about dying would ask Morveren and she'd tell them the truth. That wasn't the same as causing their deaths. She played tricks on folk who wanted to humiliate or entrap her – again, understandable.

In the following years Fenella came to understand Maw's worry and the reasons she wished her to stay away from the enchantress.

It was the night of the full moon one summer's day shortly after Fenella turned thirteen. Maw was seriously ill and had taken a turn for the worse. Fenella was the oldest, and Pa perished at sea several years ago. They barely got by on Maw's lowly income alone. Fenella was standing in for Maw at work, but the other staff were starting to get annoyed. The head maid was the only one who bothered being nice to her, as well as teaching her to be proper and to write. Some thought it reflected badly on the Thane.

Fenella decided to pay Morveren a visit. Once the bairns were all asleep and Maw took her medicine, she slipped out of bed. Already dressed for her expedition, she went out the door. Melding easily with the gentle summer's breeze.

The night was so warm that she needn't have dressed so fully. The humidity of the day stuck the clothes to her damp skin, but she wasn't bothered by the discomfort.

She was too entranced with the task ahead.

Fenella snuck across the lane, past the other shacks on their row. Lived in by people employed by the Thane; blacksmiths, launderers, maids, servants and others of the same ilk. She knew plainly where she was venturing. The burn – a small river snaking through the beautiful valley.

They say that Morveren is the most beautiful being anyone

has ever laid eyes upon. Fenella was excited to see if it was true. She hastened her speed, anxious that one of the bairns would notice her missing and raise Maw.

Bairns were known for going missing. Snatched and tricked from their beds by wealthy gentlemen with the promise of a better life.

She continued on to meet the mermaid who she hoped would be the saviour of her family. She knew why Maw hated Morveren so much. Fenella's late father drowned at sea. Mermaids were renowned for their illustrious siren song, luring men to wreck their boats at the slight chance of adultery at sea.

Fenella's shoes were thin, and rubbing before long. Maw hadn't enough money for clothing so they had to put up with quick fixes and charity from neighbours much larger than herself. She was grateful. She walked across the patchy gravel path towards the burn. Soon she was away from the village and could step freely without worrying about the noise.

She looked up at the moon, the perfectly spherical wonder in the sky. It was a clear night, not a blemish – not a cloud to be seen. She was thankful for the light. It was enchanting, like something out of a fairytale.

Fenella was too busy gawking at the moon to see the shapes lumbering towards her. Several men were stumbling back from the tavern in the next village over. The Thane frowned upon enabling such a vicious addiction such as alcoholism, Maw said. She wasn't looking at her feet, and tripped over a stone in the path tumbling down the riverbank to its edge. She had never been glad of falling before then. She heard the men whooping drunkenly. They hadn't noticed her. She waited for them to pass before picking herself up and dusting off her dress.

She started scrambling up the bank when she saw the stream next to her, which was platformed. A blessing, to walk unobserved to her secret meeting with the being she was forbidden to meet with.

Fenella thought about what her auntie said. About Maw's illness, about Morveren. About how they would all have to go and live with her and their cousins once Maw's illness took her. She didn't want to live with them. Folk say that blood is thicker than water but those folk were like ice. Fenella knew she had to take care of it.

She wished on the moon: for good fortune on her travels, success on her mission, for Maw's recovery.

She trekked along the river's bank, keeping an eye on her feet and listening out for any threats. The mermaid's seat was three miles away; the distance wasn't a problem in summer when the weather was fair and dry. After a harsh winter and grim spring, the summer was glorious. Sun warming every crevice, and flowers blooming so beautifully around the estate. Fenella felt warmed, reborn by the lighter nights and the sun on her face.

An hour later she reached her destination, the mermaid's seat.

It was empty.

There was no-one there. Fenella crashed to the water's edge, fists balled. *Was it all a lie? Something they told bairns to give them false hope? Fake miracles, to make the world seem less harsh? Was Morveren a fairytale?* Tears rolled down her face uncontrollably. Without Morveren there was no way Fenella could keep her family intact.

She dropped to the ground, knees breaking open bloodily against the abrasive shale. She sobbed, letting her tears fill the burn. Her mind kept landing back at the same conclusion: there was nothing she could do to save her family.

A wet rustling nearby brought her back to the present but she didn't see the point of reacting. So what if some great beast crawled out of the depths and pulled her under, would that be the worst thing? They were probably fake too.

"Bairn," a voice beckoned sweetly, "why do you weep?"

"Leave me be," Fenella begged, hands covering her face out of shame.

"So you didn't come to see me?" the voice sang.

Fenella looked up, expecting to see a maiden standing by the shore. About to berate her for absconding in the dead of night to make a deal with a demon. But no-one was standing on the shore.

"I don't believe it," Fenella gasped, blinking tears from her puffy eyes.

"Then why did you travel all this way, lassie?" Morveren taunted from the perfectly formed seat protruding from the gentle watercourse.

"I need your help," Fenella gushed, splashing into the shallows, reaching out for Morveren, her last hope.

She'd been too traumatised to look at the mermaid properly until then. She saw her now. Her long, straight, platinum white hair lay wet against her pale, shimmering skin. Her face was perfectly symmetrical. Timelessly beautiful. Her seafoam eyes oozed the pain of centuries past – the only indicator of her age.

Fenella observed the mermaid's body, down to the tell-tale feature, the one she'd been excited to see. Morveren's tail. *Was it rude to stare?* She couldn't help herself. It seemed to change colour with each lapping wave. Taking on the colours of the water, the crest of the wave, the silty bottom, and the moon's rays in quick succession. Fenella was entranced, unable to tear her eyes away.

"You done gawking?" Morveren inquired.

"I'm sorry," Fenella replied, ripping her gaze away from the kaleidoscope tail.

"You came here to ask for help," Morveren repeated, lounging delicately on her seat. "What do you need, bairn?"

"Maw is sick, been so for months, she is going to die."

"You wish to save her?"

"I wish to save us all."

Morveren pondered this for a moment, as if unsure. "And what do you offer me in return?"

"I have nothing but my own life to offer."

"How noble, but what do I need a child's life for?"

Fenella had heard of mermaid's humour before but didn't think she'd be so cruel. "To do your bidding on land."

"Clever lassie."

"Do we have a deal?" Fenella stuck out her hand for the mermaid to shake.

"Indeed, your maw's life for your service, it shall be so."

"How do I know you won't trick me?"

"A Maighdean-mara's word is binding." Morveren's face was stern and sincere. Fenella believed her.

"You won't own my maw's life, cure her illness and ensure she lives to a ripe old age?"

"You shall be in service to me for as long as she lives. You shall share in my riches, be under my protection and do my bidding 'til your debt is paid. Or you bring me my *cohuleen druith* – my cap." Morveren reached out and shook Fenella's hand; her cold, wet skin sent shivers down Fenella's arm.

"Deal." Fenella felt the words bind her. A warm flutter spread through the water into her bones, searing down her wrists.

Morveren slid deftly off her seat and disappeared into the depths. Fenella froze, the weight of her actions dawning on her. The promise of lifelong servitude to a trickster enchantress. There were worse things.

She waited, hoping the mermaid hadn't abandoned her. Morveren said her words were binding so Fenella felt sure she would return.

Where she felt the magic spread, she now noticed why it seared with pain as it passed her wrist. On her forearm was a mark, a brand, a three-pronged fork burned into her skin. She recalled some old tale, the King of the Sea often had one of those...tridents.

Suddenly, Morveren was back, bursting through the surface and reclaiming her seat.

"Make sure she drinks all of this, at once," Morveren extended her arm. Enclosed in her fist was a tiny vial, its contents inky black. "It will take a few hours to kick in."

"Ta, Morveren!" Fenella waded out to the seat and took the potion.

"Come back here when the full moon is next out and I will have your first task."

"I will, ta."

"Hurry along now, the night is waning." Morveren waved her off.

If Fenella looked back she would have seen the grin on Morveren's face, but she didn't look back.

She ran. All the way home.

***

Fenella's maw made a miraculous recovery, shocking everyone. Fenella didn't tell anyone about her excursion to see Morveren. Not a soul. She kept the brand hidden, telling people she'd burnt herself and covered it to keep it from infection.

When Maw was well enough to go back to work she took Fenella with her and asked if she could stay on as an apprentice. To work for free until she came of age. Free labour was never turned down – even if she was only a bairn.

So Fenella went to work with Maw. Every day and every night she'd come home to see the happy faces of her siblings. Who had food in their bellies and clothes on their backs.

Dreading the day that she had to go back and work for Morveren.

At least it is only one night a month, she told herself. It was the most wonderful month of her life. Maw was happy, the children were happy and everything was going to be okay. Fenella's auntie felt cheated. She walked around with a sour look on her face, like she was harbouring a mouthful of wasps.

***

Finally, the night of the full moon came around and, after making preparations the day before, Fenella was ready to face her new mistress. Sneaking away in the dead of night would be harder now that Maw was lucid. So she made sure to slip her a bit of homemade sleeping draught.

She didn't know what to expect. She packed a satchel with an assortment of items: bread, water, pencil, paper, knife, and an extra pair of woollen socks in case she needed to go swimming again.

The walk to the burn seemed to take longer this time, with the knowledge that some sinister tasks were ahead of her.

***

Months went by and Fenella's arrangement with Morveren was comfortable. They'd meet once a month and plan a series of tasks for Fenella to carry out that lunar cycle. These included collecting information, ingredients for potions and spells, and collecting debts.

Fenella was happy. Morveren was a good mistress. She taught her spells here and there. She shared her vast wealth so Fenella could buy her siblings new clothes and do things like fix the hole in the roof. Maw never questioned where the wealth came from, but somewhere deep down she must have worked it out.

***

It was nearly a year into the arrangement when things took a turn. Fenella was walking back from the burn like she'd done on every full moon for the past eleven months when suddenly a figure jumped out from behind a bush.

"Aha!" the figure bellowed, pointing an accusatory finger.

Fenella pulled her knife instinctively. "What do you want?" she commanded with as much force as a fourteen-year-old girl could.

"Do you not know your own flesh and blood?" the figure teased and stepped into the moonlight.

"Auntie?"

"You wicked lassie, what trouble you've gotten yourself into. Dealing with sick demonic monsters!"

"You know nothing about my life, or the company I keep."

"How dare you show your face in Church!"

Fenella laughed.

"Take her," Auntie called to the trees.

Several figures stepped out of the foliage. Wearing all black and clutching their crucifixes piously.

"What are you doing?" Fenella asked, keeping the panic from her tone.

She had no chance against four fully grown women in a fight, but in a race? That was different. She feinted to the closest woman, ducked under her arm as she went for the grab and sprinted down the path towards her home. Shouts of disgust followed her escape.

Fenella didn't stop until she reached the village, slowing down so as not to raise people from their beds with her heavy footfall. She took deep, heaving breaths to calm herself. She would tell Morveren the next time she saw her. That calmed her down. After her auntie found out about Morveren would the villagers think she was evil, too? She decided to sleep on it.

The next morning Fenella was the first up. She was too stressed to sleep for long and too anxious that the women were going to steal her from her bed. Villagers squawked. Something was amiss. Fenella dressed quickly and woke Maw, who went out to see what the kerfuffle was about. Fenella peeked through the keyhole. She saw the four women soaking wet, clutching their bibles and shouting at the top of their lungs.

"The seat is no more!"

"The mermaid's wrath is over!"

Auntie yelled with a sly, spiteful look in Fenella's direction. As if she could see her through the tiny hole in the wooden door. It was not the first time her auntie had taken it upon herself to destroy something she disagreed with. Fenella's maw had told her harrowing tales of their childhood.

Fenella's heart sank. What will Morveren do without her seat? Will she disappear? Is my servitude over? she thought, deciding that she would miss the mermaid if she was never to see her again. People whooped and cheered, people who had been wronged by the enchantress. Others stood as Fenella did, with sorrow in their hearts, for the mermaid had done them good deals.

***

Fenella laid low for the rest of the month, keeping out of her auntie's way and only going to work with Maw. She waited for the night of the full moon when she could see if Morveren would return without her seat there. It was painful, not knowing whether her life was about to change. In some ways it was a huge relief knowing that she would be able to go back to her normal life. The brand on her arm reminded her that she had been special – a part of something much more fantastical.

Fenella decided that she would go to the burn before nightfall. To see the damage the women did to the seat and if there was anything she could do to restore it to its former glory. She was almost certain that Morveren would return. There wasn't anything stopping her, was there? It was just a seat. Somewhere to sit while she waited for custom.

There was no sign that the seat had even existed. The women had done a good job of making sure the mermaid had no base of operation. Fenella sighed. She wrapped herself up in her thin shawl and sat hunched in the sand with her back against the eroded riverbank. Waiting for night to fall, for the moon to come out, for her mistress to return.

She turned words around in her head, wondering how she was going to explain the situation. Morveren wouldn't know that the women had vandalised her seat yet. The sky grew dark and Fenella became more anxious. She couldn't wait, so she waded out into the burn to where the seat used to stand.

The moon was the only source of light now, a glowing mystical orb in the clear sky. Like the night Fenella first met her mistress – there wasn't a cloud in the sky. She was glad of the warm summer breeze and that the water had been sunbaked all day.

"Morveren!" she called, standing waist deep in the gentle current.

"You called?" Morveren answered. Breaking the surface gracefully, flipping her wet hair calmly over her shoulder.

"Some of the townsfolk came and destroyed your seat, they think you're wicked," Fenella admitted, her head hung low.

"Then they must pay." Morveren hissed.

"What will happen to them?"

"Who were they?"

"I..."

"You know who the criminals are? You can't protect them. They must pay for their crimes." Morveren's expression was serious, her body rigid with anger.

"My auntie and some other pious women," Fenella confided.

"You must take me to them," Morveren ordered.

"But you don't have legs, won't you die out of the water?"

"I can walk on land if I wish."

"Then why have I been doing your dirty work?" Fenella asked.

"Because it's a horrible sensation. Legs are unnatural, and my skin gets dry out of the water."

"So you just don't like it? But it's possible?"

"I have to return to the water before sunrise, but yes, it's possible under the power of the full moon," Morveren said.

"Fine, I'll take you there."

"I need some clothes first."

"Of course, I'll be back soon."

Fenella left her bag on the riverbank and hiked up her skirts. She ran all the way back to the village and snuck into her house, being careful not to wake her family. She rifled through Maw's belongings and found a pair of her pa's old slacks and a soft linen shirt he reserved for church. She didn't feel too bad seeing her pa's old things but she did feel bad for Maw, who had kept them even when they didn't have enough money for food or clothes.

Fenella stuffed everything she needed into a burlap sack along with a hunk of bread and cheese. In case Morveren needed to eat once she took human form. She pushed her front door open and dipped her head. She ran as fast as she could all the way back to the burn where her mistress was waiting for her.

"Clothes," she panted.

"Good lass."

Fenella laid out the clothes on the dry riverbank and turned away, knowing that it wouldn't be polite to stare as Morveren transformed. Much less when she was naked in her human form. That was something Fenella didn't want to see.

"You can look now," Morveren said, her voice as sweet and hypnotic as before her transformation.

Fenella turned around and gasped as she laid eyes on her mistress. Wearing her pa's clothes that cloaked her slim figure and long, slender legs. Her fair hair was dry, pulled up into a ponytail with elegant stragglers framing her face. Her features looked less ethereal than before, probably to blend in with the humans. But she was still the most beautiful person Fenella had ever laid eyes upon.

"Ready?" Morveren asked, taking a bite of bread.

"Yes," Fenella replied hesitantly, "for what exactly?"

"Revenge, my sweet."

Fenella saw the murderous glint in Morveren's eye. She knew then that nothing good was to be committed that night. She nodded tightly and dropped her gaze.

"Don't worry, your household will not be affected," Morveren promised.

"I'm not worried."

"Then let us go."

Fenella led Morveren to her village. They walked purposefully, ready to reap hell. The summer sky was darkening and was filled with thunderous clouds. A summer storm was brewing. It was almost as if it knew what was about to happen. The thick warm rain droplets started to fall, soaking the pair's thin clothes. Fenella was glad for the coolness as she had run several miles already that night.

"So what are we going to do when we get there?" Fenella asked.

"Your auntie, and the other women, they need to suffer for what they have done to me."

"What are we going to do to them? Magic? Murder?"

"I don't know yet," Morveren admitted. "I have limited

magic in this form."

"Alright."

"I need you to tell me everything you know about your auntie and the women that aided her."

Fenella told her everything while they walked. About Auntie's life, the family, the women she controlled and their obsession with the church. Morveren listened dutifully, without interruption. Fenella found it easy to talk about her auntie because of the resentment she felt for her when Maw was ill. She vowed that she would look after her horrible cousins if anything happened to their maw.

"You have no love for this woman?" Morveren asked.

"None."

"I thought humans loved their family members fearlessly."

"We do, I do... but that woman is no family," Fenella said bitterly.

"I see." Morveren went quiet. She had grown fond of her little servant and felt doubly enraged with the woman's existence.

"The bairns, nothing will happen to them?"

"I can't promise that."

"Please," Fenella begged, clutching to Morveren, clawing her arms and pulling her to a stop.

Morveren decided to humour her human companion. "You care for them, why?"

"It isn't their fault they were raised by a madwoman; they haven't done anything wrong."

"I understand you humans less and less with every conversation we have, bairn."

"That's okay. I understand them enough for the both of us."

"You must remember to burn sage in the window of your home when we begin. My friends will know to leave it undisturbed, and valerian to ensure they stay asleep."

"I have a stockpile as you asked. What will happen to the other villagers that weren't involved?" Fenella asked.

"Call it a lesson, but I'll focus my powers on the women who wronged me. Tell me their names."

Fenella told her.

"Go now, protect your family, and meet me on the ridge once you have done."

"Will I need to hide?" asked Fenella.

"No, you have my mark. It is a protection of the highest kind. Animals and supernatural beings wouldn't dare mess with you while you bear my mark."

"Alright."

"It is with you forever, as a token of my appreciation," Morveren said with a small nod of appreciation.

"Ta, Morveren."

Fenella was sure then that the *Maighdean-mara* had come to care for her. She nodded once more and sneaked through the silent, sleepy houses to her family home.

Since her illness passed, Maw had allowed Fenella her own bed. She said that it was because she was nearly a grown woman and it wouldn't do to share with the bairns. But Fenella assumed it was because Maw knew about her full moon excursions.

Under her bed she kept a basket of dried herbs and potion-making supplies. Supplies she had used to fulfil some of Morveren's contracts. She quietly slid out the basket and selected a bundle of each herb she needed. Sage for protection, valerian for sleep - intertwining them delicately into a magical bouquet.

She grabbed some matches off the hearth and a glass from the kitchen. She began burning and wafting the aromatic protection through the rooms of the house before leaving it to smoulder in the glass on the window sill.

Fenella cracked open the window lest the fumes harm the sleeping forms within. Once she was satisfied with her work she left to meet Morveren on the ridge.

Morveren was sitting cross legged on the crisp grass, bathed in the moon's rays, her eyes closed, her hands cupped surreptitiously. Fenella dared not interrupt her, so she hovered several feet away waiting for something to happen. Morveren began singing;

"Lend your ears and send your heart

Hear my fears and let's depart

Under sharp moon rays and open skies

An army I raise, my warriors arise

Shift your bones and head my pleas

From deep unknowns and tallest trees

Follow me to battle and take your fill

I ask thee to dismantle, to feed, to kill

Seek my revenge and you shall prosper

This I pledge, this I foster

Smite my foes and spare the young

For those who oppose will die unsung."

Had Fenella not been under the protection of the singer she too would have picked up a weapon and joined the call to arms. She shook her head briskly once the mermaid had stopped her song in a bid to clear her head. It didn't take long for the warriors to arrive. They flocked in droves to Morveren. Animals seen not uncommonly on warm summer nights; pipistrelle bats, Long-eared owls, Tawny owls, hares, squirrels, Pine Martens, Stoats, wild boar. Flanked by the more vicious looking; Grey wolves in their summer ochreous coats, Lynx slinking down from their camouflaged canopies, and Adders charged with the day's warmth descended on the ridge, snarling and whooping in various tongues. All hungry and desperate after the slim pickings of the baking hot day.

Morveren hissed, clicked and snarled back at them. Fenella was both impressed and frightened. As she was about to release them upon the village an almighty roar came from the path. Morveren smiled mischievously.

"What was that?" Fenella asked, gripping her elbows tightly.

"You did not know your village had a *lycanthrope*?"

"A what?"

"A werewolf."

"I did not! Who is it?"

Morveren laughed heartily.

"Who?" Fenella repeated anxiously.

"My best paying customer," she replied finally, looking up to the Thane's castle with a glint in her eye.

"No..." Fenella gasped.

"Yes."

As the lycanthrope joined their ranks Morveren spoke briefly with the Thane in a language unknown to Fenella before sending them all off to battle. The unknowing villagers still slept soundly and unaware in their beds.

The animals swept silently down the hillside and into the village. Fenella's heart was in her mouth, her eyes fixed on her family home, willing the creatures to stay away. She was grateful to see no evil breaking down her door. She turned to her mistress.

"What did you say to him?"

"To bring me your auntie," Morveren said sweetly, "alive."

Fenella and Morveren watched from the ridge as the animals slinked through the village sniffing and snuffling, flying in through open windows, scratching at doors and lying in wait.

The animals seemed to work together. The winged ones went into the house and harassed the sleeping forms. Forcing them to flee their homes into the open jaws of the creatures outside.

It was carnage. Fenella hated every minute of it. She looked at Morveren expecting to see her grinning maliciously, but she looked tired. It must have been hard for her, living all these years away from the sea and her family because she didn't have her cap.

"Morveren?"

"Yes, bairn?"

"How did you lose your cap?"

"Lose it? It was stolen from me," Morveren's face contorted. "I was young, I thought I was in love. It was all a trap."

"In love with a human?"

"He was the most beautiful human. His black curls and amber eyes like no merperson. He was a humble crofter, he had a warrior's spirit... but a thief's heart," Morveren said softly.

"He stole your cap?"

"He asked that in return for marrying him and siring his children I would give him my cap so that I wouldn't leave him. The way he said it made it sound so romantic, like he couldn't bear for us to be apart."

"But he was lying?" Fenella asked.

"Indeed, the moment I gave him my cap, he fled, back to his home, bragging of a treasure no man had ever owned."

"Why didn't you use magic to make him never leave you?"

"Because then how would I know his love was real? I could

make anyone do anything, but where's the fun in that?"

Fenella considered this. "I guess you are right. What was the man's name?"

"Alastair Ariss."

Fenella laughed childishly.

"What?" Morveren asked, snapping her head around in annoyance.

"Alastair means protector of mankind."

Morveren laughed at the irony. "And Ariss, do you know where that originates?"

"I think it's a clan name. I can find out."

"Ta, bairn."

"How long ago did Alastair Ariss steal your cap?"

"Almost a hundred years I've kept my seat here."

Fenella thought about Morveren's tragic past and vowed to help her once all this trouble was over. She was glad of the conversation because it kept her mind and her eyes off the bloodshed before her.

People were screaming, high, guttural screams. Fires were roaring all around – a candle knocked over in the height of summer was a deadly thing. It wasn't uncommon in such close residences for wildfire to spread, especially if the foliage was crisp and dry, baked over days of intense summer sun. The perfect kindling. Fenella's family slept on, oblivious to the carnage around them. Fenella latched onto the Thane. He was dragging her auntie towards them, his jaws clenched around her shin. Her scream was bloodcurdling, she clawed at the ground, trying to get back to her house. Fenella thought that it was pathetic until she heard the words through the pain.

"*My baby!*"

"Morveren..." Fenella said quietly, looking as though she was ready to rush to her cousins.

"I told him not to harm the bairns."

"Then why is she screaming like that?"

"People will do anything to instil sympathy." Morveren hissed, her lips retracting over her teeth horribly.

Fenella brushed off her mistress' words and took off down the hill. Avoiding men wrestling with wolves, women shrieking at diving bats and lifeless bodies in pools of blood... She reached the house unharmed and tore inside, slamming the door firmly behind her. She closed the windows forcefully to exclude the flying horrors. Fenella turned around to see a horrific scene. There was blood everywhere, her cousins shaking and weeping under the bed.

"It's alright, I'm here," she cooed softly. "It's Fenella, your cousin."

"Ella!" a voice cried happily, followed by several tiny forms crawling out from under the bed.

"Where is Archie?"

"Maw's bed."

Fenella looked under the bloodied blankets and torn pillows hastily. Hoping to find her youngest cousin alive. She gasped.

"Ella?" one of the bairns asked.

"It's okay, Mair, he's alive."

Fenella looked down. Her cousin Archie, eight months old, wasn't crying, just looking at her distantly.

"Archie baby, it's okay, it's okay," Fenella cooed, scooping him up in her arms and cradling him against her chest.

Archie gave a disgruntled cry, then she looked down and almost dropped him in disgust. He had started sprouting thick hair across his face and body. His stubby baby teeth lengthened and his jaw cracked horribly. Fenella placed him down on the bed and surveyed his body. He was bleeding from his thigh. A bite from a lycanthrope, on the night of a full moon... her baby cousin was transforming. She covered him with a blanket, hiding him from view.

"Follow me." Fenella called to her remaining cousins, grabbing as many tiny hands as she could manage.

"Where are we going?"

"What about Archie?"

"Where's Maw?"

"Shush! Keep quiet, follow me, eyes on the ground. Don't look up!" ordered Fenella.

Fenella took a deep breath and kicked open the door, dragging the tiny bairns with her. Across the path towards her family home. It might have been the reflection from the burning buildings, but Fenella could have sworn the trident brand was glowing. While the cousins were near her they weren't attacked by Morveren's army. The mark of her mistress did its job. Fenella opened the door quietly and pushed the bairns in. She pulled back the covers of her bed and beckoned them over.

"Come, sleep here, it's safe," Fenella patted the bed. "See, my brothers and sisters are still asleep." Fenella pointed to the other bed where her family was snoring blissfully.

The children nodded sleepily, looking longingly between their cousins and the soft, clean sheets of Fenella's bed. Once the cousins were safely tucked up in bed and promised Fenella that they wouldn't leave until she came to get them, she left, back through the dwindling battle to her mistress.

She couldn't bear to think of Archie. He would be safely bundled up 'til morning, right?

She assumed that since Auntie had been captured and the other women were reprimanded that Morveren's revenge was nearly over.

Fenella heard Morveren singing once more. The gathered

animals dispersed as quickly as they had arrived.

"Fenella?"

"Yes?"

"The bairn. He is a wolf!" Morveren exclaimed, stroking the tiny wolf pup on her lap. He must have escaped Fenella's bed when he heard the howls of his sire in the heat of battle.

"It would appear so."

"I'm terribly sorry."

"Yeah, me too," Fenella stated harshly. She was fed up; all she wanted was for her family to be well and without want.

She looked around her – feeling ashamed and selfish, because without her none of this would have happened. She couldn't blame Morveren. She had been fair and honourable with her revenge and fulfilling Fenella's contract. She blamed herself.

"The Thane has agreed to take him as his ward," Morveren said.

"That's good news at least."

"What is wrong, Fenella?"

"I'm tired," she replied, knowing that if she said what she was really feeling she might be struck down where she stood.

"Go now, then, and sleep."

"What will happen to my village?"

"Only the criminals have perished tonight, lassie. Others have suffered, but they will live, they will rebuild, they will remember."

"What did you do to my auntie?"

"The Thane took care of that for me, after I had a few words with her," Morveren said mischievously.

"I'll find your cap." Fenella promised sleepily. She felt her eyes closing and her body relaxing. Was Morveren weaving her magic on her?

***

Fenella woke up late the next day, coated in sweat from the midday heat. Her family was busying around her, bringing items of clothing and belongings for their cousins. So suddenly orphaned.

"Good afternoon," Maw sang, "a letter for you."

Fenella stretched and rubbed the magic-induced sleep from her eyes. The letter was from the Thane. He wanted an audience.

Fenella groaned.

"What is it?" Maw asked, frowning slightly.

"I have to go."

"You be careful," she warned.

"Always," Fenella lied.

Fenella washed and brushed her hair, tying it up into a bun – a respectable hairdo. She dressed in her Sunday clothes; a smart white dress with polished black shoes.

Once ready, she walked up the gravel track to the Thane's castle anxiously wondering what he wanted. She could only guess that it had to do with Morveren. He either wanted to beg her to keep his lycanthropy secret or talk to her about her mistress. She wondered how much of last night he could remember, because she didn't know much about his condition to know for sure.

Gripping the letter tightly in her hand she walked into her employer's abode. Wondering where he would be. She was sweating by the time she reached the gates, only a short distance away from her house.

"You lost, miss?" a guard asked, looking her up and down.

"I'm to meet with the Thane," she replied, brandishing the letter.

"Follow me, then." The guard didn't question the letter.

Fenella didn't know whether this was a good sign. *Had the Thane told the guards to expect her? Was she to be arrested for her part in the slaughter last night?* The guard took her up the cold, stone staircase to the second floor. Down a long dimly lit corridor and towards an eerie looking door at the end of the corridor.

"Here we are. The Thane's study."

"Thank you."

Fenella knocked loudly on the heavy wooden door. She didn't have to wait long before a deep, hoarse voice instructed her to enter. She pushed open the door and stepped into the bright, airy study. It was lined with large, beautifully ornate windows that looked out onto the village proudly.

"You must be Fenella?" the tall, darkly handsome man behind the thick desk asked.

"I am, sir."

"I am the Thane. I understand you are one of my servants?"

"Yes, sir." Fenella replied, her eyes lowered to the Thane's feet.

"And you also work for the enchantress?"

Fenella paused before answering, wondering if she was talking herself into a trap. "I do, sir."

"Then you know about my... affliction?"

"I do, sir, but I won't tell a soul. You have agreed to look after my cousin?"

"Young Archie is my ward, yes. Thank you, bairn."

Fenella nodded dutifully.

"That is not why I have asked you here, though. Please, take a seat."

Fenella did as she was asked and sat in front of the desk like a schoolgirl in trouble. The Thane shelved the book he had been studying. He sat across from her, dropping himself carelessly into the chair. As if he was in great pain.

"Your mistress, the sea-witch, said that I could aid you in your... work. What do you need? I'm at your disposal."

Fenella was taken aback. Not only had she gotten away with last night and all the nights when she had been in the service of Morveren, she now had the Thane's full attention and resources at her fingertips?

"I'm trying to locate Morveren's cap. Do you know what that means?" She tried not to sound patronising, but she wanted to be as clear with the Thane as possible. He had to understand the gravity of the task at hand.

"I do. Morveren and I have spoken on several occasions about it, but I have tried and come up bare. What makes you so special that you should succeed where I have failed?"

"The young man that stole her cap was called Alastair Ariss. I want to locate him, follow the trail and find the cap."

"What do you need from me?"

"Ariss is a clan name. I need to know where he was from. I'm hoping that you have records here that I can read."

"Interesting." The Thane leaned back in his chair and looked at Fenella. The scrawny, feral child with a fiery glint in her eye. He wondered why he had never noticed her around his castle before.

"You understand that once Morveren has her cap she will leave?"

"I do," he replied sadly. "I have enjoyed her company and would be sad to see her go, but she does cause as much trouble as she fixes," he added with a sly smile.

"Once she is gone you will have no-one who knows your secret."

The Thane nodded.

"You will have me."

"So, you will be a companion to Archie and me?"

"Yes, the mermaid's mark will protect me, so you won't have to worry."

He pondered this for a moment, scratching his thick chin.

"Then we have a deal. You may come and live in the castle while you make use of our vast libraries and resources."

"What will you tell people?" Fenella asked.

"Damn the people, you are in my pack now. I'll see to it that you are cared for."

Fenella was speechless.

"I'll show you the library. There is a book of clans in there and a census of the village going back hundreds of years. A good start. I'll have my advisor meet with your mother and collect your things."

***

In the weeks leading up to Fenella's monthly meeting with Morveren, she spent most of her time with her head buried in books and records. Grateful that the head maid taught her to read so well. She had found out where the Ariss' hailed from but could find no trace of the thief in the village census. Morveren had claimed that he was a crofter and Fenella had hoped that meant he was going to be easily traceable. The universe had other ideas.

***

Three days before the full moon Fenella asked the Thane for a horse and an escort to Wester Ross. A journey that would take her across 300 miles of Scotland. She hoped she was right. If she was wrong then she would have missed her meeting with her mistress for no good reason and wasted a week journeying.

***

The journey was gruelling, but after several nights of riding Fenella and her escorts finally made it to The Isle of Ewe. It was too hot to travel during the day so Fenella's escorts decided it would be better to ride at night, despite the risk of bandits and beasts.

They asked around for the Ariss' and were directed to a small farm on the northern part of the isle. Armed with a letter from the Thane and a chest of gold, Fenella felt certain that the Ariss' would relent the stolen cap.

If they still had it, that was.

Fenella spoke with Mrs Ariss but she was a horrible woman. Clearly thieving had passed through the generations. She was not willing to let the cap go for the chest of gold and the assurance from the Thane that she would not be punished for possessing it. Fenella had to rethink her strategy, so she sat by the water's edge and cried. Like the night when she first met Morveren. Which got her thinking. Maybe she could call to her mistress and tell her what she had found out without waiting another lunar cycle.

She stripped off her boots and long socks and waded into the ocean, which was only uncomfortably cold rather than freezing like it was most of the year round. She let the water lap over her *trident* as she called to the sea.

"Morveren, mistress, hear my calls, I have found your cap and need your assistance."

She called it over and over again. Until her voice was sore and her body ached with cold, despite the blazing sun overhead. It wasn't Morveren who approached her but another mermaid.

"Child of the trident, you call for my sister, but she is land bound."

"I know; I'm her servant. I have found her cap but I cannot retrieve it."

"Fetch me your cloak," the mermaid ordered, flipping her copper-coloured hair over her shoulder.

She was beautiful, but looked unlike Morveren who had pale tones and an ethereal look. She mustn't have meant that they were blood relatives but sisters in kind. Fenella splashed back to the shore and grabbed her riding cloak from her horse. The mysterious mermaid returned transformed and was walking unashamedly naked towards her. Fenella shielded her eyes with the fabric and handed her the cloak.

"Thank you. I am Rubina, but you may call me Ruby."

"I'm Fenella. Morveren's cap is in that farmhouse." She pointed to the offending building.

"Leave it to me."

Fenella watched as Ruby strutted up to the door and knocked softly. She exuded an immense power that made Fenella want to cower. Ruby waited for Mrs Arris to open the door. The older woman impatiently tugged open the door. Expecting it to be Fenella and her troop returning. She was shocked to see the beautiful young woman standing there with just a cloak to hide her features.

Fenella couldn't hear the words exchanged but was giddy when Mrs Arris let Ruby into her home. Moments later Ruby exited the house holding a small bundle of feathered, red fabric. Mrs Arris was nowhere to be seen.

"What happened?" Fenella demanded once the mermaid reached her.

"I have my sisters *cohuleen druith*," Ruby smirked, "and I cursed the Arris'. If they should ever steal again then they will suffer endless misfortunes."

"Oh." Fenella was relieved. "That's fair."

Ruby handed Fenella the small bundle, not letting it go before thanking her for her service and dedication to her people.

"Morveren saved my family. I owe her everything; I'm happy to be of service."

"I will send any sisters-in-need your way if the occasion arises. If you need anything from us you know where to find us." Ruby said finally, handing back the cloak and returning to the sea.

Fenella watched the figure disappear into the waves and sank to the ground. She had finally fulfilled her promise to Morveren. She would no longer be in service to the deadly enchantress she had come to think of as a friend. It was time to head back home. Fenella stowed the cap on her person, worried that if she didn't know where it was at all times, it would go missing.

***

On the next full moon, close to summers end; Morveren wept with joy at being reunited with her cap. She returned to the sea, to her family. She thanked Fenella and reminded her that just because their contract was over, their bond needn't be.

Fenella cried when Morveren left. She didn't know why exactly. Maybe it was that the most exciting part of her life was over, or maybe it was the start of her next chapter. She learned a lot from her supernatural friends that year. Promises are sacred, hard work pays off, and never, ever piss off a mermaid.

M. J. Weatherall is one of those people who loves writing but always struggles to write about herself. She always feel like she's bragging (which in and of itself sounds like a brag according to her).

She is a young author from Sheffield who moved to the Lake District to get her BSc (Hons) degree in Outdoor Adventure and Environment. More recently she has qualified as a primary school teacher and is now fulfilling her calling as an educator.

M. J. loves climbing, kayaking and spending all her spare time in nature. A lifelong bookworm, she takes pride in growing her book knowledge (an asset to any pub quiz team to be sure!). She likes to think that she's a fun person to be around...at the very least, her cat seems to think so.

ACKNOWLEDGEMENTS
H. L. Macfarlane, editor

After Once Upon a Winter came out in November 2021 I couldn't believe I'd actually committed to a further three seasonal anthologies; organising, editing and promoting a group anthology is *very* hard work. Luckily that hard work is also incredibly rewarding. Though I delayed Once Upon a Summer from 2022 to 2023 I'm very happy I kept going with this series, because boy is this a great book.

If you're reading this then it follows that you've at least skimmed through the stories in this anthology (and preferably read a few of them!), so you know how wonderful every tale is. The authors smashed the brief of 'summer' out of the park – not surprising considering the quality of their ideas in the Winter anthology. Now I can't wait to see what they have in store for Spring and Autumn. Will we get some Eldritch horror going forward? I can only hope so!

On that note, I'd love to thank each and every author who contributed to this anthology. You're all a joy to work with, and your boundless creativity is what has kept inspiring me to continue with this series. In particular I'd like to thank Adie Hart, who going forward will be co-editing the remainder of the Once Upon a Season series with me. Thanks for listening to my meandering ramblings, sending me pictures of your cat and sharing hyper-specific memes and jokes that only I will understand.

Lastly, a massive thank you to each and every person who decided to pick up a copy of Once Upon a Summer. This book wouldn't exist without your overwhelming support. I hope to see you in the next one.

Printed in Great Britain
by Amazon